The Case of the Woebegone Widow

A Richard Sherlock Whodunit

By
Jim Stevens

Creative Inc. Publishing

The final approval of this literary material is granted by the author.

First Printing

ISBN: 978 1942424-02-4

This book is dedicated to Victor Hugo, who so well said:
"Laughter is the sun that drives winter from the human face."

The Richard Sherlock Whodunit Series

The Case of the Not-So-Fair Trader

The Case of Moomah's Moolah

The Case of Tiffany's Epiphany

The Case of Mr. Wonderful

The Case of the Woebegone Widow

The Case of the Missing Milk Money

Also by Jim Stevens:

WHUPPED

Hell No, We Won't Go,
A Novel of Peace, Love, War, and Football

CHAPTER 1

It's freezing in here. To make matters worse, I'm sitting on a cold slab of marble. The only thing that could make this more uncomfortable is to have my tongue stuck to a flagpole. I'm wearing long underwear, two pairs of socks, an additional T-shirt, muffler, gloves, and a pair of lace-up duck boots. I'm wearing so many layers underneath my suit I can't button my coat. To top off my frigid wardrobe, I've donned my Russian Ushanka trooper hat. I look like an overdressed Siberian Gulag commandant on his day off. And even with all the clothes I'm wearing, my knees are still knocking to the beat of "Nearer, My God, to Thee."

Chicago is in the middle of a cold snap that could freeze the life out of a woolly mammoth. When I was a kid, the TV weathermen called these cold weather calamities "Canadian Clippers;" now they refer to them as polar vortexes. Call it what you want, but when it's nineteen below, I call it unbearable. And to add more injury to the insult of subzero temperatures, toss in the Chicago wind, which chills the air to minus forty, and suddenly minus nineteen feels downright balmy. There should be a law forbidding air to get this cold.

The twelve or so people sitting in front of me look as if they're in a competition to become the next Michelin Man. They're all wearing so many layers of clothing I can't tell if they're grossly obese or skinny as a rail. Everyone has their heads covered; a few even wear ski masks. I can't say I blame them. Nobody, except the one lady in the front row, looks familiar. She lives in my building, and she's the one who asked me to do this.

Why can't I learn to say no to people?

The audience is so old they're shivering in slow motion. The average age must be close to eighty. It would be ninety, but there's one guy who looks about my age—or at least his face looks middle-aged since that's all the skin I can see. Everyone's sniffling, not because they're sad or feel bad, but because their noses are running faster than the thousands of busted water pipes in town this week. A couple of the old guys are as bald as billiard balls, and I swear I can see steam rising from their slick skulls. The assembled sit on wood benches with weird grins on their faces as they listen to the emcee of the event go on and on about valleys, flowers, dust, and more dust. I came all this way to hear a speech about dirt? For the assembled, this show is a rerun of a rerun of a rerun. They've all been here before, and they'll all be here again, if only in spirit. Maybe the only reason they've come is to get ideas on how best to throw one of these parties for themselves.

The guy playing the tunes in the way, way back of the room must have frostbitten fingers because he's missing more notes than he's hitting. I can only hope he's making hazard pay. I stomp my feet to his beat, not to keep the rhythm but to keep the blood flowing to my toes. The music is muffled because I have the flaps of my hat covering my ears, putting my face in furry parentheses. After the end of the depressing dirge, the main man starts up again and goes on and on about the everlasting. The only thing everlasting is this shindig lasting forever.

You'd think a place that has more gold trim in its walls than Fort Knox could afford a little heat, but they probably don't turn it on until Sunday when they get you nice and comfortable to hit you up for big bucks. Obviously, this group has no money, and the powers that be know it, so "No tickety, no heaty," as my buddy Detective Lester Oland would say.

It's so cold my teeth knock together in a staccato equal to a tap dancer on pep pills. I wonder if the fluid in my eyes has frozen because I think I'm hallucinating. I look to the back of the room and see heads pop up over the rows of benches like gophers coming out of their holes to see the sun, then descend downward as fast as they arose. If I had a big mallet, I could go back there and play "Whack a Frozen Mole."

I ask myself the same question over and over, "What am I doing here?"

I should get up and move around. If I don't, I may become an ice sculpture.

The only guy who seems to be enjoying all of this is the man of the hour, Mr. Roscoe Jarbeaux. There he is, as comfortable as a cat in a cradle, looking better than he has in years. He's got a smirk on his face. It's as if he's laughing at the suckers who've showed up for his frigid festivities. I used to see Roscoe walking around in the neighborhood, poking his cane at mothers pushing strollers who got in his way, teaching youngsters his favorite swear words, and puffing on big, thick cancer sticks illegally imported from Cuba. I did my best to avoid him. And now he's the center of attention, literally resting in the center of the big, cold room without a care in the world. The speaker speaks of him as if he didn't have a mean bone in his body, "He wasn't blessed with a family, but he made all of you his family. Down deep, he felt so much for all of the people around him."

What? Who is this guy trying to kid? This is hardly the setting to be telling whoppers. Roscoe's bones are so far past mean they're in the cruel category. And he didn't have a family because they couldn't stand to be around the old coot. His one second cousin twice removed in the front row must be cashing in later, or I'm sure she wouldn't be here either.

"And Roscoe's professional life, spending over fifty years in the credit department of the Illinois Financial Retrieval Company," the big, burly main man continues, "his work touched so many, many people." Oh, yeah, Roscoe touched a lot of people with his slimy and sneaky methods of collecting past-due bills. I heard stories where Roscoe would turn off people's water while they were in the shower, call them on the hour, every hour, starting at 2 o'clock in the morning, and follow unsuspecting debtors to their bank on payday to see if he could scoop some of their hard-earned cash. I wouldn't be at all surprised if he had my number on his list a few times. This fact alone makes it all the more absurd that I'm up here doing what I'm doing.

After another song is butchered beyond even God's recognition, I get the nod from the emcee. They have saved the best for last. I stand up, and my knees buckle. The fluid inside me must be frozen. I find my balance and stumble to the podium. I look out over the scattered people in attendance. If they were smart, or better friends, they'd be huddled together to keep warm. Nobody looks sad. They all look totally miserable. And I can't blame them. On the side aisles, their walkers and wheelchairs are parked haphazardly, resembling the abandoned cars on Lake Shore Drive earlier this week when a lake-effect blizzard added a thirty-minute whiteout to the lives of the already agonized North Side citizens. The traffic that day backed up all the way to the parking lots underneath Grant Park, where so many motionless cars were idling noxious fumes if you cracked your window an inch, you'd be asphyxiated in moments.

I take one more look at Roscoe, and I swear his smile has widened. Somewhere, somehow he's enjoying every minute of this.

I remove my Ushanka hat out of reverence. The cold air hits my head like a blast of liquid nitrogen. My hair freezes in place. Thank God I don't use mousse, or it would freeze and shatter like a wine glass dropped on a tile floor. I begin, "Good morn—" My vocal chords lock up like brakes on black ice. I try to swallow but only swallow air. I can see my breath; it hangs in the air like gas coming off dry ice. I take my gloves off and blow into my fists. I put my hands to my face and rub around my nose to break up the frozen mucus inside. I exercise my jaw, moving it back and forth. I begin again, "Good morning."

The faces in front of me don't move. They are either freeze-dried or don't agree with my assessment. I might as well continue. "Roscoe Jarbeaux, what can you say about Roscoe Jarbeaux?" I pause. I'm not waiting for a reply, but if one came out of the peanut gallery seated before me, it would be welcome. I do see one man lift the middle finger of his right glove and hold it up to answer my question. I pretend to ignore his silent comment. I continue from my notes, "I remember once asking Roscoe, 'In your more than nine decades in Chicago, what wisdom have you learned that you would like to pass along?'"

"'Not a damn thing,' he replied."

"In ninety-three years, you didn't pick up anything?"

"'Naw,' he said as he spit his cigar butt into the street. 'Except maybe pay your bills, so you won't have to deal with a mean old cuss like me.' And if that doesn't say it all, I don't know what does."

There is not one reaction in the bunch. Maybe these people have become ice cubes; the human body is 98% water.

I try another tack. “Roscoe did list a few requests. He said he didn’t want any moving tributes. So, I hope all of you who purchased decals for the back windows of your pickup trucks are able to get your money back.” I wait for the laughter, but none comes. They should have scheduled a warm-up man to go on before me.

One more attempt to thaw this crowd. “This day reminds me of the time the famous choreographer, Mr. John Hoki, was in the same place as Roscoe Jarbeaux is today. John Hoki, as he was carried in, was dropped by his buddies, fell out of his box and onto the floor, and no one knew how to get him back into his place. His friends and family gathered around him in a circle, perplexed on what to do, until finally, someone sang out ‘You put his right foot in, and his left foot out ...’”

I even sing the last line, but the only reaction I get is a loud rumbling from the mass of a dozen. Their senses of humor must also be frozen. I hear growls. The natives are getting restless. They are squirming in their seats to show their impatience or trying to shake off the ice pellets that have formed on their extremities. I decide to toss the notes I scribbled on the back of a Walgreen’s receipt and wing it from this point on. “Is there anything anyone in attendance would like to add; a thought, memory, or anecdote about Roscoe Jarbeaux?”

“Can we poke him to see if he moves, just to make sure?” one woman shouts out.

“He borrowed my snow shovel years ago, and I want it back,” another yells out.

“The only thing I can say is I wish we coulda done this years ago.”

“Wouldn’t you know it, he’s in hell nice and warm, and we’re up here freezing to death.”

I interrupt to quell the irreverent comments. “Please, we should all show some respect.”

“Why?” one voice yells out. “He didn’t show us no respect. He once busted my kid’s piggy bank open.”

“I’ve been picking up his cigar butts off my lawn for twenty years.”

“He smelled bad.”

This is getting out of hand.

“The invitation said ‘lunch will be served.’ When does it start?”

"I'm hungry," another yells out.

"Only reason I came is to make sure he's really dead."

Just as the audience is about to become a mob and desecrate the life and corpse of dearly departed Roscoe Jarbeaux, I hear the words that will no doubt be the cause of my untimely death: "Oh, Mr. Sherlock."

I look up to see a human snowflake prancing up the church's center aisle. She wears knee-high leather boots, thick, pink leggings, and a white mink coat with a hoodie that makes her face look as if it's encased inside a giant snowflake.

"What are you doing up there, Mr. Sherlock?" She stops to peer inside the coffin. "And who's the stiff?"

"Tiffany!"

"Is he dead or just frozen?"

"Tiffany, we're in the middle of the funeral right now."

"I don't think it's going to bother him much," Tiffany says, nodding towards Roscoe.

"Tiffany, could you wait until this is over?"

"No, Mr. Sherlock. My daddy needs you right there and now."

"Why?"

"We got a big case to investigate. It'll be a lot more fun than this."

"I'm busy."

"When Daddy says jump, Mr. Sherlock, you got to say, 'Up or down?'"

"But I'm right in the middle of a eulogy."

"You lo-gee, later, Mr. Sherlock." She takes me by the arm, pulls me from the altar, and into the middle aisle. "Oh, come on, you know there's no fun in funerals."

I get dragged out of a church in the middle of a memorial service by a person who can't spell.

Is it any wonder why I hate my life?

***

My name is Richard Sherlock. I spent nineteen years in the Chicago Police Department, sixteen as a detective. I got kicked off the force due to an uncharacteristic temper tantrum. My fist collided with the face of my commanding officer after he OK'd a plea deal for a guy I spent ten years trying to put behind bars. I lost my job and my pension and couldn't find another job. Not a lot of suburban, Chicago police departments were in need of a guy with a right cross aimed at his superior. I ended up as an on-call investigator for the Richmond Insurance Company, where I am forced to investigate settlement frauds or any settlements that can be proven fraudulent.

I hate my job.

I am also a divorced dad of two girls, twelve and fourteen going on twenty. I have a bad back, no savings, and an ex-wife that hates me. I live in a crummy, currently freezing, one-bedroom apartment. I'm a lousy dresser. I can't find a steady girlfriend, and I drive a 1992 Toyota Tercel. To make matters worse, it's now dropped to twenty-one below with a wind chill of minus fifty.

Am I having fun?

No.

A big portion of my job with the insurance agency is mentoring (aka babysitting) the twenty-something, spoiled heiress of the Richmond fortune, Tiffany Richmond. On the surface, Tiffany is a vapid, spoiled-rotten, rich, self-centered, egotistical girl who will never experience an "I can't afford it" moment in her life. Deep down, Tiffany is a vapid, spoiled-rotten, rich, self-centered, egotistical girl with a good heart. I have found in life if you have one of those, all other frailties diminish. Plus, my kids think the world of her. I suspect they like her more than they like me. I really can't blame them because even I like her more than I like me.

***

On the way out of the church, I see I wasn't hallucinating. Those heads I was seeing popping up over the pews were homeless guys trying to sleep through a loud, boring memorial service. Life's tough enough without being blasted out of bed by a pipe organ.

"Tiffany, what's this all about?"

"Daddy's getting sued. He says this is a case that could blow the lid off the insurance company can."

"I don't think you got that right."

"Whatever, Mr. Sherlock. All I know is we gotta hurry."

We stop in the vestibule of the church, and before we head

outside, Tiffany pulls this Hazmat mask contraption out of nowhere. She puts it on as if it were a WWI gas mask and tucks its flaps in under her mink. She cinches the waist sash on her fur, flips the hoodie up, and speaks to me through the mask, sounding like E.T., "I can't let any freezing air hit my face because it will throw my skin emollients out of sync, and I could get a zit."

"Oh my God, perish that thought, Tiffany."

She opens the door, we step outside, and we get hit with an arctic blast straight from the North Pole. It's so bitterly cold I'll bet Santa let his elves off for the day.

My *slightly used* Navy bridge coat, which I bought from the Army/Navy Surplus store and was "guaranteed to keep you warm in the Aleutians," is failing on its promise. The wind goes through it like it was a piece of cheesecloth. The exposed skin on my face painfully stings from the cold air. I put my gloved hands against my face, opening my fingers slightly so I can see to follow Tiffany running ahead of me. Luckily, we don't have to go far since she parked half on the sidewalk and half on the church steps. Her Lexus is idling. There must be heat inside. I lunge for the passenger side but can't open the door because my fingers can't get underneath the latch. I have to take off one glove, which freezes my hand immediately. In sheer agony, I grasp the cold metal door latch, pull up, and the door opens. I tumble inside because with so many clothes on, it's tough to maneuver a graceful entry. I pull on the door, but it won't close. The wind howls inside the car.

"Shut the door, Mr. Sherlock," Tiffany orders, now sounding like Roseanne Barr in the middle of a hissy fit.

I pull my coat up and out of the doorframe, squish my body to the left, and slam the door closed. I unbutton my coat and stuff my now almost frostbitten hand inside and under my armpit. Tiffany flips the heat control to the "hotter than Hades" setting, and a blast of hot air hits my face like a slap from an angry girlfriend. After the shock wears off, I breathe in the warm air and start to feel a thawing from my nostrils to my frontal lobe. In about three minutes, I'm breathing normally. "I hate winter," I tell Tiffany.

"I kinda like it. There are so many more fashion choices with cold weather."

We have to wait for the window defrosters to do their thing

before we can move. “Where are we going anyway?” I ask.

“See Mr. Twitchell.”

“Who?”

“Mr. Houston Twitchell.”

“Let me guess,” I say to my protégée. “We’re going to tell him, ‘Houston, we have a problem’?”

“Wow, Mr. Sherlock, you are one smart detective.”

CHAPTER 2

The law firm of Hickle, Belittle, Twitchell, and Mitchell takes up the entire forty-seventh floor of the AT&T tower in the Loop. Thank the Lord the skyscraper has heated underground parking, where Tiffany pulls into the first handicapped space available.

"If you ask me, Mr. Sherlock, this is the best driving invention since the garage door opener." She's referring to the blue and white handicapped placard she's hanging from her rearview mirror.

"You know how I feel about you using that sticker, Tiffany."

"No, I don't."

"I've told you time and time again that I don't agree with you using something meant for people who need assistance."

"I wasn't listening."

"Why not?"

"Why would I want to hear something I know I don't want to hear?"

Ah, yes, mentoring someone who refuses to listen to my mentoring, yet another aspect of my life so near and dear to me.

We take the elevator to the forty-seventh floor. The reception area of Hickel, Belittle, Twitchell, and Mitchell is three times the size of my apartment and twice as warm.

Seeing Tiffany, one of the two receptionists comes out from around her desk and helps her off with her mink. "Gorgeous," the woman remarks.

"Yes, it is," Tiffany concurs.

"We'll keep yours behind the desk," she tells Tiffany, taking the coat. "Yours," she says to me, "can go in the closet over there."

Where I hang my coat, there's a pail and mop to keep it company.

"And who are you here to see?" the receptionist asks.

"I'm Tiffany Richmond, this is Mr. Sherlock, and we have an appointment with Houston Twitchell."

The woman moves back behind her desk to check her computer screen. "Your appointment was for eleven."

"Yes," Tiffany says.

"It's eleven forty-five."

"Okay, so maybe you didn't hear me. I'm Tiffany Richmond of Richmond Insurance. We have an appointment with Houston Twitchell."

The receptionist looks up at me with an odd look on her face.

"Welcome to my world," I tell her.

"Have a seat, please."

By the time we sit on the plush couch, I'm sweating.

One of the problems of winter in Chicago is you dress for the worst. You wear all the extra layers to protect yourself from becoming an icicle when venturing outside. But when you go inside, you discover many stores and businesses jack the heat up to summertime highs. Since you're all bundled up, your body starts to perspire as if it were in the middle of a Louisiana swamp in mid-August.

"Gee, Mr. Sherlock, you look like you're sitting in a sauna," Tiffany remarks, no doubt watching the beads of sweat roll down my face.

"It's hot in here."

"Really? I think it is quite pleasant."

Tiffany, who looks fresh as a spring daisy, doesn't have this problem. Once her thick fur is off, she resembles a winter nymph. No extra layers on her.

"Excuse me, Miss Richmond, you'll be in conference room sixteen," the receptionist announces.

We stand. "How many conference rooms does this place have?" I have to ask.

"I'm not supposed to say, but there's four."

Image is everything.

We follow the lady inside the legal sanctum sanctorium and walk by about thirty offices. The offices to our left each have a window with a spectacular view. On each outside door there is a nameplate with Esq. after the person's name. The offices in the middle of the floor are the smallest, but as you head down the hallway, they get bigger, culminating in the corner offices being the biggest. I'll bet Hickel, Belittle, Twitchell, and Mitchell each have one of these. If they ever add another partner, they'll have a problem.

"Mr. Twitchell will be right in," the receptionist informs us as we enter an interior conference room. “There are refreshments in the cooler. Please help yourself,” she says before leaving us alone.

Tiffany heads straight for the cooler, where she removes a bottle of water, opens the cap, pours a little in her hand, and uses the fingers of her other hand to spritz droplets of water onto her face. “With all the processed heat blowing on you, it’s important to moisturize, Mr. Sherlock.”

“I prefer my moisturizing to come from the inside out.”

We wait. I sweat. Tiffany spritzes. We both have beads of moisture on our faces, one natural, one not, when Mr. Houston Twitchell, Esq. and his two-person entourage enter after a few minutes.

Houston is a little guy, maybe five-five, and tipping the scale at one-fifty tops. He has wispy, thinning hair, a pair of cheaters resting on his nose, and ears that don’t fit his face. He wears a three-piece, vested suit, starched white shirt, and a black and white, checkered bow tie. He forgot to take the rubbers off his wingtips this morning. Behind Houston is a very attractive, middle-aged woman, conservatively dressed, who is at least a head taller than her boss. She carries a steno pad in her left hand, a Tiffany pen in her right, and a stern, all-business expression on her face. Following her is a younger man, who could wear custom Armani but would still look disheveled. Calling him nerdy would be a compliment. He carries a laptop computer, an oversized cell phone, and some other computer peripherals I don’t recognize and probably never will recognize.

“Hello, Houston,” Tiffany says.

Houston leans over toward Tiffany, who holds back far enough to ensure the greeting is only an air kiss.

“This is Mr. Sherlock,” Tiffany introduces me. “He’s our in-house detective.”

Houston thankfully holds off on another kiss and shakes my hand. “Yes.”

I respond with, “Nice to meet you.”

Houston waves his hand toward the others in the room as if he’s the circus ringmaster presenting the elephant act.

They each nod in an automaton fashion.

Houston sits at the head of the table, flanked by his people, and starts the meeting. “Yes.”

"Didn't Daddy call you?" Tiffany asks.

Houston turns his head to his female counterpart, hears her whisper, and says, "Yes."

Jamison Richmond, III never calls me. The closest I get to the big guy is through his voice mail or through his daughter, which is probably detrimental to any purpose I might have in trying to communicate with him.

"Okay," Tiffany says.

Houston's male counterpart hurriedly types onto his computer, waits, and pushes the laptop in front of his boss. Houston reads the message silently and pushes the laptop in front of Tiffany, who gets the idea and reads, "Everyone at Hickel, Belittle, Twitchell, and Mitchell will do everything in their power and spare no expense to cease and desist this absurd, totally preposterous, venal, and unlawful lawsuit before it sees the legal light of day."

Houston and his people listen intently with assured looks on their faces.

"That sounds super," Tiffany says as she finishes.

The better looking half of Houston's people taps him on his sleeve, pulls him toward her, and again whispers in his ear.

Houston listens, nods in agreement, and stands up. "Yes." Houston spreads his hands as if he's Jesus dismissing the heretics from the temple.

Houston's people rise with him. Tiffany follows the crowd.

I stay seated and ask, "You got me out of a funeral, just before the free lunch, for this?"

"What do you mean, Mr. Sherlock?" Tiffany asks.

"If I'm going to be involved, shouldn't I know what this is all about?"

"Oh, yeah."

Tiffany sits, Houston sits, and his people sit.

"Tell him," she orders.

The nerdier of Houston's people pushes his laptop toward his boss, hits one key, sits back, picks up his smartphone, and starts punching its screen. As the correct page comes up, he pushes the cell phone in front of me.

I read, "A plaintiff, who goes by the name of Vilma Kromka, a Richmond Happy Health HMO customer, has filed a lawsuit against Richmond Health Incorporated for denying her claim for a forty-two thousand dollar yearly sum of money to be paid to her, on what she claims is her incapacitation, due to what she refers to as PTGD."

I stop, look up, and ask, "PTGD?"

"Yes," Houston says.

"I never heard of PTGD," I admit.

"It sounds like something you'd text," Tiffany says.

"No," Houston replies.

Thank God Houston said no. I was beginning to think of him only as a yes man.

"PTGD, I bet a lot of people get it mixed up with PITA," Tiffany says.

"What's that mean?" Of course I have to ask.

"Pain In The Ass," Tiffany answers.

ISHK, I Should Have Known.

The nerdy guy takes the laptop back, pushes a few keys, waits, and points the new screen at me. I read the screen aloud, "Post-traumatic grief disorder."

"Yes," Houston says and sits back to listen.

I continue reading, "Vilma Kromka claims she has become mentally and physically distraught over the loss of her husband, whose life was also insured by Richmond Life Insurance Incorporated; that she is now incapable of holding down suitable employment in her career as an oil change specialist and part-time professional dog walker."

I stop reading. "When did her husband die?" I ask and hand the computer back to the nerd.

Houston waits until he hears the whisper in his ear and lifts six fingers into the air.

"Six months ago?" I question.

"Yes."

"And how much did she get from the life policy?" I keep the questions coming.

Another pause and the laptop comes my way again, "Half million."

"Yes."

"Why would she have to work if she just got a half million?" If I had a half-mil, I'd quit this gig in a heartbeat.

"A half million isn't what it used to be," Tiffany informs me.

Another tug on his sleeve, another whisper, and Houston speaks again, "No."

I read, "If PTGD is introduced, and heaven forbid, Vilma

wins, a legal precedent will be set, and post-traumatic grief disorder will become a recognized disease. From that point forward, every spouse, partner, live-in, and one-night stand who precedes the other in dropping dead is going to fake symptoms, file a lawsuit, and expect a free ride on a never-ending insurance company gravy train. The lineup will be longer than the tollbooth backup when the automatic lanes aren't working. A negative judgment, in a case of this magnitude, could put Richmond Insurance out of business."

"And we certainly don't want that," Tiffany says. "Do we?"

Houston, this time without prompting, says, "No."

"What do you want me to do about it?" I ask. "This sounds more like a matter for an attorney than a private detective."

Houston gives me an odd look then a different odd look to his help. In a few seconds another new page fills the screen. I read, "Find her, assess the situation, study her, and dig up enough dirt so we can bury her deeper than a pirate's booty. We need to come up with so much trash on this woman, she'll look like a toxic waste dump on the stand. We need you to find fraud, fakery, philandering, falsification of facts, and enough phoniness in this floozy to make her next year's poster girl for frivolous lawsuits." I come to the end of the page. "Well, that certainly sounds like a fun time to me," I say in a sarcastic tone.

"Yes," Houston says.

"Me too," Tiffany agrees.

Houston stands, his entourage stands, we stand. Everyone smiles, and the meeting ends for the second time.

"Nice meeting you, Mr. Twitchell," I say, bidding him goodbye.

"Yes."

In the lobby we retrieve our coats. "I'll bet Houston Twitchell is a real bulldog in a courtroom."

"Yes," Tiffany replies.

In a few moments, we are once again sitting in Tiffany's car.

"So when do we begin to break this woman in two, Mr. Sherlock?" Tiffany asks as she removes the gimp sticker from her rearview mirror and places it in the Lexus' glove compartment.

"Why don't you get her address," I suggest.

"How am I going to do that?"

“All you’d have to do is look up her policy.”

“Or get somebody to look it up for me.”

“Yes, Tiffany, you could delegate the activity to a lesser person.”

“You know, Mr. Sherlock, I’m starting to think I was born to manage.”

Well, it’s good to know she’s starting to think.

Tiffany fires up the Lexus. “Where to now, Mr. Sherlock?”

“Drop me off at the ‘L’ station on Wacker.”

“Why?” she asks. “We have a case to investigate.”

“I can’t.”

“Why can’t you?”

“It’s Tuesday.”

“So?”

“Tuesday is my kid day.”

CHAPTER 3

During cold snaps like the one we're in, the Chicago Transit Authority, the CTA, makes the wise decision to keep the trains and busses running 24/7 even if they're not leaving the station during the post-midnight hours. They do this in fear that if they turn off the power, the engines might freeze, and nobody will be going anywhere in the morning commute.

Keeping the engines running also keeps the heaters running inside the vehicles, which is both good and bad. It's good because when the train or bus is moving, it's warm and toasty inside. It's bad because a lot more people commute by train in subzero weather, which overflows the cars and drives the body heat quotient sky-high. Commuters, when packed like sardines, rub against each other and produce massive amounts of hot, kinetic energy, which they are forced to share. Also, the cars stay toasty until the train or bus comes to a stop, and when their doors open, arctic air swoops inside, reversing the microwaved heating effect into a blast of ice-cold Eskimo air. Winter is especially unkind to rush-hour commuters in Chicago.

I'm on the Brown Line on my way home, and it's not too crowded. I sit in a front-to-back row next to the door and watch as people try to maneuver the turning of newspaper pages wearing thick mittens. The Sun-Times is much easier to read than the Tribune. It is only a couple of blocks to walk from the station to my apartment, but with ice packed inches thick on the sidewalks, the trip is as treacherous as jumping ice floes to get across a raging river.

My Toyota is parked in front of my building. It hasn't moved in three days. I am not a praying man, but I say a quick one before I unlock its door, climb inside, and fumble the key into the ignition. I say a second prayer before I turn the key.

The car starts up on the first try. Thank you God and Japanese engineering. I turn on the defroster and let the car run as I retrieve the ice scraper from the back seat. Out of the car, I go to work on the windows, scraping the ice in long rows with the hard edge of the tool and then sweeping the ice off with the brush end. I do all the windows, not just front and back. Visibility is one of the most important aspects of driving safety. By the time I am back in the car, the interior is warm. I slip out of my coat but use it as a seat cover. I put the car into gear and pull out slowly into the street. Once in the traffic lane, I stop the car, set the brake, get out of the car, go back to the parking space I just vacated, and put up the old kitchen chair I am using to reserve the space for my future return. I'm the one who shoveled the space, so I'm the one to use the space, according to the unwritten law of winter street parking in Chicago.

It takes me forty minutes to get to the schools and into the queue to pick up my kids. I'm right on time. Luckily, Care's grammar school and Kelly's middle school are located next to one another. For the pick-up in the afternoon, the driving lane is one way, with the grammar school first in line. The rule is to keep the line moving because if you stop for too long a time, everyone has to stop behind you. I see Care standing on the sidewalk, patiently waiting. She wears calf-high rubber boots, a thick down coat down to her knees, mittens, an oversized, knitted wool muffler, and a knit hat. If I didn't know the outfit, I wouldn't know it was my daughter. She sees me and hustles to climb in the car, so I don't stop the traffic behind me.

"Hi, Care."

"Hi, Dad."

"Did you learn anything in school today?"

"No," she answers and asks, "Can we stop at McDonald's?"

"No."

Kelly is up ahead, paying no attention to the cars slowly cruising by. She is in the middle of a gaggle of girls chitchatting each other up like a barrel of chattering monkeys. She's wearing her latest fashion-conscious hat, which doesn't cover her ears, a pair of jeans tucked into her leather boots, and only a ski parka, which she has left wide open in the front. I have to honk the horn to get her attention.

She pretends not to see me and keeps talking away. The horns start honking behind me. I roll down my window and shout, "Kelly, let's go."

She ambles over after waves of goodbye and plops into the backseat of the Toyota. "God, Dad, what's the big hurry?"

"Kelly, how many times have I told you to zip your coat up.

You're going to catch pneumonia."

"I'm not cold."

"It's twenty below out."

"I got hot blood, Dad."

"I don't need to hear that, Kelly."

"Can we go to McDonald's?" Care asks again.

"You already asked me that and the answer is no."

"Why not?"

"Because fast food is terrible for you."

"Mom takes us to McDonald's."

"Well, I don't. And someday you're both going to thank me for teaching you good eating habits."

"Until then, can we go to Burger King?"

"No."

"Are you going to take us to do something fun today?" Kelly asks.

"No."

"Why not?"

"Because it's Tuesday, and you have homework to do for tomorrow."

"Let's go to the mall and buy new clothes."

"Did you bring money, Kelly?"

"No, that's your job, Dad."

"Well, I guess I better start looking for a new job because I'm sure not doing very well in this one."

"You got that right, Dad."

"I think you're a great dad, Dad," my younger daughter says, more to disagree with her sister than to compliment her father. I don't care, I'll take it anyway I can get it.

"Thank you, Care, I appreciate your heartfelt appreciation."

"You're welcome," Care says. "Now, can we stop at McDonald's?"

"No."

***

Our apartment is as drafty as an Alcatraz prison cell. Being on the third floor of an old building with ancient, rotted casement windows, the cold air whips through like a Siberian squall. Two of the four radiators work great, but they are no match against a polar vortex. The ones in the kitchen and bathroom pump out the most hot air, but the front room and the bedroom units are not so hot. When we enter this afternoon, the temperature must be below fifty. I go immediately to the kitchen and turn on the stove's burners and start the oven. Once it heats up, I'll leave the oven door wide open. Next, I take a small hammer and bang on the two deficient radiators. I don't know why this works, but it does seem to increase the available hot air. I make sure the heavy, sand-filled doorstops are pushed flush against the bottom of the front and back doors to block cold air from coming in the door cracks. I have already sealed the windows shut with a clear caulking material, which smells like airplane glue, but it doesn't seem to be working too well. I can hold my hand up to the glass and feel the cold air rushing inside. I've got to come up with a better solution for this problem because I'm losing a ton of heat.

Within thirty minutes the apartment is as cozy as a five-star ski lodge with a roaring fireplace.

The girls do their homework, comment that my turkey tetrazzini casserole would be food "fit for a king if we had a dog named King," and take their showers.

We watch a TV show about a single writer who gets to play policeman each week helping a gorgeous female detective solve crimes in an hour. Yeah, like that's going to happen. Tiffany calls right before bedtime.

"Let me talk to her," Kelly says when she realizes who's calling.

"Me too," Care says.

"What's up, Tiffany?"

"I have the Vilma lady's address, Mr. Sherlock."

"Good."

"Are we going to stake her out, arrest her, or put her in a hot room and sweat the truth out of her?"

"None of the above."

"Well, then what are we going to do?"

"Talk to her."

"Talk to her? I thought we have to dig in her dirt, flaunt her fraud, and mentally break her until she grovels at my feet."

"No. We'll start by talking to her, Tiffany."

"That sounds boring."

"Most of life is boring, Tiffany. Get used to it."

"Not my life, Mr. Sherlock."

I take down the address, tell her I'll meet her there at nine after I drop off the kids at school, and hand the phone to my daughters who chat with her until I tell them "it's time for bed."

Next morning I awaken a half hour earlier than usual to heat up the place. At six thirty, I rouse the girls out of bed and tell them we are leaving fifteen minutes early because snow is falling. I fix lunches while they get ready and dressed. At 7 a.m. we're outside getting in the car.

"Think it will start, Dad?" Care asks.

"If it doesn't start, can we blow off school and go shopping?" Kelly asks before I get a chance to answer.

"Get in the car and zip your coat up, Kelly."

The Toyota kicks over on the first try.

"Darn!" Kelly says.

I'm glad we left early because the snowflakes increase in size and severity, and the going is slow-and-go at best. I take Western Avenue north because it is one of the first streets to get plowed.

When we reach their schools, the drop-off line is as empty as a car wash on a rainy day.

"What's going on?"

"Snow day," the girls call out in utmost glee.

Oh jeesh.

The Chicago School District has a system where, if the weather is intense, you call a special number, punch in the school code, and a recorded voice will tell you if your school has been closed for the day. You can also access the service on your home computer or smartphone. Of course, I do none of the above.

"It's barely a dusting, and they call off school? I can't believe this."

"Let's go shopping. Sledding. Movie. Bowling. Manicure. Pedicure. Spa. Laser tag." For my kids the possibilities are endless.

"No."

"Why not?"

"Because Dad has to work."

"So, take the day off, Dad."

"I can't."

"Why not?"

"Economics. Or lack thereof in my case."

"Gee, Dad, you're no fun."

"For once, Kelly, I agree with you."

CHAPTER 4

Vilma Kromka lives off Belmont, west of the expressway. I know the neighborhood. It used to be Polish, until the Hispanics moved in, and then it went gay when the gays couldn't afford Boystown any longer. Now it's yuppie since developers came in, bought up apartment buildings, cheaply refurbished them, jacked the prices sky-high, and sold them as hip urban condos and townhomes. This is progress? I liked it better when the kielbasas hung in storefront windows.

We arrive about nine thirty. I find a parking spot one condo building away from the intended visit site. I told Tiffany to be here at nine, so we should only have to wait fifteen minutes for her to show up. During the interlude, Care tells me about "Buggers" Reagan, a kid in her class that picks his nose so much he can get all his fingers going at the same time. The kids find particular interest in watching "Buggers" perform, what they call, the Reagan Reaper. When it is Kelly's turn, she tells me all about Helen "Tugboat" Tognari, who has a helicopter mother that buzzes around her like an obnoxious fly. I love talking with my kids.

Vilma's house is the last holdout on Ridgeway Avenue. It's the worst house on the block, a mishmash of wood, concrete, and brick, an architect's testament to the cheapest materials available at the time of construction. There are burglar bars on the windows, the front steps are cracked at the edges, and the house looks multicolored, not in a hip modern art design, but because the outside paint is peeling just about everywhere, revealing the bright blue, lime green, and scarlet red colors of previous paint jobs. I'll bet every yuppie in the neighborhood hates the place.

Tiffany arrives right on Tiffany-time, parks in a red zone, and hangs her sticker on her mirror. I hate that.

We all get out of our cars at the same time.

"What are you doing here?" Tiffany asks, seeing my girls.

"We had a snow day, so we came along to help," Care informs her.

"Then we want you to take us shopping," Kelly adds.

"No," I interject.

"Manicure?"

"No."

"Pedicure?"

"No."

"Eyebrow plucking?"

"Want your eyebrows plucked, Kelly? Let me do it for you," I suggest.

"I prefer a licensed aesthetician, Dad." Sometimes, Kelly is too smart for her own good.

I lead the crew up the unshoveled sidewalk of the house. "Now, I want you people to be quiet and let me do the talking."

"No problem, Mr. Sherlock," Tiffany replies, and the girls nod.

Their answer assures me there's going to be a problem.

I knock on the front door. No answer. I hear voices inside arguing. I knock again. A light goes on in the front room but no answer. The arguing increases. I knock for the third time.

A voice is heard. "I don't want any."

"We're not selling anything," I assure her.

"What do you want?"

"Is this Vilma Kromka?"

"Why do you want to know?"

"We're from the Richmond Insurance Company and want to discuss your recent claim."

"Did you bring my money?"

"Maybe," Tiffany calls out.

The front door unlocks from the inside.

Tiffany taps her index finger on her temple to self-proclaim her quick-thinking intellectual capabilities.

The door opens wide. "I'm Richard Sherlock—"

Vilma cuts me off, "Like the detective?"

"Yes, he is a detective," Tiffany informs her. "How'd you know?"

"Are you Watson?"

"No, I'm Tiffany."

Vilma peers down at my kids. "Who are you?"

"I'm Kelly."

"I'm Care."

"The insurance company uses child labor?"

"No, these are my kids. They had a snow day today."

"Can we come in? It's cold out here."

The house is smaller inside than it looked from the outside, probably because it is filled to the brim with furniture. The only item less than forty years old in the room is a forty-inch flat-screen TV set, haphazardly set up on the widest wall.

In my years as a detective, I've been in hundreds of people's homes, and no matter how bad the house, how awful the neighborhood, or how dirt poor the occupant may be, there's always a new, oversized, modern HDTV in the front room. Vilma's Panasonic is turned on to one of those shows where people suing other people take their case to a TV judge and let him rule one way or the other. The lady on the left in this case is suing the guy on the right for breach of promise, after he spent her six-hundred dollar wedding reception down payment on a set of spinners for his pickup. The man is countersuing, claiming he wasn't sure she would perform her duties as a wife due to her current state of "no-lay, mai-laise."

"I do love you," she responds to the accusation, "but since I'm the only one with a job, my mojo is no go."

Vilma Kromka wears a terry cloth robe, has curlers in her hair, and furry slippers in the shape of kitty cats on her feet. We're catching her at a bad time, at least I hope this is a bad time. Vilma's face sags like an almost empty balloon, with so many wrinkles she could pass for a roadmap. The whites of her eyes are streaked in red, as is the bridge of her nose. Her teeth are yellowed beyond the help of any whitening strip. Her third or fourth chin rests on her mole-spotted chest. She snacks on a big bag of Megawat Chili Cheese Flavored Doritos.

"Sit," she says.

I don't count, but there must be six or seven end tables, coffee tables, or table tables squashed into the room. If that isn't enough clutter, on top of each are hundreds of knickknacks and bric-a-brac, all in some way, shape, or form of a cat. Calico, feral, Manx, alley, and many more in all shapes and sizes. Cats sipping milk, Halloween cats, black cats, scaredy cats, and cats in a cradle. There is enough cat paraphernalia in the room to fill a feline museum.

The place gives me the willies. I'm not big on cats.

We find seats and all end up sitting next to a different live cat. The room is warm due to a portable propane heater set up under the fireplace mantle, which is also filled up with cat stuff and an eight-inch-high, silver container. The fumes of the heater mix with the stale cigarette smoke, Vilma, and cat odors, making the room a far cry from Chanel N°5. The interior walls are all the same color, a dirty yellowish tint, caused by the trapped nicotine and smoke residue. The drapes, which were once white, are past yellow and on the edge of brown. Vilma's interior designer was either R.J. Reynolds or Felix the Cat.

The cigarette resting in the overflowing, large glass ashtray on the coffee table is close to butt stage. Vilma lights up another, evidently not wanting to break the chain.

"You got my money?" she asks.

"Not yet," I tell her. "We need a little more information."

"Like what?"

"Like, how you feel."

"About what?"

"Your husband passing."

"Was he a quarterback?" Care jumps in to ask.

"No."

"Then what did he pass?" Kelly asks.

"Gas?" Care guesses.

Tiffany jumps in, "That's a big red flag. Nothing's worse than a guy filling up your Egyptian cotton sheets with his own brand of hot air."

So much for me doing all the talking.

"My husband's dead," Vilma announces.

"Oh," Kelly says. "That's not cool."

Back to me doing the talking. "And we want to express our condolences."

"You could have sent a card."

"Dad's not a *card* person," Care tells her.

"We are sorry," I add.

"You don't know what it's like to go through," Vilma says. "It's like a piece of my heart has been removed, and there is nothing to replace it except sorrow. You know how that feels?" Vilma twists the huge diamond she wears on her fourth finger as if it is a screw top on a beer bottle.

"Yes," Tiffany says. "My mother died during a botched liposuction operation."

"It's not the same," Vilma says. "You hadn't waited your whole life to meet the man of your dreams. You didn't feel the magical connection of a man and a woman falling into a deep and unstoppable love. You didn't establish a bond of love so unbreakable only death could pull you apart."

"Well," Tiffany says, "I guess if you put it that way."

Vilma sniffles as she tells her story. "Sergai and I had a bond so strong it superseded time. It pushed the boundaries of our emotions to heights we never could have imagined. And then, in the blink of an eye, it was over."

Tiffany is now sniffling.

"It was like someone reached inside me and tore my heart out," Vilma explains. "Has that ever happened to you?"

Kelly, also sniffling, says, "Once."

What is she talking about? She's in the eighth grade.

"You know what the name Sergai means?" Vilma asks me.

"No," I admit. I'm not big on names.

"Sergai means 'attendant.' A person who caters to your every need, answers your questions, and fills the voids in your life you can't fill yourself. Sergai is a Russian saint; my Sergai was a saint to me."

Vilma is laying it on thicker than my kids pouring syrup on pancakes. "I never knew love until I loved Sergai."

At this point, the only life form in the room not in tears, besides me, are the six sleeping cats scattered about. The waterworks are going full blast with the rest of them. On the TV, a commercial comes on. A lawyer in a three-piece suit, wearing an oversized pair of boxing gloves, comes out swinging and says, "I'm Eddie Floyd, and I'll fight for you!" Eddie continues to spar as the announcer repeats a phone number to call, and then he says, "If you need a real fighting champion in your corner, I can throw the knockout punch and settle any fight once and for all. I'm Eddie Floyd, and I'll fight for you."

Everyone in the room, except me and the cats, continue to weep as Vilma continues her tale of woe. "He was warm, honest, loving, and kind. A gentleman's gentleman. A prince among paupers. When we made love, Sergai would take me to the moon, back to earth, and back to the moon again."

I should go over and cover Care's ears.

"Our lovemaking drove our bodies and souls into such orgasmic climaxes the earth would rumble beneath us."

Call me a cynic, but I'm having a problem with a fifty-something, dumpy, curler-wearing woman munching Chili Cheese Doritos using the term "orgasmic climaxes."

"I can feel your pain, Vilma," Tiffany says, dabbing her wet eyes.

"So can I," Kelly says.

"You don't know pain until you've lost the man of your dreams."

"I slammed my finger in a car door once," Care tells her. "That really hurt."

"Pain to the body is nothing compared to pain to your soul."

There is a break in the action while everyone weeps. On the TV, the judge rules the future groom has to recoup his fiancée the six hundred, plus interest, and the two of them attend a "How to be Married" course before they tie the knot. The guy rolls his eyes upward to express his displeasure. I'm pretty sure if his fiancée didn't have a job, the guy would announce on national television, "I'm outta here and outta here right now."

"How did Sergai die?" I ask.

"It's too painful to replay. I have vowed never to voice in words what happened to my love."

"Could you give me a hint?"

"A broken heart."

"That's what I was going to guess," Tiffany says.

I ask, "And his death has affected you physically?"

"Look at me."

Unfortunately, we don't have much choice.

"I can barely get up and out of bed some mornings," Vilma says.

"Neither can I," Tiffany agrees, but her malady is due to the amount of alcohol consumed the night before.

"I can't sleep. I can't go out. I have no appetite."

By the amount of Dorito dust around her mouth, her last claim is debatable.

"The pain is so great I can no longer perform even the simplest tasks."

"Such as?" I ask.

"Cleaning, getting dressed, and bathing."

Evidence is everywhere, especially the latter.

"It's like my mind can no longer tell my body how to perform the mundane duties of everyday life. I'm constantly exhausted, depressed, and stuck in neutral."

"It's been six months since he's been gone; are you getting any better?"

"Worse."

Tiffany rises from her spot on the couch, waking the cat next to her. She's weeping a bit less as she moves to the mantle and comments on the silver piece amidst cat cornucopia. "This looks interesting. Is it real silver?"

"It's him," Vilma says.

"Huh?" Tiffany doesn't understand. She picks the item up, brings it down to her, and fiddles with the top. "What's inside?"

Vilma shrieks. "Don't spill him."

Tiffany pops the top of the urn open, looks inside, and takes one whiff, which almost curls her eyebrows. "Whew!" She slams the top back on. "What's in here?"

"Sergai."

Vilma quickly rises from the couch and grabs the urn back from Tiffany. "That's all I have left of him."

"He smells like an old ashtray."

Vilma cradles the urn in her arms like a newborn. With tears in her eyes, she screams, "Why are you people doing this to me? Can't you see I'm in enough pain already?"

"Maybe we should be leaving," I announce.

Vilma's anger continues. "Do I look like a healthy person to you? One who could hold down a job, live a normal life, and ever find happiness again?"

I don't answer, but Kelly and Care do, "No."

"Why can't you just pay me my money? Stop harassing me, forcing me to go see your shrinks, treating me as if I am a criminal?"

"I'm just trying to do my job," I tell her.

"Haven't I suffered enough?"

"Maybe," I say, knowing it is not the answer she wants to hear.

I stand and signal my crew to exit stage left. I scan the entire room before leaving and tell her, "We'll be in touch, Vilma."

Even before the front door closes behind us, Tiffany says, "The woman's living in a cat kennel. I wonder if she pees in the litter box."

"Quiet."

"Did you see that ring?" Tiffany can't shut up. "Was that hideous or what?"

I lead the females off the porch and head for Tiffany's

Lexus.

"I thought it was really sad," Care says.

"Me too," Kelly agrees with her sister for maybe the second time in her life. "I think you should give her the money."

"Let's not get carried away here," Tiffany says, a chip right off her father's block.

We climb into the Lexus, adults in the front, kids in the back. Tiffany fires it up and blasts the heater. We're warm in no time.

"It doesn't make sense," I comment.

"It certainly doesn't," Tiffany agrees. "A woman with that many cats never gets married."

"Maybe Sergai was a cat lover too," Care suggests. "And that was what brought them together."

Kelly says, "I want to fall in love as deeply as Vilma and Sergai."

"Please wait until after you get your learner's permit, okay, Kelly."

"God, Dad, you're so unromantic."

"Did anyone notice anything strange in the room?"

"The whole room was strange," Tiffany says. "I thought I was in the middle of Catatonia."

"Dad, can I get a cat?" Care asks.

"No."

"Why not? I'd like to have a pet."

"I can't afford kids, how could I afford a pet?" I tell her.

"Darn."

"Didn't you people notice anything missing from the room?" I ask for the second time.

No one speaks.

"Tiffany?" I single out my so-called protégée.

"Ah, I'm thinking it over."

I give them a few seconds to redeem themselves and give up. "There were no pictures anywhere. On the walls, on the counters, on the mantle, none."

"What do you mean?" Tiffany asks. "There were cat pictures everywhere."

"Pictures of the two of them, Vilma and Sergai," I explain. "Don't you think if you lost the love of your life, you'd have his picture all over?"

"Maybe she had them all in another room?" Care says.

"Where he was taking her *to the moon*," Kelly says. A comment I don't need to hear from her.

"Maybe in the bedroom they had some boudoir photography," Tiffany says. "She's in a little slinky, silk harem girl outfit, and he's a half-naked, invading Mongol warrior."

"I certainly hope that image never enters my photographic memory."

"Dad, that's mean. Sergai and Vilma were in love, and you have to respect that," Kelly tells me.

"Something is wrong, and I don't know what," I tell my group.

"Probably Vilma in the harem girl outfit," Tiffany says.

I sit and contemplate for a few seconds.

"Dad, I'm hungry," Care announces. "Can we go to McDonald's?"

"No. You go to McDonald's, Care, you'll end up looking like Vilma."

"I bet Vilma eats cat food," Kelly says.

"I bet she eats cat," Tiffany says as she pulls a manila folder from the space between her seat and the console. "Here, Mr. Sherlock. The lady who found Vilma's address gave me this."

I open the file. It is a summary of the pertinent paperwork concerning the dispersal of Sergai's life insurance payout. "Did you go through it, Tiffany?"

"No, I knew you would, so what would be the point of me doing it too?"

"Another management decision of yours?"

"Yeah, I guess you could say that."

I open the file and start reading, but I'm interrupted. "Where are we going now, Dad?" Kelly asks as if I'm the camp counselor for the day.

Tiffany answers for me. "I don't know about you people, but I could use a spa treatment. I can still feel all that cat creepiness creeping all over my skin."

"Me too," Kelly says.

Probably not a bad idea. "You girls go with Tiffany; I'll meet you later."

Shouts of joy erupt from the backseat.

"Where are you going to go, Dad?"

"One of us has to make a living."

"And we're glad it's not us, Mr. Sherlock."

CHAPTER 5

I drive east and stop at the Merlo Public Library on Belmont, not far from the lake. The place is packed, more with people wanting a break from the cold than wanting to improve their minds. I find a spot way in the back stacks, take off my coat, sit, and open the Kromka file.

Vilma and Sergai were married eleven months ago in Las Vegas, Nevada at the Hunka-Burnin' Love Chapel. The pastor performing the service was Reverend Elvis Aron Priestly, and the official witness was Maralyn Monroe. There is no mention of a best man or maid of honor being present. A copy of the license of matrimony, complete with drawn-on sequins, is stapled to the bill for services, which totaled three hundred thirty-two dollars. Vilma and Sergai chose the Hound Dog package, which included one rose, three songs of Elvis' choice, ten digital photos, and an upload of their "I do's" to YouTube, "So all your friends can share in your happiness."

Touching.

According to the document, Vilma's birthdate was May 31, 1960, which makes her a fifty-something Gemini. I didn't suspect after seeing her she was a cougar, but evidently she is/was one because Sergai's birthday was July 29, 1970. He's a Leo.

Sergai Levenchenko was born in Moscow when it was the old USSR, or CCCP if you're a native. With a name like Levenchenko, I don't blame Vilma for sticking with Kromka. There is a Russian birth certificate, marriage license, and death certificate in the file, completing the circle of life. From the report from the mortuary where the after death services were performed, the cause of death is listed as myocardial infarction, better known as a heart attack. The dates match with Vilma's account. His remains were cremated.

What isn't in the file, concerning Sergai, are any naturalization papers, green card, citizenship record, passport, or driver's license. All I find is a copy of an immigration form partially filled out.

There is a stack of paper from the Richmond Insurance Company. A copy of the policy, which was executed three months after they were married, copies of checks Vilma sent to pay for the premiums, and the medical exam records revealing a physically fit Sergai. There is no name or address of the clinic where the procedure was performed. Sergai's blood pressure was 140 over 86, which is much better than mine. He was six feet tall, weighed 180, had type O blood, had no history of cancer in his family, and didn't smoke. A picture of health. Although I would not expect to see one, there is no photo of Sergai in the file.

The last piece of paper in the file is a copy of the check for $500,000, made out to Vilma Kromka.

I close the file, get up, and go to the front desk to sign up for the next available computer. I'm told I am thirteenth on the list. The people who came into the library to get warm must also be looking for ways to stay busy. I go back to my chair and reread the entire file.

There is a guy in a small storefront on a side street off Belmont who makes the best Philly cheesesteak sandwich this side of Philly. I don't eat a lot of meat, but I decide to walk over and splurge. I order a six-inch special, watch it being prepared, pay my tab, and find a spot to chow down. Eating one of these sloppy sandwiches is an art. You eat standing up, your feet spread wider than your hips, a foot or two behind the high-top counter. You lean forward, resting on your elbows, with the wax paper the sandwich is wrapped in spread out beneath your chin. You grab half the sandwich with one hand, steady your leaning body with the other, and attack your lunch like a lion at an antelope buffet. Bits of bread, meat, and lots of juice come squirting out and splatter on the paper beneath. You don't care if the juice runs out of your mouth and down your chin because it is part of the culinary experience. The Philly tastes great. You can't stop eating. And, because of the position you're in, no juice, grease, or crud of any kind stains your clothes or coat. You finish the first half, straighten up, burp, take a deep breath or two, have a sip of whatever you're drinking, and position yourself for the second and final round. Delicious. I leave the place stuffed and satisfied. The walk back to the library in the cold air is the perfect antidote for feeling drowsy once I sit down. I only have to wait fifteen minutes when I return to the library to be assigned a computer.

I Google Sergai Levenchenko and get zilch. I change the spelling a few times, and the closest hit I get is a tennis store in Southern California named Levchenco, which closed a few years ago. I find a death records site and put in Sergai's name, but the site asks me for money, so I log off. I Google Vilma Kromka and get the same zilch. I Google the name Sergai and discover the guy who started Google was named Sergai. I bet he gets Googled a lot. I have six minutes of computer time left, but I'm bored, so I give up my seat to a homeless guy who doesn't impress me as being tech savvy, but ya never know, maybe he's an out-of-work programmer working on a new app that lets homeless people know where its best to set up camp for the night.

I get my things, go outside, and call Tiffany. She doesn't answer. I leave a message: "Please tell my kids their no-fun father is on the way to get them and drive them back to reality."

***

The Re-New-Me Spa is on Oak Street. It's trendy, expensive, and caters to women who have little to do except reach new heights of relaxation on a weekly basis. The spa's customers are people who don't have jobs, don't do housework, and have live-in nannies to watch their kids. The only amount of stress they have in their lives is the stress their personal trainers put on them during their gym workouts. Tiffany is a regular at the place. As the front desk staff sees me enter, I feel as welcome as a liver spot. I announce to the perky, tanned receptionist my reason for being there and take a seat in their well-appointed lobby. I pick up a magazine and read how the latest monumental breakthrough in breast enhancement surgery is making it "almost impossible for your friends or loved ones to detect." The article's before and after pictures are especially revealing. The next article I read concerns "the challenges of attaining perfect cleavage." Just as I get to the page with the pictures, I'm interrupted.

"Dad, this place is heaven," Kelly tells me as she comes out into the lobby. "We have to find a way of adding a massage to my weekly routine."

"We?"

"I'm feeling so renewed."

"Wish I was."

"Dad, aren't you happy I'm feeling wonderful?"

"Not really."

Care and Tiffany follow.

"Hi, Dad."

"How was the massage, Care?"

"It was okay although I wasn't wild about getting naked in front of that lady."

"Don't worry, you'll get used to it," Tiffany assures my youngest.

"There's no hurry on that, Care."

I stand and put on my coat. "You two thank Tiffany for paying for your session." I give these instructions for two reasons.

"Thank you, Tiffany."

"You're welcome, little dudettes."

As we exit the spa, Tiffany asks me, "What are we doing next with Vilma?"

"Tiffany, to be honest with you, I haven't the faintest idea."

CHAPTER 6

I drop the girls off at their mother's, tell them I love them, and start on my way home. I get about three blocks and change direction. Something is bothering me.

Most good cops I've known either have or have developed a certain "cop" sense about people. A patrolman can be riding down a street, see someone walking along, and just know that person is guilty of something or up to no good. For a detective, the sense comes in the ability to instantly read people. A good detective can chat with a stranger for only a few minutes and immediately "get" what the person is all about. It is not an accumulation of facts or knowledge being revealed that triggers the sense, but more of an ethereal feeling coming from the person a detective recognizes. In my years as a CPD detective, my sense wasn't right 100% of the time, but I bet it was close to ninety.

I bring this up now because after my meeting with Vilma Kromka, my cop sense has been pretty much knocked senseless. The woman was a walking, talking, loafing mass of contradictions. She hardly looked the babe/lover type, but she talked like a character in one of those chick lit, bodice-ripper novels. She had a house full of cats and cat crud, but she walked dogs as a sideline. She didn't look like she could lift anything heavier than a cigarette, but she claimed to be an oil change specialist. I would love to see her in her Jiffy Lube uniform. Most bothersome is why a fit and trim guy, ten years her junior, would fall for her, much less want to take her to the moon and back.

I drive back to her place, park across the street, leave the car running, sit back, and watch. The sun sets before five, and a light goes on in her front room. At five thirty, the light goes off. I wait for Vilma to exit out the front door, but after a few minutes, I pull out of the spot, drive down the block, and enter the alley. Sure enough, out of a driveway mid-block, a new Buick backs out of a garage. I follow, but the rut in the alley is so high the bottom of my Toyota scrapes the ice and snow of the long, high ridge in the middle of the alley, and my car grinds to a stop like a snowplow up against an iceberg. By the time I back up, get two wheels of the car on the left side tire track, and get the right side two wheels riding on the high ridge, the Buick has sped up and driven out of my sight. I proceed up the alley at a forty-five-degree angle, get back on Ridgeway, and re-park in my previous parking space. I wait another thirty minutes, realize Vilma's trip was no trip to the Jewel, pull out of the space, and drive home.

The apartment is freezing when I step inside, and I go through the usual procedure to warm it up. My gas bill for the month is going to rival the national debt. I have the leftover tetrazzini for dinner, make a cup of green tea, and sit down to go over the Kromka file one more time. In this review, I gain less than I gained the first time around, which was pretty much zilch.

***

The weather lets up a bit Wednesday morning; it's only nine below zero with a wind chill of minus twenty. I can almost feel spring in the air.

Tiffany picks me up at ten. I asked her to pick me up at nine. She's fifteen minutes past picking me up on Tiffany time.

"Where are we going, Mr. Sherlock?" she asks, driving down my street.

"See a shrink."

If she hadn't had her seat belt fastened, she would have jumped right out of the front seat. "Did my dad call you and tell you to do this?" she screams my way.

"No, your father never speaks to me."

"Well, I'm not going." She stops the car in the middle of the block. "If I have to tell one more person how I feel, my brain is going to explode."

"Tiffany ..."

"You know how many couches I've had to lie on? How many inkblots I've had to describe? How many words I had to associate?" She pauses. "Do you?"

"No."

"I don't either because I never counted, but let me tell you, it's a lot."

"Tiffany, we're not going to your shrink," I inform her.

"We're going to see Vilma's shrink."

"Vilma has a shrink, too?"

"Yes."

"Well it's about time the foot's wearing the other Jimmy Choo."

***

The offices of Dr. H. Oliva Lunay, Psy.D. are on South Michigan Avenue, one street south of the Chicago Cultural Center. The building, which is filled with psychiatrists and psychologists, has been referred to as Anxiety Asylum, Treatment Tower, and Analysis Avenue. Dr. H's office, the only office in the offices of Dr. Lunay, is on the thirty-second floor.

"I'm Richard Sherlock, and this is my assistant, Tiffany. Thanks for seeing us on such short notice," I start off our meeting.

"You're late."

"Sorry."

"You know that a pattern of arriving late is a clear sign that the person has a strong dislike for the task they have been sent out to perform."

If that's the case, I should exist on Tiffany time. "I didn't know that Doctor. Did you know that, Tiffany?"

Tiffany says, "I wasn't listening."

"Refusal to listen would be in the same category of aversion behavior," Dr. Lunay adds.

"I'm still not listening," Tiffany tells her.

Tiffany seems a bit on the edge of an edge.

"Dr. Lunay, we're here to talk about Vilma Kromka."

"I can't."

"Can't what?" Tiffany asks, obviously listening.

"Speak of a patient."

"Why not?" Tiffany takes charge.

"Doctor-client confidentiality. What's said in here, what happens in here, stays in here."

"This place doesn't look like Vegas to me," Tiffany says.

"I am sensing a suppressed release of repressed animosity," the doc says to Tiffany.

"And I'm sensing you ain't making sense," Tiffany barks back to her.

"I have a special program for anger management," Dr. Lunay informs her. "I call it my 'How to manage your anger without getting angry' program."

"I can mange my anger to get angry on my own," Tiffany snaps at her. "Thank you very much."

This is certainly a side of Tiffany I haven't seen.

"Revealing anger when the topic of anger arises is an angry sign of agitated aggression," Dr. Lunay responds.

"Yeah well, you want to make something of it, Doc?" Tiffany puts up her manicured and moisturized dukes.

I get between the two like a referee, "Shall we return to the topic at hand?" I pause for the two to cool down. "Since we both are representing Richmond Insurance, and the discussion concerns a Richmond client, we are keeping it in the Richmond family."

"I'm sorry, I have sworn an oath of privilege and have my reputation to protect." Dr. Lunay sits back in her chair as if she is not going to speak another word the rest of our session.

"We're not here to hear the intimate details of your meetings with Ms. Kromka," I calmly tell her. "What we need to know is why you approved her disability claim due to post-traumatic grief disorder."

Dr. Lunay takes her thumb and forefinger, pushes them together, and pretends to zip an imaginary zipper across her lips.

"We're not asking you to divulge any conversation, or personal revelations, about Ms. Kromka."

Dr. Lunay sits statue still. Her expression reminds me of the famous picture of Sitting Bull sitting silently.

"We just want to know why you voted yea instead of nay."

Dr. Lunay holds her non-response position like a kid playing freeze tag.

"Start talking, lady," Tiffany says. "We don't got all day."

Dr. Lunay breaks her silence to bark at Tiffany. "You wouldn't want me to talk about you, if you were the topic of such conversation, would you?"

"People like you only wish people would say about them what they say about me."

"Personally, I could care less," I tell the two. "If I spent time thinking about what people say about me, I wouldn't get any sleep."

"It is obvious you are transferring your unresolved anger to people and objects not responsible for your subliminal feelings," the doc challenges Tiffany.

Tiffany, who has taken out her phone and is punching the screen, either making a call or playing Angry Birds, informs Dr. Lunay, "The only transferring I do, lady, is between savings and checking."

Dr. Lunay gives Tiffany a stare that could melt 24-karat gold. Tiffany returns in kind.

"Can we please return to the subject of Ms. Kromka?" I plead.

Dr. Lunay's face again stiffens like quick-drying plaster.

"You heard him, toots," Tiffany tells her. "Talk, or I'll make you talk."

Not only is this a side of Tiffany I've never seen, it's a side I have no interest in seeing again.

"Doctor," I break in again and try to reason with the doc. "We're not asking for personal details, but we need to know why you made the decision you made."

"My lips are sealed."

Tiffany is now texting faster than a neurotic thumb twiddler on uppers. She stops, waits, and a *boing* boings from her phone.

I continue, "I have to find out what I'm dealing with here—"

Tiffany interrupts. Facing the doc, she reads what's on the screen. "How much money did Richmond Insurance pay you last year?"

Dr. Lunay doesn't speak, but I see a few new cracks in her plaster.

"Would eighty-seven thousand four hundred thirty-seven dollars and seventy-three cents sound about right?" Tiffany continues.

Dr. Lunay's face shatters.

"And you are on the preferred list of Richmond doctors?" Tiffany continues her interrogation.

"How do you know such information?" Dr. Lunay nervously asks.

I hate it when people answer a question with a question.

"My financial records are privileged information," the doc states.

"Well, lady," Tiffany says, "if you don't start talking,

starting tomorrow the future amount you're going to get is going to be real easy to figure."

"Says who?"

"Says me, Tiffany Richmond."

"Richmond, as in Richmond?" the doc asks.

"Blood is thicker than money, Doc."

Dr. Lunay's zipper unzips quicker than an ADHD sufferer acting out an aggression. "There are seven stages of grief: shock, denial, anger, bargaining, guilt, depression, and acceptance. Vilma is stuck on number six. She shows numerous signs of severe depression including weight gain, poor eating habits, sleep deprivation, exhaustion ..." Dr. Lunay is going on as if she's the guest on a radio talk show. "... sadness, breaks from reality, inability to perform daily tasks, and hallucinatory behavior."

"Could any of that be caused by hanging around too many cats?" Tiffany asks.

"I would doubt it."

"I hate to be the cynic, but could she be faking it?" I ask.

"In my years as a doctor, health care professional, and seeing hundreds of cases of both severe and mild depression, there is no possible way she could fool the trained eye of *this* professional."

Dr. H. Oliva Lunay certainly has no problem with self-worth.

"Could it only be a question of time before she gets better?" I ask.

"These cases sometimes go on for years."

"She was only married to the guy for a few months," I toss in.

"It doesn't matter," the doc says. "It is the intensity of the relationship which matters."

There's the "taking her to the moon" thing again.

Tiffany asks, "Let's say she met another guy and started getting some action; you think that could cure her?"

"No."

"I realize there is a grief factor when one loses another, but allowing a price tag to be put on it could be 'big trouble in River City' for an insurance company, Doc," I explain.

"Loss of love to the emotions is like loss of blood to the heart," Lunay explains and adds, "Vilma's distress is like the river in River City running dry."

"How's she going to get over this?"

"Therapy, lots of therapy."

"Maybe I should ask some of the guys I've dumped how they got over me," Tiffany suggests, "and pass along some tips."

"Interesting take on psychiatric research," Dr. Lunay says with her tongue firmly in her cheek.

"You have to understand, Doctor, you could be opening up a big can of worms here," I say to make the point clear.

Tiffany adds, "And Richmond Insurance doesn't want to be inviting a lot of people to go fishing with 'em."

"As a medical professional, all I can say is ..." Dr. H. Oliva Lunay pauses for dramatic effect. "That's my prognosis, and I'm sticking to it."

CHAPTER 7

We are in Tiffany's car heading north on Lake Shore Drive.

"I never knew you had such an aversion to people in the mental health field, Tiffany."

"The reason shrinks become shrinks is so they can talk to people who are loonier than they are."

"Not a very positive attitude, Tiffany."

"All I know is every appointment I ever had with a shrink, I felt worse coming out than I felt going in."

"Then why did you go?"

"I think it was easier for my dad to send me to a shrink than to talk to me after Mom died."

"I'm sorry to hear that, Tiffany."

"My dad doesn't talk to me because he thinks I'm some screwed-up, air-headed idiot." She fishtails around a slow driver like Jeff Gordon on a wet NASCAR track. "That's why we have to solve this case, Mr. Sherlock. So I can show my dad who I really am, what I'm capable of, and make him proud to be my father."

Oh jeesh.

"Get off at Belmont."

"Back to the cat lady? Haven't we already been there and done that already, Mr. Sherlock?"

"It ain't over until the fat lady sings, Tiffany."

"Oh my God! Vilma with a karaoke machine? That'll drive me right back to the shrink."

***

The building immediately to the south of Vilma's is a restored three-flat. There is no one home on the first floor, but a young mom answers the door on the second. Her baby is in a playpen in the middle of the living room.

"Yes?"

"Hi, my name is Richard, and this is Tiffany, and we're from Lincoln Park Real Estate."

The woman cuts me off. "We moved in a year ago; we don't want to sell."

"No," I cordially say, "we're not here to talk about your property." I chuckle and pause. "We're here because we've had a difficult time reaching your next-door neighbor—"

She cuts me off again. "That awful house? The agent who sold us this place told us 'she was as good as gone,' but I haven't seen a sign go up."

"What can you tell us about her?"

"She doesn't shovel snow, clean up her yard, and her cats crap all over the neighborhood."

"I hate that," Tiffany says.

"Do you see her much?" I ask.

"Not now."

"When the weather's better?"

"She's not very friendly."

"Does she live alone?"

"Probably."

"No husband?"

"I don't think so."

"Boyfriend?"

"I doubt it."

"Not even six months ago?"

She pauses, then asks, "Have you seen her?"

"Yes," Tiffany answers, "unfortunately."

"You ever see any other cars besides hers using her garage?"

"No."

The woman gives me an odd look, and I can't say I blame her.

"So, you don't know her well enough to maybe introduce us to her?"

"No."

The next neighbor we find at home lives directly across the street from Vilma.

"Can't you people leave us alone? We don't care what its worth, whether or not you have buyers ready to buy, or that you can put us in a bigger place for less money. We don't want to sell. We want to stay. You real estate people are leeches. Leave us alone." The lady finishes by slamming the door in our face.

"That went well, Mr. Sherlock."

Before the third homeowner on our neighborhood canvass opens the door, Tiffany says to me, “Let me handle this one.”

A middle-aged guy with a jowly face and extended love handles takes one look at Tiffany and says, “Whatever you’re selling lady, I’ll take two as long as you come along with it.”

“I’m not selling anything,” Tiffany says without emotion. “We’re from the City of Chicago Department of Health, and there has been a complaint about the number of stray cats in the neighborhood.”

“It’s that crazy loon across the street. She must have thirty cats,” the guy says, his eyes transfixed on the opening of Tiffany’s mink coat.

“She live alone?”

“No, I just told you she’s got like thirty cats living with her.” He pauses. “Would you like to come in? I’ve got a new martini recipe I’d like to try.” He gives me a *Not you buddy, only her* stare.

“Sorry, I’m on duty.” Tiffany continues, “Have you seen men entering the home, husbands, boyfriends, or male cat sitters?”

“Not lately.”

“Six months ago?”

He doesn’t answer. Instead he says, “I bet you’re the kind of woman who likes a real man’s man.”

“Oh, yeah,” Tiffany tells him.

“Well, I was the lead singer in a rock band my junior year in high school.”

“I’m not a bit surprised.”

“Stop by later and I’ll show you my *Macarena*.” He gives her a toothy smile.

He has salami stuck in his teeth.

“I’ll bet you could really shake it down,” Tiffany says.

“Shake it down, shake it down, shake it down to the ground,” he says.

“Maybe when I’m more in a musical mood, I’ll stop by.” Tiffany gets back on topic. “Anything else you can tell us about the cat lady across the street?”

The guy performs a few moves as he sings, “Heeeey Macarena.”

I consider telling the guy, “Don’t quit your day job,” but I don’t because I doubt if he has a day job.

We leave.

It seems pretty pointless to continue questioning the neighbors, mainly because it's too darn cold out. My feet feel like I've been walking barefoot behind a Zamboni machine.

We go back to Tiffany's car. She fires it up, turns on the heat, and I begin to thaw. "Doesn't it make you crazy when all these slime balls put the hit on you, Tiffany?"

"Naw, you get used to it after a while."

"If it were me, I don't think I could handle it."

"I don't think you have too much to worry about, Mr. Sherlock."

Tifffany pulls the Lexus into the street. "Where to next?"

"Get on the Dan Ryan going south."

"Where are we going?"

"Since we didn't have any luck with the bride, we'll start in on the husband."

"Are we going to question him?" She asks.

"No."

"Why not?"

"He's dead."

"Oh yeah."

CHAPTER 8

Chappie Foote lives with his mother and aunt in the Mt. Greenwood neighborhood on the South Side. The house is an old bungalow with two bedrooms and one bath on the first floor. Downstairs has a full basement and bath. This is where Chappie lives. His aunt takes care of his mother, and his mother takes care of him. It is about the only thing his mother can remember how to do. Funny how the mind works.

Chappie, now probably fifty, grew up in this Catholic, German/Slav, blue-collar neighborhood and was destined to be a pipe fitter or steelworker, until he contracted a weird disease at the age of ten. It started with black marks appearing on his neck beneath his jawbone. The doctors had no idea of the cause. Within a year, the black marks became black bumps, and in another six months, they became black marbles. Any chances of Chappie becoming a male model or a member of a boy band were dashed. He was ugly and getting uglier by the day. His neck resembled an oblong bag of lumpy ugli fruit.

Chappie was taken to a number of doctors and finally to Children's Hospital in Lincoln Park, where they diagnosed the condition as Proteus syndrome, a malady named after the Greek god Proteus, who could change his shape at will. Chappie went through a battery of procedures. None worked. Specialists saw him. The marbles grew into golf balls and started working their way up into his face. The doctors operated, slitting open his throat and cutting out the tumors as if they were welders removing dingleberries off a welded joint. After the surgery and lab sample analysis, the diagnosis was changed to neurofibromatosis type 1. When giving Chappie the news, the doctor told him he didn't have the exact disease Joseph Merrick, the Elephant Man, had but a lesser strain of the malady. Chappie replied, "So I have baby Elephant Man's disease? Wow, what a relief that is."

From that point on, every couple of years, Chappie goes under the knife and has his tumors removed. Not fun. He's got more scars than a subpar sabermaster who refuses to give up the sport. Soon Chappie got sick of people staring at him as if they were watching the movie *Mask*. His mother pulled him out of school, his father took a powder, and Chappie moved into the basement, where he still resides thirty-some years later.

Around eighteen years of age, through a friend of a friend of a friend of the family next door, Chappie got hired at a local Chicago radio station. His one and only duty was to sit in his basement, listen to his radio station's competing stations, and write down the names of every commercial that came on over a week's time. A couple days he would listen to the morning and afternoon drive times, other days he would listen from 6 p.m. until midnight, one night a week he would stay up all night. He was reliable. He worked cheap. Word spread and other radio stations employed his services. It was tedious, boring, mind-numbing work, especially when he had to listen to a station he didn't like. He grew to especially hate the big band sound. But it was a job and gave Chappie a bit of self-worth.

After about three or four years, the radio monitoring jobs petered out, but with the money he was able to save, Chappie bought himself a shortwave police scanner and graduated to monitoring emergency police and fire department bands. He quickly learned to pick out the good calls from the bad and sell the information to slimy lawyers who wanted a leg up on their ambulance chasing competition. He didn't enjoy the work, but it was work. The biggest problem he had was the amount of time between the emergency calls. Some nights he'd sit and not get a one, but instead of getting angry and frustrated, he used the time to study how it all worked. He was fascinated with the intricacies of communicating through the airways. Chappie studied the engineering, the history, and the current developments in the business. Radio led him to shortwave, which led him to television, which led him right into the exploding world of silicon technology. What Gates, Jobs, and Packard were doing blew Chappie away. He couldn't get enough of this new world. He read every book, pamphlet, and magazine article he could find. He'd send his mother to the library to borrow manuals. He'd call universities and asked questions. When the Internet arrived, Chappie was one of the first to sign on. And, for the first time in his life, he was an equal. As long as he was on the World Wide Web, it didn't matter that he was stuck in a basement with tumors growing on his neck like weeds after a rainstorm.

From one AM/FM radio and police scanner on one small table, the basement was filled with computers, routers, screens, keyboards, and whatever else computer geeks use. He loved every minute of it. He communicated with other geeks like himself through cyberspace and found the closest thing to actual friends. Word spread on what he could do, and he started to get assignments, jobs, and problems to work on, and it was bye-bye to the slimy lawyers. Chappie started to make some real money. He'd never be Bill Gates rich, but he could help support his mother and himself. He bought an antenna for the back yard, installed small satellite dishes on the roof, and ran enough wire and cable to equal a telephone switching station.

I found Chappie when I was investigating a murder-for-hire case. A soon-to-be ex-wife thought she would be invisible buying an ad on Craigslist for a cheap hit man. She was wrong. With the help of Chappie's technical forte, we set up a sting and caught the idiot woman, making for a slam-dunk divorce for her husband. I liked working with Chappie. I found that once you got over the initial shock of his looks he was a nice guy. And smart, really smart. I used him to find missing persons, cases where the police computer system was inadequate, and in situations where information was needed from deeper inside other systems. I was in awe of his skills. He could handle an Internet keyboard better than LeBron dribbled a basketball. I could give him a name or a topic, and in a day, he'd have enough information to make the entire search team at Google jealous.

I don't mention any of this to Tiffany.

We arrive at the house before noon.

"You sure he's going to be home, Mr. Sherlock?"

"Positive."

His mother answers the door.

"Is Chappie home?"

"Who?"

"Chappie Foote."

"You sure you got the right house, Mr. Sherlock?" Tiffany joins the question parade.

I ask the woman, "Is your sister home?"

The aunt comes up from behind, "Oh, hi."

"Remember me?"

"I think so."

"I don't," Mom says.

"Richard Sherlock."

"Of course, please come in."

"We shouldn't let just anyone come in the house," Mom says.

"He's a cop," the aunt explains.

"Well, he used to be," Tiffany corrects her.

The two women lead us to a door and point us down a rickety stairway. "Chappie doesn't get out much anymore; he'll love seeing you," the aunt tells me.

The dark stairway before us would be the perfect setting for a slasher movie's slasher scene. Tiffany is hesitant; she stands behind me at the top and cowers like a small child. "Maybe you should go down, Mr. Sherlock, and call me when the coast is clear."

"Oh no, Tiffany." I pull her behind me as I start down, clearing the cobwebs with my hand as the wooden staircase eerily creaks on my every step. "This is going to be fun."

"It isn't so far."

"Don't you enjoy meeting new, interesting people?"

"No."

When I'm halfway down, I hear "Hey, dude." For some reason, Chappie calls me dude.

"Chappie."

I have to strengthen my grip on Tiffany's wrist because once she sees Chappie, she almost levitates back up the stairs.

"Oh my God."

"Chappie, this is my assistant, Tiffany."

He turns to give her his full frontal. "Don't be scared. I know I'm ugly. When I walk in the bank, they turn off the camera."

Tiffany is speechless.

"How you been, Chappie?"

"Good, dude. Guess what. I can now turn milk into yogurt just by looking at it."

Tiffany stares at him as if he's the measles virus. "Don't stare, Tiffany," I tell her.

"It's okay; I'm used to it," Chappie says as he sits behind his massive console. "I have a feeling Tiffany is too."

"What are you doing?" I ask.

"I'm working on a new website named *Hermit*. It's going to be an antisocial networking site."

Tiffany remains in suspended shock. Her mouth open, jaw slack, eyes fixed on Chappie's scars, misshapen face, and bad haircut.

"Hope you don't mind us dropping in unannounced," I say.

"Dude, you're a sight for sore eyes, and my eyes get real sore staring at these screens all day." Chappie removes a pair of coke-bottle thick eyeglasses.

Tiffany must think she is in the middle of a comedic, science fiction monster movie with a melodramatic storyline. She doesn't know whether to scream, laugh, or cry. She stands in front of a small man who's uglier than a deformed catfish.

To break her stare, I give her a quick tour of the place. To the left is a bathroom, to the right a bed. The remainder of the room is filled with something electronic. Home sweet home. "What do you think of the place, Tiffany?" I ask. "Want me to get you the name of Chappie's decorator?"

Tiffany's lips move, but no sound emits from her mouth.

"The place is getting so crowded I barely have room to change my mind," Chappie says.

"Chappie, I got a job for you."

"Do you have any money, dude?"

"No."

"Money is the root of all evil, but a man needs roots."

"Tiffany, do you have any money?" I ask. This is an excellent time to ask Tiffany to foot the bill. No pun intended.

"Ah." The shock is slowly wearing off.

"What do you need?" Chappie asks.

I open the folder I brought along, remove a few of the pages on Sergai, and lay them in front of Chappie. "I need you to *chappie* this guy." I turn to Tiffany to explain. "When Googling doesn't cut it, Chappie will *chappie* him."

"Who is the guy?"

"Russian, Latvian, or whatever-an."

"These guys can be tough to trace," Chappie warns.

"Husband of a lady named Vilma Kromka, who lives on the North Side."

Chappie takes the file and finds the Vilma pages. "When were they married?"

"Eleven months ago in Vegas."

"People get married, then have to solve problems they never had before they got married." He looks up from the pages. "What are you looking for?"

"I have no clue; that's why I'm here."

"Dude, you're as clueless as a detective with amnesia."

"Don't laugh; I've been there."

Chappie types into his computer something he reads from the file.

"I'll need some up-front cash, dude."

"How much?"

"A thousand bucks," he announces. "But for you, dude, seven fifty."

"Tiffany?"

Tiffany takes out her phone and finally speaks, "Do you take PayPal?"

"Of course."

After the money has flown through cyberspace, Chappie turns to Tiffany, "Thank you."

Tiffany tries to smile.

"Also, thanks for coming down. It's not often I get to see the total antithesis of myself."

Tiffany looks to me for explanation.

"Antithesis means opposite, Tiffany."

"That's quite a compliment coming from you," she says, breaking her silence.

"Beauty is only skin deep, but I have very thick skin."

I tell Chappie, "I also need to borrow a tracking device."

"Why?"

"It's just too darn cold to do a stakeout."

"How cold is it?"

"Is this a joke?" Tiffany asks.

"No, I haven't been upstairs in three months."

***

"Why didn't you tell me what I was in for, Mr. Sherlock?" are the first words out of Tiffany's mouth once we're in her car. "Your friend gave a whole new meaning to the word *butt ugly*."

"I thought the shock might do you good."

"Why?"

"You have to start seeing people for who they are and not

just what they look like, Tiffany."

"The guy has to sneak up on his own mirror, Mr. Sherlock. He's scarier than a failed face-lift."

"It wasn't his fault that he looks worse than Freddy Krueger on a bad day."

"Compared to Chappie, Freddy Krueger's a stud muffin."

"He's also a very nice guy, Tiffany. If we all had a fraction of some of Chappie's good qualities, the world would be a much better place."

"Not in the looks department, Mr. Sherlock."

"Look past his face, Tiffany. Give the poor guy a chance."

"Are you kidding me? 'Look past his face.' The guy could scare blind kids."

CHAPTER 9

The offices of the Richmond Insurance Company take up six floors of the Aon Center on East Randolph Street. Years ago when Richmond moved in, the building was called the Standard Oil Building, a few years later the name changed to the Amoco Building, and in 1999 became the Aon Center, named after the Aon Insurance Company, which is based in London. For Richmond, being an insurance company housed in the 'Center' of a competitive insurance company was a bit disconcerting at first, but Aon must have made some adjustment on the rent, because Richmond never moved.

The Aon Center is the third tallest structure in Chicago. The Willis Tower, which used to be the Sears Tower and the "World's Tallest Building," is now only "Chicago's Tallest Building." Evidently, if you want to be the tallest, you have to keep subtracting from the total area you include in your survey. I find it interesting that two of the three tallest buildings in Chicago are namesakes of London-based insurance companies. I wonder what Mr. Sears and Mr. Rockefeller would have to say about that.

Tiffany and I sit in the lobby area of the Richmond Claims Department.

"What's the matter, Tiffany?"

"Nothing."

"You're pouting."

"No, I'm not."

"Are you mad at me for not warning you about Chappie yesterday?"

"No." She pauses for three seconds, then says, "And don't ask me if it's female 'cause I'm mad because I hate that."

"I thought you said you weren't mad."

"I'm not."

A woman comes out from behind the reception area and says, "She'll see you now."

Before we rise, Tiffany gets one more shot in, "You're going to get me a lot madder if you don't stop telling me I'm mad if I'm not mad, Mr. Sherlock."

Why do I bother?

As we walk through the maze of cubicles on the floor, our guide asks, “How are you, Tiffany?”

“Why are you asking?” Tiffany snaps back. “You think I’m mad, too?”

The nice lady sees me shrug my shoulders and lets the conversation drop.

We are escorted into a corner office. The woman behind the huge desk rises to come around. She’s quite attractive, dressed in a perfectly tailored, corporate suit in the Hillary Clinton mode. Her subtle diamond earrings sparkle, her lipstick is perfect, and there’s not a hair out of place. Her body is striking, quite heavy on the top but sleek and thin from there south. Wow.

To our escort’s surprise, Tiffany jumps the introduction, “Mr. Sherlock, this is Antoinette Bisonette.” Tiffany puts special emphasis on the “nettes,” pronouncing it “Ann-Twon-NET Biz-Oh-NET.”

The woman pretends not to notice the comment and puts out her hand for me to shake. “It’s pronounced Bis-o-Nay,” she explains. “My friends and you can call me Bree.”

“Hi, I’m Richard Sherlock.”

“Hello, Tiffany, your father told me you’d be in this morning.”

“When?”

“This morning.” She pauses and adds, “Early this morning.”

Tiffany gives her a stare that could defrost a frozen porterhouse in seconds.

“Shall we sit?”

Bree takes the power seat at the conference table. Tiffany and I flank her.

“How may I be of service?”

I speak as Tiffany growls. “We’re working on the Vilma Kromka case.”

Tiffany interrupts, “Where I happen to be the lead investigator.”

“Oh yes,” Bree says, “I’m sure you are.” She gives Tiffany a smug smile. “Please continue, Mr. Sherlock.”

“I—“

“We,” Tiffany interrupts again.

"We," I repeat slowly, "need access to both the current file and the file concerning the life insurance payout on Vilma Kromka's husband's death. After visiting the woman, there seems to be some loose ends I—we—can't seem to get a handle on."

"Loose ends which I detected," Tiffany adds.

"Are you sure those weren't split ends, Tiffy?" Bree asks, twirling a hank of her hair.

"Positive, because I don't waste my time watching football," Tiffany snaps back.

"That's too bad because Jamison and I have room in the skybox this Sunday for the Bears game. I thought maybe you'd like to bring one of your playmates along."

"I'm busy."

"You might want to reconsider; it's going to be fun watching all the people in the stands freezing to death."

"And if I wasn't busy, I'd get busy," Tiffany adds.

I, not we, better get this back on topic before two sets of overly manicured nails are used as weapons. "Is it possible to get copies of the files, plus any information or correspondence pertinent to the case?"

"As the Executive Vice President of the Richmond Claims Department, I can assure you I will bend over backwards to provide anything you need to perform your duties."

Bree rises from her seat and walks behind her desk. With such a different weight differential between top and bottom, I'm surprised she's so nimble.

As I can't keep my eyes off Bree, Tiffany leans over and assures me, "If there's one thing she's good at, it's bending over."

"Would you please have Ms. Warma come in," Bree speaks into her speakerphone.

VP Bree returns to her power chair. "What else can I do for you?"

"Please freeze all payouts, make no mention of the case in any external correspondence, and no statements to the press," I say.

"And," Tiffany tosses in, "bring anything suspicious or suspect to my attention whenever someone suspects some suspicion."

"Will do, little Tiffy."

A knock comes on the outer door. I turn to see a woman waiting for the okay to enter. She's tiny, maybe five-one on a good day, wearing a pair of ski pants and a thick sweater. She either has circulation problems or hasn't stripped down a layer from her morning commute.

"Yes, Ms. Bisonette?"

"Selma, please come in," Bree says, motioning her into the room. "Selma Warma, please meet Mr. Sherlock." Bree says to me, "Ms. Warma was the administrator on the case."

"Nice meeting you."

"Nice meeting you." It may just take a lot of clothing to keep Selma Warma warm-a.

"Mr. Sherlock and his lead investigator, Tiffy, will need the files and any subsequent information connected with the Vilma Kromka case."

"And the case of her husband, Sergai Leftachunkof," Tiffany adds.

"Whatever you need, I would be happy to supply," she says.

"Until next Friday, correct?" Bree asks Selma.

"Yes."

"Selma is retiring after—how many years at Richmond?"

"Thirty-five," the lady says with pride.

"Congratulations," I say.

"Thank you."

The way my career is going, the only retiring I'll be doing is to my Toyota.

"If you give me an hour, I could have the copies made and the information boxed," she says assuredly.

"That would be very kind of you," I say with a smile.

Selma looks to Bree and hears, "That will be all."

The tiny woman leaves the room. Bree stands to put an end to our meeting. "Anything else?"

I stand, "No, thank you."

"Tiffy," Bree says as we make our way out of the office, "is there anything you'd like me to pass along to your dad? I'll be seeing him this evening, although we won't be getting together until quite late."

"No," Tiffany replies, "and please don't you pass along anything antibiotics can't handle."

"Oh, Tiffy, you're so adorable when you try to be clever."

I pull Tiffany out of the room and the verbal fray. "I think we're done here."

***

Tiffany is huffing and puffing like the Big Bad Wolf as we sit in the coffee shop downstairs in the Aon Center.

"I hate that biotch."

"Tiffany, calm down."

"Those breasts aren't hers, Mr. Sherlock. And I'm sure she's lipo'd her butt. She used to have more chins than a Japanese email list."

"Well, it certainly explains why you weren't mad when you were so angry before the meeting. Why didn't you tell me?"

"My dad's just using her for sex. I know he is."

"Tiffany..."

"What else could he want with Nettie-Net-Net?"

"She didn't seem that bad of a person."

"She's evil, Mr. Sherlock. I can see it right through those blue-colored contact lenses she's wearing."

"Tiffany, do I sense a little green monster resting on your shoulder?"

"No."

"Do you know the connotation of a little green monster?"

"No."

"It means Tiffany is a little jealous."

"No."

I pause.

"If they ever outlaw Botox, she'll have to change her name to Shar-pei."

We sit for a moment in silence.

"Your dad has the right to have a girlfriend, Tiffany. Your mom's been gone long enough; he needs a relationship."

"You don't have one; why should he?"

"Anybody who uses me for comparison, doesn't have much of an argument, Tiffany."

"She's the one who tells him I'm nothing but an empty, air-headed, spoiled, rich brat whose main function in life is to spend his money."

I don't agree or disagree with her self-assessment. What would be the point?

"That's why this case is so important, Mr. Sherlock. This is my chance to show my dad and that disgusting Bree Bitch-o-nay who I really am, what I'm capable of, and that I can do something else besides buying the perfect pair of shoes to match a purse."

"Okay."

"And you have to help me, Mr. Sherlock."

"I do?"

"Yes."

Oh jeesh. The pressure's on.

CHAPTER 10

There are only six pages in the file on Vilma and Sergai. I'm paging through each as Tiffany heads up the drive.

"I can't believe that biotch." Tiffany's still stuck in her "hate Bree" mode. She mimics her, "'You're so adorable when you try to be clever.'" Returning to her own voice, she tells me, "I wish she'd fall on her face and it shatters along with her cheap jewelry."

"Give it a rest, Tiffany."

"I bet she wears knockoffs she buys at sidewalk sales outside Walmart."

"Enough, Tiffany."

Tiffany stews.

"When we go see Vilma, one of us has got to get into her bedroom."

"You want to get into Vilma's bedroom? Mr. Sherlock, you must be really hard up."

"No." Although I'm so far past the point of being hard up I resemble Lot's wife. "We have to see a picture of Sergai."

"Why?"

"It's always nice to know what a dead guy looked like." I say this as I page through the files, none of which have a photo of her dearly departed hubby.

"Why? Are you going to do another of those eeeuuu-logy things?"

"No," I answer. "And one of us has got to get into the bathroom."

"I'm telling you right now, Mr. Sherlock, I'm not going to go anywhere Vilma's gone before."

"We have to get into her medicine cabinet and see what medications she's on."

"Why?"

"If she's not on any antidepressants, that'll tell us a lot."

"A lot of what?"

"I'm not sure."

"Me neither."

As we approach the Ridgeway block with Vilma's house, there isn't a spot to park.

"Can you believe that guy? He can't park there without a gimp sticker." Tiffany points out a black Chevy sedan parked illegally in front of a fire hydrant. Its windows are fogged up from the inside and exhaust spews from the tailpipe. "I should call 9-1-1 and have that guy towed."

"Drive around the back."

Tiffany goes down the block, turns left, and makes another left up the alley. When we get mid-block, Vilma's garage door is open. Many Chicagoans leave their garage doors open during bad weather because they're scared they won't open or get too heavy to open.

"Pull up behind the Buick."

We have to trudge through a foot of snow on the side passageway to get into Vilma's small back yard and then proceed all the way around to the front porch. I should have worn snowshoes.

I knock on the door.

From inside, "Who is it?"

"It's Richard Sherlock from Richmond Insurance again. Can we come in?"

"No."

"Please, it's really cold out here."

"Too bad."

"Why not?"

"My lawyer told me not to talk to you."

"But I just need a couple of questions answered."

"Forget it."

"Please."

"Go away."

I'm at a loss for words all of a sudden. I hesitate.

Tiffany takes up my slack. "Vilma, this is Tiffany. Remember me?"

"Yeah."

"Can I come in? I got to pee really, really bad."

The door opens.

"You can come in, but he can't." Vilma announces.

Tiffany enters. I shiver. The door slams shut.

I can sense Vilma's standing at the door. "Who's your lawyer?" I shout.

"Eddie Floyd, Esquire." I doubt if Vilma realizes "Esquire" is a title not a name, but this is no time to school her; it's too cold.

I continue to shiver, and hearing Eddie's name, I add a shudder. "And, by the way, when you and Sergai were married, is this where you lived?"

"No. We lived in Plainfield Estates," Vilma says. Then she adds, "Darn it. Forget what I just said because I'm not supposed to say anything."

"No problem." I pause. "And by the way, I didn't happen to have come across any immigration papers on Sergai."

Silence.

"Vilma?"

"No, I'm not falling for that one again," she says through the door. "You tricked me the first time."

"No, I didn't."

The door opens. Tiffany says to Vilma, "Thanks, I really needed that."

"When you got to go, you got to go," Vilma says.

Tiffany joins me on the porch. The door slams shut behind her. "Now get off my property," are Vilma's last words.

"Oh, Mr. Sherlock, you wouldn't believe what I just saw."

I pull Tiffany off the porch before she starts blabbing away in earshot of Vilma. We trudge back through the snowdrift to the garage. "You get in the car, Tiffany. I'll be there in a minute."

I take off my glove, reach into my coat pocket, and pull out a small metal object. I enter the open garage. Tiffany stays with me. "What are we doing?"

"I thought I told you to get in the car."

"Yeah, so?"

Nobody listens to me.

I go to the front of the car, reach inside the grill, and insert the magnetized device to the biggest piece of metal I can feel, which is hard to do because it's so cold I can barely feel my fingers. I blow on my bare fist before putting my glove back on.

"What was that?" Tiffany asks.

"We're bugging her," I confess.

"I know. That's why she wouldn't let you in her house."

"Okay, we're bugging her in more ways than one."

"You still haven't told me what that thing was," Tiffany

scolds me. “How am I supposed to learn if you keep things from me?”

“Don’t you remember I asked Chappie for a GPS tracker?”

“No.”

“It will tell us where she goes.”

“Oh wow, that is so James Bondish.”

Back in her Lexus, with the heater blasting hot air, I ask, “Did you get into her bedroom?”

“Yes.”

“And did you see any pictures of Sergai?”

“Yes.”

“What did he look like?”

“Well, there were two pictures. One real big one,” Tiffany puts her arms out wide. “It was right over the bed, and there was another one on the other wall, about this big.” She cuts her arms to a small distance.

“And, what did he look like?”

“Well, first of all, it was, like, really shiny. Like, it was on this material that was shiny. Not like Thai silk shiny, but shiny, shiny.”

“The guy, Tiffany.”

“It was just his head. He had black, wavy hair, brushed back with a few strands falling onto his forehead. He had ugly sideburns, thick, pouty lips, nice eyes, no tattoos; and it wasn’t that he looked old, but it was kinda like an old picture.”

“How about the other picture of him?”

“This was a picture, picture. Same guy, but in this white, silly looking jumpsuit with a lot of, like, shiny stuff on it; not like the shiny material in the other picture, but like cheap, cubic-zirconium shiny.”

“Did he look familiar?”

“Kinda.”

For years there’s been a rumor floating around that the twin brother of one past Memphis, Tennessee resident did not die at birth, as was reported, but lived and is now living with his famous recluse brother in Kalamazoo, Michigan where they frequent their neighborhood Dunkin' Donuts on a daily basis. I have an odd suspicion Tiffany saw the picture of one of these guys.

“Tiffany, did the picture at all resemble Elvis Presley?”

“You know, it did look a bit like him.”

"And the material the big picture was on, could it have been velour?"

"What's velour?"

"Tell me about the bathroom, Tiffany."

"You better sit down, Mr. Sherlock; this gets a bit graphic," she says, driving the car up the alley.

"I am sitting down, Tiffany."

"Okay, so I walk in there first, and it like smells like a litter box landfill. It reeks. I want to hold my breath, but I don't want to take in a breath and hold that dirty, gross air inside me, so instead I grab a whole mess of toilet paper and put it to my face so I can breathe. And I do have to grab a whole lot since its single-ply. In the bathtub, which hasn't been cleaned since the disco era, there are five litter boxes lined up. Each has little cat poops popping up over the top. Disgusting."

"Were there any pictures on the walls?"

"Cat pictures."

"Sergai pictures?"

"How would I know, Mr. Sherlock? Until I got into the bedroom, I didn't know what Sergai looked like."

"Were there any pictures of humans in the room?"

"No."

"What was on the vanity, next to the sink?"

"Cat stuff. She has a kitty-cat toothbrush holder and a kitty-cat soap dish."

"Any medicine vials?"

"Not that I saw."

"Did you look in the medicine cabinet?"

"No. Was I supposed to?"

"Yes. Wouldn't you think that's where she'd keep her prescriptions?"

"I probably didn't think of that because I was oxygen deprived having to breath through all that toilet paper."

"Was there anything in the bathroom or bedroom that seemed odd to you, Tiffany?"

"Yeah. There was this funny looking horseshoe necklace hanging from the mirror with a plastic thing on the end, covered with gold, diamonds, and four-leaf clovers. Ugly. It was definitely something I would never wear."

"Was it expandable?"

"Like a pair of fat girl sweatpants?"

"So to speak."

"I'm not sure; I didn't want to touch anything."

"I don't blame you, Tiffany." I take a moment to figure out how to process such information.

The Lexus is back on Ridgeway driving north. "How'd I do, Mr. Sherlock?"

"Nobody, but nobody can secretly scout out a scene like you do, Tiffany. Nobody."

"Thanks. I love being complimented." She beams. "And don't forget to tell my dad how good I was."

"No problem," I say, knowing I've never had a conversation with her father and probably never will. "Next time we chat, I'll make sure to mention it."

"And tell Daddy to mention how good I was to Bay-o-net Bree."

CHAPTER 11

Thankfully, the roads are clear, and Tiffany is able to break the speed limit all the way south on the Stevenson. There is some road construction a little past Romeoville. I've always wondered why there isn't a Julietville nearby Romeoville. I guess there was only one Shakespeare-loving city father around at the time of incorporating Illinois farm towns.

Plainfield, the next big town past Romeoville, is well named. It has quite a few plain fields surrounding it. The downtown area is quite quaint, homey, and all-American. On the City Hall electronic bulletin board, there is a Meet and Greet with the Mayor on the seventeenth, a Severe Weather Warning class scheduled for the twentieth, and sign-ups for Little League to begin March 1st.

Plainfield was pretty much a rural farming community up until the mid-1990s when the Chicagoland suburban housing boom sprouted south. Today, the biggest Plainfield crop is houses, cheaper to buy than the ones sold in Romeoville.

I check the address Chappie found on Google, and we drive west out of town. It's flat, there isn't a hill to be seen for miles, so it amazes me we have such a difficult time locating the Plainfield Estates housing development. We find the Estates of Plainfield and the Field Estates with no trouble, but no Plainfield Estates. We keep driving until we stop in The Fields of Plainfield and ask a guy shoveling snow, "Excuse me, could you tell us where the Plainfield Estates are?"

The guy gives me an odd look, "I think what's left of them are thataway." He points in the direction from which we came.

"Thank you."

We continue on the rural road until it turns to mushy ice and we see an askew sign reading "Pl–nf–el E–tat–s."

"That Russian?" Tiffany asks, reading the sign.

"No." I point. "Go that way."

I personally do not believe there is a more fickle woman than Mother Nature. Why would she design a tornado that can blow away one doublewide trailer but leave the one across the road untouched? I'm not sure when this particular tornado hit, but the majority of the estates in The Plainfield Estates no longer exist. On some of the properties, the cement slab is visible, but little else. We drive by the address I found in the Sergai files, and there isn't even a slab remaining.

"Nice place to visit, but I wouldn't want to live here," I tell Tiffany.

"People actually live here?"

***

Traffic is horrible going back into the city. By the time we get to Harlem Avenue, it's already dark, and we're moving a car length at a time.

"I hate traffic, Mr. Sherlock."

"Everybody in traffic hates traffic, Tiffany, but they're all part of the traffic, so they only have themselves to blame."

"That makes no sense, Mr. Sherlock."

I am about to attempt to explain, but what would be the point. We continue on for a mile or two. The traffic starts to ease up about a mile before we hit the interchange.

The small receiver in my coat pocket begins to buzz.

"What's that?" Tiffany asks.

"Elvis's wife is leaving the building," I explain as I see a red dot moving on the small screen map. "Good, she's coming this way."

I pause.

"She's on the ninety-four." I watch the screen. "Get in the right lane, Tiffany."

We take the Dan Ryan south. Vilma is only a mile ahead of us as we pass the Sox Park exit. Tiffany is cutting through traffic like the bad guy in a police pursuit.

"That's her." I point to the new Buick about six cars ahead of us. "Don't get too close."

"This is really fun, Mr. Sherlock; let's do it again real soon."

Vilma takes I-90 south, and as we follow, I just happen to glance in the rearview mirror and see a black Chevy sedan right behind us. I watch for about a mile. "Drop back a car length."

"I don't want to lose her, Mr. Sherlock."

"You won't."

Tiffany does as told, what a switch. I see the Chevy drops

back one car along with us. Indiana isn't far off. My eyes stay on the rearview mirror.

"What are we doing?" Tiffany asks.

"I'm trying to figure out if we're following, being followed, or both."

"She's going toward Gary," she informs me. "I hate Gary."

The black Chevy stays far enough behind that I can't make out who's driving. "Get in front of her, Tiffany."

"Why? I do that, I'll lose her."

"Do it. Not only do I know where she's going, we have a tracking device."

"Oh yeah."

Tiffany speeds up and zips past Vilma like an Indy car on Memorial Day. The black Chevy stays behind the Buick. "Where am I going, Mr. Sherlock?"

"Follow the casino signs. We'll meet everybody there."

"How do you know Vilma's going there?"

"Her jewelry."

About twenty years ago, someone had the great idea that what the Midwest needed was another casino. Plans were made with the city of Gary to develop a plot of Lake Michigan lakefront land for a hotel and gambling mecca. Donald Trump even got involved, building a multistory hotel adjacent to the floating riverboat. Realizing steel town Gary, which has ranked as the Murder Capital of America for a number of years, is hardly synonymous with wealth and class, the area is now referred to as Buffington Harbor. The new moniker was meant to add the necessary cache to convince the big money gamblers from Chicago to drive twenty-five miles to lose their hard-earned paychecks. They named the floating casino the Majestic Star.

Despite the fact that the riverboat has gone through a number of owners and bankruptcies, the Majestic Star is still floating with the dice rolling and slot machines spinning.

We arrive five minutes earlier than our fellow caravaners and wait in the parking lot.

"What happens if they don't show up?" Tiffany asks.

"Don't worry, they'll be here."

"Who do you think was following us?"

"I don't know."

"How are we going to find out?"

"Wait for them and ask, I guess."

"Sounds like a plan," Tiffany concludes.

Five minutes later, the Buick and Chevy arrive. Vilma parks first, gets out, locks her car, and hurries into the casino. Her necklace hangs like a Derby winner's horseshoe around her neck, with her diamond and gold, four-leaf clover Player's Card proudly attached to its lowest point. The Chevy parks a row behind her, but no one exits the car. We park a row behind the Chevy. I wait about thirty seconds, hit the handle, and open my door. "Tiffany, you wait here."

I jump from the car and hurry in the direction of the Chevy, approaching from the rear.

Tiffany follows.

"I told you to stay in the car."

"Backups never sit in the car; they always get out and back up."

The rear and side windows of the Chevy are heavily tinted. I can't see inside. I tap on the driver's side window. The electric window rolls down.

"Oh jeesh. What are you doing here?"

"Hey, Sherlock, long time no see."

Just my bad luck, it's Alibi Al Landeen.

Al Landeen has been a CPD detective for more than twenty-five years. He's worked in every station, every department, and with every other detective on the force. There isn't a detective in Chicago, suburban Chicago, or the state of Illinois who hasn't or wouldn't ask for a transfer after working with Alibi Al. I'm included in the Landeen ex-partners' roster. I lasted six weeks with the guy. The only person who has ever driven me crazier is my ex-wife. Now that I think of it, maybe she and Al should be paired up.

"I'm working cold cases now, Sherlock."

"It's thirty below, Al, every case is cold."

"Well, that's not my fault."

"Do you have a partner?"

"I had one, and it wasn't my fault he quit. He came down with some kind of twitch and took a leave of absence."

Tiffany must decide I'm no longer in need of backup and comes to my side. "Everything all ten-four, okay, Mr. Sherlock?"

It's all just super, Tiffany." It's not, but I say it is. "Mind if we join you, Al. It's cold out here."

"Sherlock, you and your little lady can come on down."

I get in the front and Tiffany in the back of the Chevy.

"It stinks back here," Tiffany says. "What's all this gunk?"

"Oh, that's not my fault. Some kids must have broken in and left their Burger King wrappers."

I make the introductions, and Al is impressed with my partner. "You've certainly come up in the world, Sherlock."

"You have no clue, Al."

"No, I don't."

"Don't feel bad, Mr. Landeen," Tiffany says. "Neither do I most of the time."

"What are you doing following Vilma Kromka?" I ask.

"She's attached somehow to a case I'm working on," Al tells us.

"Al Landeen" and "working on" is an oxymoron if there ever was one.

"Attached how?"

"A number of searches popped up on a Russian mobster named—"

"Sergai Leaveatipfor," Tiffany interrupts.

"No, it's Sergai Leftachinkoutof, isn't it?" Al says.

"Levenchenko," I correct all.

"It ain't my fault I got it wrong; them Russians should have names like other foreigners."

If nothing else, this tells me Chappie Foote is hard at work.

"And?" I ask.

"This Vilma person was alongside Sergai's name."

"Vilma Kromka?" I say for a positive recognition.

"Yeah."

"Do you know why?"

"No."

"They were married," I inform Al.

"How'd you know that?"

"Mr. Sherlock is really smart," Tiffany informs him.

"Really?"

"And guess what else," Tiffany says to Al.

Al shrugs his shoulders.

"Sergai's dead."

"He is?"

"Yep." Tiffany says proudly.

"Well, it ain't my fault I didn't know. Somebody must have forgot to add me to the email list."

I can only shake my head back and forth as these two of equal intellectual capacity chat it up.

"I don't know about you people," Al says, "but I haven't had a chance to have dinner. What do you say we go in and grab some grub?"

"I don't know," Tiffany says. "These Burger King wrappers have ruined my appetite."

"Let's go inside and see if we can get it back."

In the casino, we find a bar where we can also order food. Tiffany and I sit with our backs to the slot machine floor where Vilma is sixty feet away, sitting at a Wheel of Fortune machine, her garish green Players Club card plugged into the slot in the slot machine. She pushes down on the electronic spinner button faster than a one-fingered typist in the steno pool. Since the casino world has gone high-tech, I can only imagine the amount of elbow and shoulder problems eradicated by the absence of the one-armed bandit. The push-button slot machine should be placed in the same category as the Salk vaccine.

Al orders two beers, a steak, baked potato, and mac and cheese on the side. I go with a Cobb salad, but hold the bacon. Tiffany orders carrots and celery stalks.

"So, why are you looking for Sergai?" I ask.

"He's a crook."

"What kind?"

"Pretty much a run-of-the-mill mobster. Extortion, leg-breaking, runnin' drugs, usual stuff."

"You have a picture of him?"

"Yeah." Al pulls out an old rap sheet. The guy in the picture isn't much older than twenty-five.

"He sure doesn't look like the guy in the picture in Vilma's room," Tiffany says.

"How old is this picture?" I ask.

"Beats me," Al says. "It's a cold case, don't forget."

I glance behind me, as I have done at three-minute intervals since we sat down, and see Vilma get up from her machine. "She's moving."

Tiffany turns around to see.

"Don't turn around."

Tiffany turns around anyway. "She's going the other way."

"Al, does Vilma know what you look like?"

"I don't think so."

"See what she's doing."

Al takes two big bites of steak and a big gulp of beer before he rises from his chair and takes chase.

Tiffany and I sit. For some reason we stare at the mostly eaten hunk of meat and bone left on Al's plate. "Did you know, Mr. Sherlock, that almost a pound of red meat fat can become lodged in your colon?"

"No, I didn't know that, Tiffany, but thanks so much for informing me."

"You're welcome."

Al returns a few minutes later, sits, and immediately starts to gnaw on the steak bone.

"What did she do, Al?"

"Went to the window and put more money on her card."

"Cash or charge?"

"Cash."

"How much?"

"Four hundred."

"You got close enough to count?" Tiffany asks.

"I only had to count four bills."

This is interesting.

Al orders another beer to help wash down the mac and cheese. When the bill comes, he picks it up. "Hey, it's on me."

This is really interesting.

Al plops down his credit card and hands it all back to the waiter.

By the time the waiter returns, Vilma is back at her wheel trying to win a fortune.

"I'm sorry, sir, but your credit card has been rejected," the waiter informs Al.

"You're kidding?" Al does his best to elicit surprise.

"I'm sorry, sir."

"Well, it ain't my fault. That wife of mine puts all her charges on it. Runs it over the limit, doesn't tell me, and I'm left holding the bag." Al looks my way as he hands the bill off. "Can you help me out here?"

They don't call him Alibi Al for nothing.

CHAPTER 12

In Canada, if you file a lawsuit against another person and the case goes to trial and you lose, you would then be responsible for paying the legal fees of the guy you sued. They call this the *Canadian System*. In America, we don't subscribe to this system and have in its place millions upon millions of frivolous lawsuits filed. There has been everything from the guy who sued the beer company for false advertising because when he drank a lot of beer, he never did as well with the ladies as the guys in the commercial, to the guy who sued the strip club because of the whiplash he suffered when he reached up to insert his dollar into a g-string and a silicone boob came around and whacked him upside of the head.

I'm not saying the Canadian System is better than the American or vice versa, but I will say that if we had the Canadian System in operation, there wouldn't be the offices of Eddie Floyd and Associates.

"Richard Sherlock to see Mr. Floyd," I say to the receptionist.

"And Tiffany Richmond," Tiffany adds.

"Do you have an appointment?"

"No, we're investigating a possible fraud with one of his clients." I pull out my somewhat official private eye badge and flash it before her eyes.

"Which Eddie Floyd do you want to see?" she asks.

"There's more than one?" Tiffany asks the question I'd ask if I didn't make it a rule never to answer a question with another question.

"Eddie, TV Eddie, and Eddie Jr."

"The case concerns a Ms. Vilma Kromka."

The receptionist scrolls through the listings on her computer. "Oh," she says, obviously impressed, "that would be TV Eddie, Saul Rabinowitz."

We only have to wait ten minutes before TV Eddie Floyd comes out to greet us. "Mr. Sherlock?"

Eddie is much shorter than he looks on TV, much older too. If you saw him on the street, you probably wouldn't even recognize him as the guy on TV unless he was wearing his boxing gloves.

We shake hands. "Saul Rabinowitz."

"I thought you were Eddie Floyd."

"I am."

"But there are two other Eddie Floyd's."

"Well, not really," Saul/Eddie tells us.

"Why?"

"We thought Eddie Floyd and Associates sounded better on TV than Rabinowitz, Rabinowitz, and Rabinowitz."

Saul's got a point. Image is everything.

"Call me Eddie."

He leads us to his richly appointed office.

"Now, what can I do for you?"

"Vilma Kromka."

"Oh, yes. PTGD." Eddie has an ear-to-ear smile across his face. "We win that one, we'll open up a whole new division and all be playing golf in Florida in a year or two."

"There's enough holes in the case, Mr. Floyd, to fill every country club in Miami," I tell him.

"We have already deposed Vilma's Richmond Insurance shrink, have extensive medical records on Ms. Kromka, and a statement from her past employer saying she can no longer change transmission fluid without breaking into tears. We have an open and shut case."

"I wouldn't be tacking the lid down too quick," Tiffany tells him. "My daddy will fight you with teeth and fingernails."

"Who are you?"

"I'm sorry," I apologize. "This is my assistant, Tiffany Richmond."

"Richmond as in Richmond?"

"That's me."

"Well, that should make things much easier," Eddie says. "Our client would be amenable to listen to any offer you may have." Eddie says, leans back, and folds his hands as if he's praying in temple.

"What we are here for is to exchange discovery information."

"You're not here to settle?"

"No. We need the supporting documents you have on the deceased husband, Sergai Levenchenko."

"Why?"

"We'd like to see what he looked like to begin with."

"What discovery documents have you brought along?" Eddie asks.

"We're in the process of putting our packet together."

"So, you don't have any?"

"So to speak."

"Well, Mr. Sherlock, I can tell you that Mr. Leva-whoever was a very attractive fellow."

"Did he look anything like Elvis?" Tiffany asks.

"The young or the old Elvis?" Eddie asks.

"You pick."

Eddie leans forward in his oversized leather desk chair. "Once we have a court date, Mr. Sherlock, I assure you a full and complete discovery file will be turned over. I expect the same from you."

"No problem."

"And, Mr. Sherlock, until then, I have to ask that you cease visiting my client."

"We were just there to see her cats," Tiffany explains with a whopper.

"Ms. Kromka remains in a very tenuous state of mind. She could snap at any moment."

The only thing that is going to snap on Vilma is her Majestic Star Player's Club Card if she forgets to unplug it before she leaves her Wheel of Fortune slot machine.

"Now, if we both would like to avoid yet another devastating development to the health and well-being of my client, Ms. Kromka, I would suggest we begin discussing a settlement to the case."

"Although I'm not the one to make that decision, I don't see that happening any time soon, Mr. Floyd," I tell him.

"Why not? Better to settle now than be very sorry later," Eddie speaks from his heart and wallet.

Tiffany sums it up quite succinctly, "The only thing my dad ever settles for is a cheap, floosy biotch for a girlfriend."

***

I'm more of a coffee shop/diner diner than an expensive five-star restaurant patron, but since Tiffany is buying, I'll suffer. We're sitting in the Club International, looking down on an icy Michigan Avenue.

"Mr. Sherlock, do we have anything I could tell my dad I've done so far that will impress the heck out of him?"

"Right offhand, nothing seems to be coming to mind."

"There has to be something, Mr. Sherlock. What I want to do is keep feeding Daddy bits and pieces of all the good stuff I'm doing, and then when I—I mean we—solve the case, he'll be so blown away with my work he'll have a whole new respect for his daughter."

"Tiffany, I hate to tell you this, but we're, right now, actually worse off than when we started."

"We are?"

"Dr. Lunay has already signed off on Vilma's side, her neighbors did us no good, Vilma looked horrible when we visited her, and she went and lawyer'd herself up so we can't visit her again."

"How about her gambling addiction?"

"Lots of people gamble, and just because we saw her gamble once, doesn't mean she's addicted."

"Could we say she's gone cat crazy after living around all the overflowing litter boxes?"

"They'd argue her cat mania is a symptom of her grief, and one cat lover on the jury would vote to give her more money than what she's already asking."

"For my daddy, that would be adding insult to the jury's injury."

"I don't know what to tell you, Tiffany."

Tiffany is quiet. I finish my walleyed pike, grilled in a lemon caper sauce. Delicious.

"Mr. Sherlock, We have to come up with stuff that's gonna make Daddy stand around and take notice."

"I'm trying."

"What can you—I mean we—do next?"

"Go back and see Chappie."

"Oh my God, I don't think I can take another visit with Mr. Ugly on an Ape."

"Tiffany, don't be mean."

***

"What's the difference between this case and D.B. Cooper?" Chappie asks as we enter his underground bunker.

"D.B. Cooper is easier to find," Chappie answers his own query

"Who's Debby Cooper?" Tiffany asks.

"D.B. Cooper was the guy who skyjacked a plane, got two hundred grand, parachuted out, and was never found."

Tiffany can't believe it. "He did that all for just two hundred grand?"

"You look tired," I say to Chappie.

"How can you tell, Mr. Sherlock?" Tiffany asks, although I wish she hadn't.

"I've been up all night." Chappie sits in the captain's chair of his Internet space station. "Finding Sergai is tougher than trying to make me look presentable."

"Wouldn't that be impossible?" Tiffany asks.

"Remember, Tiffany, I'm just as normal as you are on Halloween."

"Chappie, did you find anything?" I ask.

"I ran every search I could, found little or nothing, then I searched for other searches. The problem is that when the USSR broke up into pieces, information was lost, misplaced, or erased completely. The birth certificate you supplied didn't match any existing records, but there were a few close matches when I changed the spelling."

Chappie pulls up on his screen two official-looking documents, one with the name Sergie Levenchenko, and the other with Sergai Levchenko.

"Don't forget I had to translate the names from Russian to English."

"I thought a name was a name was a name," Tiffany says.

"They have a different alphabet in Russia than we do," Chappie informs her.

"Isn't ours good enough for them?" Tiffany asks.

I ask, "Did you check the Russian visas lists."

"Yes, there's lots of Levenchenkos, Levchenkos, and Lecenchenkos. It's actually a pretty common name in the Soviet Union."

"Passports?"

"Can't access those."

"Any green cards issued in the name?"

"Plenty."

"Could you check each of those?"

"I could," Chappie says, "but I'm not sure how much good it is going to do. Green cards are about as good an ID as a driver's license."

I hate to be the bearer of bad tidings, but a state-issued driver's license is one of the easiest documents to get, replicate, or counterfeit. I busted a guy once who had thirty-seven different Illinois licenses; each had the same picture and physical description, but different names, addresses, and numbers. Why retail stores ask for a driver's license ID for positive assurance is a mystery to me. Stores would be better off asking, "Excuse me, but before I can take your check, I have to know: Are you a crook?"

"How about the marriage license?"

"That checked out."

"Good," Tiffany says. "Anything else?" she asks.

"Nope."

"Bad," Tiffany says.

"I ran into a CPD detective who tells me Sergai was a local leg-breaker for the Russian mob."

"He must have been a good one because he's never been arrested."

"You see a picture of any of these guys?" I ask.

"These guys aren't very photogenic as a rule, Sherlock."

I can only hope Tiffany isn't thinking, *It takes one to know one.*

I sit back and rest my elbows on my knees and my chin on my folded fingers. Chappie knows I'm at a total loss.

"Here's an idea."

"Please."

"The going rate for a foreign wedding is about ten grand," Chappie starts to explain.

Tiffany interrupts, "Nobody gets married for ten grand. You have to figure at least four hundred a head, and with three hundred people, that's, like ..." She pauses. "A whole lot more than ten grand."

"He's not talking about the cost of the wedding ceremony, Tiffany."

"Okay, then bachelorette party can run at least seventy-five hundred, up to twenty if you go to Vegas."

"Chappie's referring to the current going rate for a marriage payout."

"Nobody gets divorced for a crummy ten grand either."

Certainly not my ex-wife.

"What Chappie is referring to is the cost of exchanging a ring for a green card."

"Well that hunk of cubic zirconium on her finger is worth no ten grand," Tiffany informs us.

"What a foreigner will do is pay an American citizen to marry him, which makes him eligible for immediate permanent status," I tell Tiffany.

"Certainly explains why Sergai would put up with all those cats."

"You prove Vilma did that, you're troubles are over," Chappie says.

"And hers would be just beginning," I add.

"And that awful Bree Boobalacious Bare-o-nette would never look down her sculpted nose again at me."

"Let me poke around immigration and see what I can come up with," Chappie says. "If you could find out if she made any major bank deposits after the honeymoon, that might answer the question."

"Thanks."

"It was nice seeing you again, Tiffany," Chappie says as we rise to exit.

"It was nice seeing you too," Tiffany says, then backtracks. "Well, not really, but you know what I mean."

"Chappie, you got to get out more often," I tell my friend. "It's not healthy to be holed up here so long."

"I know, as soon as I get through your case, I'll go on vacation. I hear the island of Molokai is nice this time of year."

"Thanks, Chappie."

Back in the car, but before we leave Chappie's, I say to Tiffany, "You weren't being very nice in there, Tiffany."

"What do you mean?"

"Nice to Chappie."

"It's hard for me being around someone who looks like him, Mr. Sherlock."

"That hardly gives you the right to be mean to him."

Tiffany stares off, avoiding my eyes.

"Tis better to have an ugly face than an ugly mind."

"What is that supposed to mean, Mr. Sherlock?"
"You figure that one out. It might do you a lot of good."

CHAPTER 13

This is a time I could really use the help of my obese, computer hacker buddy Herman McFadden. He could hack into Vilma's account, see a big deposit, trace it back to Sergai, and Saul Rabinowitz/Eddie Floyd, wouldn't get thirty percent of anything. Problem is Herman is currently in Russia interviewing potential brides-to-be. I can only imagine how that's going.

It's Thursday night. Once I get the apartment out of its ice age, I call my girls. It's my divorced dad weekend coming up, so I ask each what they want to do. The polar vortex is supposed to take a hike east, and Chicago will be at least somewhat bearable for the next few days. Care suggests we should go out and do something fun. Kelly suggests shopping. Why I bother asking is a mystery even to me. I do inform them that I am on a case, and if something comes up, it will take precedence. They both offer their services in helping me solve whatever I'm trying to solve.

For dinner, I find an old cottage cheese container in the back of my freezer but can't tell what leftover delicacy is inside. I defrost it in the microwave and still can't discern what it may be. I heat it up on the stove, eat it sitting in front of the TV news, and decide if I can ever remember what I'm eating, I will never prepare the recipe again.

After washing the plastic container, pot, fork, and glass I used, I reach into the top kitchen cupboard and take out my small metal recipe box. I go through the cards with recipes on them. None seem to match what I just ate. I put those back and remove a stack of blank 3x5 cards and a box of pushpins, and take them all into the living room. I sit down on the couch and look up at what I refer to as *The Original Carlo*, a horrendously bad painting of a red-roofed, dilapidated, brown barn with four mailboxes, set against a bright yellow sky. An art connoisseur I'm not.

I label two cards, Sergai, and Vilma. I pin the pair in the center of the picture, just above the roof of the barn. I stand back, stare, and realize I don't have any other suspects or direction in which to consider, no more cards to fill out. My usual method of push-pinning the entire case across *The Original Carlo* and seeing it all laid out before me is dead on arrival. I sit back on the couch, grab the remote, turn on the TV, and spend the next twenty minutes channel surfing to find something interesting to watch. You would think with the hundreds of cable channels out there this would be easy, but it's not.

Even considering I can only afford the *basic,* i.e. cheapest cable package available, I think it's unfair I have to pay for channels I never watch. I don't care about home shopping, travel, cartoons, Congress, preachers, or screaming political pundits. The only function these 24/7 networks serve is to make my channel surfing a lengthy experience and put undo pressure and stress on my thumb.

I end up watching a program on MTV 12, or VH 18, or ESPN 34 about the reality of being a divorced wife of an NBA player. I wouldn't be surprised if I was the only guy in America watching this dumber than dumb show. The show opens with five overly dressed, blinged out, twenty-something ex-wives sitting on a couch commenting on their recently divorced husbands' cheating ways. Their renditions of the trysts are not only graphic but also filled with cynical opinions and labels for the women doing the trysting. Although it's easy to understand their feelings, it is difficult to understand their sentences since so many words are being bleeped out. Thankfully, a commercial comes on. When the show returns, the topic changes to how they met their ex-husbands. These stories are quite similar, as all the women met their future NBA hubbies in dance or strip clubs when the player's teams were on the road, and the boys just happened to be away from their then-wives. After another commercial, there is a lot of screaming, crying and gnashing of perfect teeth from the divorced women, but absolutely no mention of the *everything that goes around comes around* theory. The show ends with a preview of next week's episode, in which two of the ex-wives discover they once were dating the same NBA player, not only at the same time but on the same night. Can't wait.

I turn off the TV and go to bed.

***

The mortuary business is one of the few remaining businesses in America that is almost exclusively a family enterprise. As far as I know, there are no "Mortuaries "R" Us," "Decease Depots," or "WalMort-uaries" in existence. The neighborhood funeral home is as alive and kicking today as it was a hundred years ago.

The Pyre/Lament Family Funeral Home, Masoleum, Crematorium, and Cemetery offer a full range of services for the recently dearly departed. It is located northwest of the city, adjacent to the end or beginning of the O'Hare Airport runways, dependent upon which way the wind is blowing. The noise from takeoffs and landings of the hundreds of jumbo jets doesn't seem to bother the permanent residents of Pyre/Lament. Not a single complaint has ever been registered.

"This place gives me the willies, Mr. Sherlock."

"I don't know why it would. Seems pretty peaceful to me."

Only a few of the headstones are tall enough to pop out from under the two-foot layer of snow.

We drive on the curvy road past the dearly departed.

"What's that smell?" Tiffany asks with her nose sticking skyward.

I take a whiff. Whatever it is, it certainly isn't lilacs.

"Why are we here again? she asks.

"According to the file, this is the last place Sergai was seen."

"Alive?"

"No, dead."

"What good is it going to do us, Mr. Sherlock? It's not like we're going to pick up any quotes from the guy."

"We have to take what we can get, Tiffany."

Tiffany parks her car in front of the main building. A maintenance man sees us get out of the car and tosses salt pellets on the path we will take to go inside the building as if they were rose petals up the aisle for a church wedding. "Thanks."

"You're welcome," he says. "And I'm sorry for your loss."

The moment we step into the ivy-covered brick building, we are met by music designed to take the fun out of any funeral. It's probably off the popular pallbearer's album *Dirge for a Miserable Day*. Only a person in a drugged stupor could dance to such tunes.

A middle-aged woman, dressed entirely in black with what

seems to be a permanent scowl on her face, approaches us. "Yes?"

"We'd like to see the owners."

"Is this concerning a relative?"

"We're from the Richmond Insurance Company."

"Is this concerning a group plan?"

"Did you say 'plan' or 'plant'?" Tiffany asks.

I intervene. "My name is Sherlock." "Like the famous detective?"

"Not really."

"Are you bereaved?" she asks.

"Only when I consider the state of my career," I confess. "It concerns a past client of Pyre/Lament."

"Dead one, not a live one," Tiffany helps explain.

"We are extremely busy at the moment. Let me see what I can do." The lady in black leads us to a small chapel, complete with altar, pews with kneelers, and stained glass windows. "You can wait in here."

The already depressing atmosphere of the room is heightened by a cold chill, which permeates from all the faux marble lining the walls and floor. The moment I sit down, I flashback to my Roscoe Jarbeaux morning and start to shiver.

"This place is totally creepy, Mr. Sherlock. I wouldn't want to be caught alive in this place. Their interior designer must have been someone from *The Walking Dead.*"

"Or the Grim Reaper."

"Who?"

"Maybe you should talk to them about a feng shui of the place." I suggest one of Tiffany's best capabilities.

"No amount of feng shui could shui the bad vibes out of this place."

We wait another five minutes, and the lady in black returns. "It's going to be at least an hour and a half before anyone can see you," she tells us. "Because of the weather, we're very busy."

"An hour and a half in this place would be like an eternity," Tiffany tells her.

I try to ignore Tiffany's poor choice of words. "We'll only be a few moments. Is there any way we can see them sooner?" I ask.

"Well, if you don't mind talking while they work ...."

The room she leads us into is all white and silver. White linoleum floors, white floor-to-ceiling tile, and a white ceiling. The stainless steel furniture, for lack of a better term, consists of two bed-like tables and two wider tray-like platforms, which tilt up and down. The pairs are positioned on opposite sides of the room. The room is especially crowded because in every available space is a haphazardly parked, rolling gurney bed carrying a current customer.

"Oh my God."

The only thing keeping Tiffany's eyes from popping out of her head is the smell of formaldehyde that permeates the air.

"Hello," the man dressed in a semi-surgical outfit says. "I'm Titus Pyre, and over there is my wife, Thelma Lament."

"Nice to meet you," the woman, dressed more like a schoolmarm than a medical tech, says from the opposite side of the room.

"We're a little stacked up," Titus explains. "With the weather, the ground's frozen, and we can't get anybody planted."

It is easy to discern that Titus is in charge of the client's interior, and Thelma is in charge of the exterior. At the present time, Titus stands next to a guy on the tilt. His fluids, the guy's not Titus's, are draining into a receptacle. Thelma is putting the finishing makeup touches on a woman who probably hasn't looked this good in years.

Tiffany gravitates toward Thelma. "What are you doing?"

"Eyeliner."

"Why?"

"You only get one chance to make a good last expression."

"I'm sorry to break in on you like this," I say to Titus.

"I don't think anyone will get too shook up over you being here."

"We're investigating a case concerning one of your former customers," I inform him, being careful not to get too close to his work. "His name was Sergai Levenchenko."

"Doesn't ring a bell."

Tiffany edges ever closer to Thelma, being careful not to upset any of the still-life patrons.

"From the records in the insurance company file, your facility cremated the body."

"What do you need to know?"

"Anything you could tell us."

"In the mortuary business, we make a habit of not discussing the particulars about our clients," he says and adds, "What goes on in the embalming room, stays in the embalming room."

"Why?"

"We sometimes discover aspects, which the deceased may not have wanted to share."

"Like what?"

"Hidden tattoos, implants, toupees, untreated diseases, and size of certain organs."

"But the guy's already dead," Tiffany says. "Like he'd care."

"It is the family, not the client we have to be concerned about," Thelma says.

"I've been in this business my whole life, Mr. Sherlock," Titus says. "And if there is one thing I've learned, it's not the dead ones that give you problems, it's the live ones."

"Please?"

Titus adjusts the tilt of the now drained, drainee to a ninety-degree angle, pulls off his latex gloves, and says, "Come into the office."

To my surprise, Tiffany doesn't follow, but stays at Thelma's side. I hear her suggest, "I think she could use a little more blush."

Titus's office is more of a storeroom than an office. He has a metal desk and file cabinets on one wall. The other three walls are floor-to-ceiling shelves with hundreds of black shoeboxes, each wrapped with a single red ribbon.

"What are those?"

"Unclaimed remains."

"How quickly they forget, huh?"'

Titus is at the file cabinets, "Spell his name for me."

I recite Sergai's letters slowly and add, "But I might be a letter or two off."

"Age?"

"Mid-thirties."

Titus pulls out a few files, reads, and puts them back in. "Not here."

He sits at his desk and turns on his computer. "Spell it one more time."

He types as I spell. "Sergai might be with an 'e' instead of an 'a.'"

"Here he is." He reads. "Sergei—that's with an 'e'—Levenchenko." Titus spells it out.

"He's got more ways to spell his name than there are plots at Arlington," I try unsuccessfully to liven up the conversation.

"He wasn't here," Titus says reading. "The procedures were done at our associate home off Belmont."

"This was the only Pyre/Lament I could find."

"For a short period of time we had a semi-partnership with the Hollerback Funeral Home in the city."

"Should I be speaking with them?"

"I'm not even sure they're still in business," Titus says. "We dissolved the partnership months ago."

"May I ask why?"

"Let's just say we had different philosophies in running a business."

Titus continues to read through the computer file. I sit and wait.

"Is there a picture of the guy?"

"No."

"Anything missing or odd about the file?"

"No, pretty standard stuff."

"Autopsy?"

"No."

"Does it list a cause of death?"

"Yes."

"What?"

Titus reads on. "Heart attack."

"Awful young for a heart attack," I say.

"It happens."

"Where did he die?"

"Doesn't say."

"Hospital report?"

"No," he answers and adds, "We didn't do the embalming or the services; we only cremated him. We do this for a lot of the smaller homes. We have an extra-large oven."

"Lucky you."

"You wouldn't believe the amount we save on our heating bills during these arctic blasts."

"I can only imagine."

Titus must reach the end of the file. He looks up. "I'm sorry

I couldn't be more help, Mr. Sherlock."

"Would your associate mortuary have anything else on the case?" I ask.

"Might."

"Could you give me the address of the other home?"

"Certainly."

While he writes the address on an old prayer card, I ask, "Wouldn't you have seen what was left of Sergai in the casket when he was delivered here for his burn?"

"He doesn't come in a casket. He's delivered in a cardboard box."

"UPS?"

"He comes in the hearse, transferred to the oven, burned, scraped out, crushed to a fine ash, and fit into an urn or cardboard box. Kinda pointless to dress him up for all that, don't you think?"

I get up slowly. The news on Sergai is bothering me.

Titus doesn't have much else to add except, "What a way to go."

"Crushing de-feet," I say.

"There is a big cluster of Russians living outside of O'Hare," Titus says in the hallway. "They seldom go for our premium packages. They're more 'in the ground with no money down' customers."

On our way back to the embalming room, we make a stop at Titus's oven. He flips the switch to Off. The casserole must be done. "Cremation is getting more and more popular, Mr. Sherlock, and not just for humans." He opens the oven door and points inside. "This was a load of cats."

I'll be sure not to mention this to Vilma.

Re-entering the embalming room, I see Tiffany and Thelma haven't moved.

"I think it gives her a much fresher, livelier look," Tiffany says, with hairbrush in hand, as she and Thelma stand back to judge the new 'do.

"I think you've done wonders for her," Thelma says, nodding her head. "If she could, I'm sure she'd thank you."

"Tiffany, we can go."

Tiffany hands the brush back to Thelma, smiles, and says, "And easy on the hairspray, you don't want her to look too made up."

CHAPTER 14

I call Al Landeen.

"Did your cold case have anything on the way Sergai died?"

"I don't think so."

"What do you mean you 'don't think so'?"

"It means ..." and he begins to speak very slowly and distinctly, "I don't think so."

"Why not?"

"Because I couldn't read the file," Al explains.

"You're on a case and you didn't read the file?" I question.

"It wasn't my fault I couldn't read it. The guy before me or the guy before him must have been eating a hot dog and spilled ketchup all over the pages. So, don't be getting your panties in a big knot, Sherlock, for something I didn't have a thing to do with."

I know he's lying. No Chicago police detective I've ever known puts ketchup on a hot dog.

"Why are you on the case, Al? Why is a low-level, dead crook so important?"

"He got detained at O'Hare once."

"What did he do, set off the TSA scanner when he forgot to take his belt off?"

"They thought he might be a terrorist."

"A terrorist, why?"

"They thought he was smuggling stuff onto the plane."

"What?"

"Six eggs of Silly Putty."

"What?"

"He had it in his carry-on bag."

"Why?"

"He probably didn't want to pay to check a bag. People hate those fees."

"It's against airline regulations to travel with Silly Putty?" I ask.

"Think about it, Sherlock. Who would carry on six eggs of Silly Putty onto an airplane in a tote bag?"

"A guy whose kids like to play with Silly Putty?"

"I didn't know he had kids."

"Al, what happened?"

"So, the TSA questions the guy until it was ten minutes before his flight, but Sergai can't speak English, and they can't find a translator who speaks Russki. So they have to let him go, but they confiscate the stuff, saying it's a liquid, more than three ounces and not in a quart-sized, plastic bag."

I hate to admit it, but almost every time I fly, I lose my toothpaste and shampoo too. Why do they require a quart-sized bag for a three-ounce tube of toothpaste?

"Then what happened?"

"A couple of TSA employees take the eggs home, their kids complain the stuff is lousy Silly Putty, and bring it back the next day. A week later, it gets analyzed, and they find out it isn't Silly Putty."

"What was it, a Silly Putty knockoff?" I ask.

"No. Possibly plastic explosive."

"Possibly?"

"Silly Putty can be tricky, Sherlock."

"They go after the guy?"

"I would assume they did."

"But they couldn't find him?"

"That I'm sure of because if they did, it wouldn't have become a cold case, and I wouldn't be on it."

I consider the information for another two seconds and say, "We better get together, Al. I need to see that file."

"When?"

"Now."

"I'd like to, Sherlock, but I can't. And it's not my fault either, my wife called, and she needs me home immediately."

"Is she sick?"

"No, she's got her own mystery, and she needs to find out who did it by eight tonight."

"I didn't know your wife was also a detective."

"She's not. She's got book club, and she still has a hundred pages to read, and she's got nobody but me to put out the munchies."

"Goodbye, Al."

"See ya, Sherlock. Have a good weekend."

The instant I hang up my cell phone, Tiffany says, "You know, Mr. Sherlock, maybe we're spending too much time on the husband and not enough time on the wife. Isn't she the one we got to prove is a disgusting, money-grubbing, awful human being?"

Tiffany has a point. I check my watch. I have just about enough time to make one more stop. "Get back on the expressway, Tiffany, and get off on Fullerton."

"Where are we going?"

"To get lubricated."

"Sounds good to me."

Tiffany puts the Lexus into overdrive, and we're at the bottom of the off-ramp in ten minutes.

"Go right," I tell her.

"There's no good bars that way, Mr. Sherlock. We have to drive toward the lake if you want hipper places to drink."

"Go right, Tiffany."

"If you say so, Mr. Sherlock."

We travel about ten blocks.

"That's the place over there."

"Doesn't look to me like a place that would serve martinis, Mr. Sherlock."

Vilma didn't work at Jiffy Lube. She worked at Lube-in-a-Jiffy.

"Park right in front of that big door," I direct my protégée.

"Let me tell you, this isn't my preferred brand of lubrication."

A uniformed Lube-in-a-Jiffy lube-ista runs up to Tiffany's side of the car, waits for her to roll down her window, and asks, "Can I get your mileage?"

"In what sense?" Tiffany asks.

I interrupt the overly aggressive grease monkey as I get out of the car. "We need to see the owner or the manager."

"He's in the office. We don't accept competitor's coupons anymore, if that's what you want to know."

"I don't do coupons," Tiffany informs him.

I make my way into the store, leaving Tiffany to fend for herself.

The man behind the counter has a sewn-on name badge reading, Will Spurts, Mgr. "What can I do for you?" he asks and adds, "We have a special on our nine-point bad weather inspection and a discount on our six-quart lube and oil if you buy three in advance."

"I need some information on one of your past employees," I tell him.

"Who?"

Before I can answer Will Spurt's question, Tiffany runs in panicked. "That guy asked me if he could 'pop my hood.' A little personal, don't you think, Mr. Sherlock?"

"One second, Tiffany." I turn back to Will. "Vilma Kromka."

"I fired her."

"Why?"

"She couldn't sell an electrical charge to a dead Chevy Volt."

The In a Jiffy crewman/lube-ista who first approached us comes in the office holding a piece of cardboard with two blotches of oily liquid side by side. He says to Tiffany, "I'd like to show you the difference in your transmission fluid and new transmission fluid." He pushes it right in front of her nose. "Would you look at that corrosion?" He pauses. "It's a lot cheaper to replace the fluid than to replace the tranny."

I put up an index finger to the guy, "One second, please." I turn back to Spurts. "You didn't fire her because she was depressed?"

"If anyone was depressed, it was me 'cause of the money I was losing."

"How long did she work here?"

"A couple of months maybe."

"I checked the brake fluid, and it was on the low side," the oil-ista/lube-ista tells Tiffany. "Remember, you don't get a second chance to hit the brakes."

"Why did you hire her?" I ask the manager.

"I didn't. My brother-in-law did. He's the owner."

"And when was the last time you had your system flushed?" the guy asks Tiffany.

"Listen, buddy," Tiffany says, "what I do at the spa, stays at the spa."

"Why'd he hire her?" I ask Will.

"Beats me."

I check my watch. I'm running out of time. "Tiffany, we got to go."

"You mean you're not getting lubed?" the salesman asks Tiffany.

"Well, at least not in the sense you're thinking."

CHAPTER 15

Tiffany drops me off at my apartment and heads downtown for happy hour. I make a pit stop inside and hurry back outside where my Toyota starts up like a sprinter at the sound of the starting gun. I pick up my girls from school right on time.

"Dad, can we stop at McDonald's on the way home?" Care asks.

"No."

"Why not?"

"It would ruin your dinner."

"No, it won't."

"Dad's the one in charge of ruining dinner," Kelly tells her sister and quickly asks me, "What fun things do you have planned for us to do this weekend?"

"Nothing."

"Why not?"

"Do I look like a camp counselor to you?"

"We wouldn't know," Care says. "You never let us go to camp."

"You know, when I was a kid, I never got to go to camp."

"So this is like a tradition?" Care asks.

"I bet when you were a kid, Dad, the only camp they had was next to the wagon train you were riding in."

Everybody laughs except me.

"Can we go shopping?" Kelly asks.

"The weather's supposed to let up. I thought we'd go play in the snow."

"Yeah," Care says, "that would be fun."

"Before or after we go to the mall?" Kelly asks.

"And another thing, Kelly, when I was a kid, I never got to go to the mall, ever."

"Because they hadn't invented the mall yet. You were still trading stuff with the Indians."

"And how many times do I have to tell you to zip up your coat, Kelly?"

"I'm not sure, but I'll let you know."

I make spaghetti for dinner, using ground turkey instead of ground beef in the sauce. I thought it was quite tasty. They each heap a pound or two of Parmesan cheese on top, then complain it's too gooey and hard to eat.

The next morning, I make pancakes, which they drench with enough syrup to drain a Vermont forest. The temps are in the mid-to-upper thirties, but after subzero weeks, it feels like a sauna. I can't waste this opportunity.

Within an hour, I get the kids bundled up and down to the car, which kicks over smoother than a soccer player in the World Cup.

"I can't believe your car starts in this weather," Kelly says.

"Keep putting oil in these Toyotas, and they'll run forever."

"Stop, and you'll put it out of its misery."

"Maybe when you're sixteen, Kelly, I'll get a new car, and you can have this one."

"Or you could get me a new car, and you can keep putting oil in this one."

I surprise the pair when, instead of dragging them along on my usual Saturday morning runs to the market, drugstore, cleaners, etc., we go to Toys "R" Us.

"What are we doing here?" Care asks.

"We don't do Barbie dolls anymore, Dad."

While other parents spend hundreds of dollars on fancy sleds, ski equipment, and snowboards, I buy three plastic ovals for a grand total of $29.75. And off we go.

Mount Trashmore in Evanston is actually a trash dump covered over, hence the name. During a snowy winter, the mountain becomes a sledder's paradise. You trudge up and you sled down; how simple can it get. Because it's early, the crowds haven't shown up, and the snow isn't yet packed down into ice. It's still fluffy, making for a fantastic, whoosh and shush ride down. The three of us have a blast. We must take thirty runs. We do spins, try to knock each other off, and fall on our butts attempting to go down standing up. By noon, we're exhausted. It is the best thirty bucks I've spent in years.

There is a cheap diner on Howard where we warm up, have lunch, and laugh at the silliness of our morning. A light snow begins to fall on our way out the door.

"I have one stop I want to make," I tell the kids as we get back into the car. "I promise you it won't take more than a half hour."

"Then can we go shopping?"

"We already went shopping this morning, Kelly."

"Toys "R" Us isn't shopping, Dad."

The snow starts to pick up as we drive south. The address I'm looking for is a few blocks from the square in Logan Square. We pull up and park next to where there was once a sign.

"What's this place, Dad?" Care asks.

"It looks like somebody's weird house," Kelly says.

"You guys want to wait in the car?" I ask.

"No."

The place is on the corner and takes up two lots. There is an extra-wide driveway leading to a garage that's attached to the middle of the property instead of the side. There is a dumpster off to the left of the driveway; it's full.

The girls follow me to the extra-wide, double front doors. I ring the bell. A man answers, dressed more like a carpenter than a mortician.

"Excuse me, is this the Hollerback Funeral Home?" I ask.

"We're referring to it now as the Hollerback Manor," he says, welcoming us inside.

We stand in a very wide hallway. To my left, I see a door labeled Men and to my right a door labeled Ladies. In the middle is a big hole in the wall, wide enough to push a wheelbarrow through, which is currently parked in the space. Overall, the place is a half-renovated disaster.

The man leads us into the building, going into what seems to be a rehearsed spiel, using his arms to direct our eyes. "Bedroom, bedroom, bath, bath. This will be the main hallway to the kitchen and great room."

We follow him through the hall to the back portion of the building. "The chapel is going to become the media room. The old workroom ..." He uses his fingers to put quotation marks around the word. "Is going to be the great room with a new gourmet kitchen, dining room for eight, and three additional bedrooms off the back of the house. If you'd want a sunroom, we could do that instead of a fifth bedroom. Fifty-six hundred square feet of living space, five bedrooms, five baths; it's a steal for four million."

"It's quite impressive," I tell the guy. "Is there anything left from what was here before?"

"Not much."

"What happened to the prior owners?"

"Somebody said they moved to Belize."

"Can't blame them for that."

"How did you find out about the place?" he asks. "We haven't put it on the market yet."

"I was almost in the real estate business once."

"But he flunked the test and didn't get his license," Kelly so kindly fills in.

"Did the Hollerback people leave anything, like records or files."

"I found a couple of CDs."

"Anything else?"

"There's some junk downstairs," he says and immediately follows with a question of his own, "How long have you been looking?"

"For what?"

"A new house."

"Oh. We really just started."

"It's going to be a perfect house for a growing family." He removes his tool belt, digs into his pocket, and pulls out a business card. "Why don't you give me a call in a month, and you'll be able to see the place really starting to take shape."

"I'll give you a holler back."

The snow has picked up quite a bit when we get back to the car. "Are we going to move here, Dad?" Care asks.

"No."

"Why not?"

"I can think of four million good reasons right off the top of my head."

By the time we travel six blocks, the heavy snow turns into a blizzard. Another eight blocks and it becomes a whiteout. It takes almost two hours to go the remaining four miles home. Thank God, the girls didn't have seconds on the hot chocolate at the diner.

Whenever Chicago experiences a deluge of snow, two things are sure to happen. The second thing is: Everything that can stop, will stop. Deliveries, school, sporting events, birthday parties, church, bridge clubs, sewing bees, and quite a few burglaries. Since nobody can get anywhere, why bother? People hunker down, stay inside, and wait for the storm to pass. The first thing that happens, before the stopping happens, is people run, sled, or snowshoe to their closest supermarket, Walgreens, corner store, liquor store, or snack stand and buy every perishable item they can get their hands on. Milk, bread, cheese, meat, vegetables, fruit, brewskis, chips, pretzels, and pizzas frozen on ovals of cardboard, which will taste like cardboard after they're heated up. Whatever is immediately edible is sold, bagged, and out the door. From the time the snow begins to fall, it takes about an hour for every store shelf in every Jewel to become as empty as a school playground during an electrical storm.

By the time I make it to my corner store, there isn't a can of sardines left, not to mention a snack cracker to put one on.

"What are we going to eat, Dad?" Kelly asks. "Are we going to end up like that Donner Party?"

"We'll find something, Kelly."

"Who's the Donner Party?" Care asks.

"They were these people who got caught in a snowstorm, then trapped in a cabin, and ended up eating each other to stay alive," her older sister informs her.

"Like cannibals?"

"Yeah."

Care doesn't quite understand. "Why would they have a party while they were eating each other?"

"They were also very bored," I explain.

At home, I enlist the girls' help, and we scavenge the kitchen fridge and cupboards to find our sustenance. For dinner we have two baked potatoes, one can of corn, and seven ounces of tuna "tartare" with tarter sauce. For dessert they each have a purple popsicle, found tucked into the back corner of the freezer, behind what is either a hunk of very bad meat or very old cheese. Oddly enough, I hear fewer complaints on this dinner than I do when I make my famous chicken drumstick flambé cassarole.

After dinner and clean up, instead of wasting our time arguing about which TV show we'll watch, then watching the dumb show and arguing how dumb it was, I suggest we play "Hurry Up Monopoly." The difference between Hurry Up and regular Monopoly is in the beginning of the former, each player gets to draw three property cards, sort of like an inheritance without estate taxes. This jumpstarts the rent collections and gets the business flowing. The next three hours fly by. We have a great time. We wheel, deal, trade, get into jail, and pay our way to get out. We build houses and hotels, get rich, go broke, and laugh at our fortunes and misfortunes.

I love these times with my kids.

I saved my last three eggs and half loaf of bread to make French toast the next morning. The sun is up, the snow has stopped, and a snowy, white blanket covers the neighborhood like a pristine, untouched, unwrinkled, white blanket. It's beautiful.

As soon as I get word that the main arteries in the city are clear, we bundle up, go outside, dig out the car, and drive on a tilt until we hit a plowed Western Avenue. We go north, and we're back on Mount Trashmore in twenty minutes and spinning downward in fresh powder.

"Whee!"

The girls do their homework in the afternoon, and I have them back at their mother's house right on time. This was one great weekend. It just goes to show that there is a silver lining for every Chicago blizzard.

***

Returning home, my first sight is of *The Original Carlo*. The two crummy, tacked-up recipe cards look as lonely as two solo diners in an empty restaurant. I take out blank recipe cards and a pen, and sit to contemplate the case. After twenty minutes, I'm all contemplated out, and have not filled out one additional card. I came up with nothing. I get up, find a legal pad, flip to a blank page, and list the letters of the alphabet from top to bottom. It takes me about an hour to come up with the following list.

A.
B. Buick, Bree
C. Cremation, Cats, Casino, Cash
D. Deceased, Depression, Dr. Lunay
E. Eddie Floyd, Elvis, Embalming
F. Foreigner, Funeral, Face
G. Gambling, Garage, Green Card, GPS
H. Hollerback, Heart Attack

I.
J.
K. Kromka, Kittens
L. Levenchenko, Lawsuit, Lousy Weather, Lube-ista, Life Insurance
M. Mob, Murder, Mafia, Mayhem, Marriage
N. No Pictures
O.
P. PTGS, Payoff, Photo-less
R. Russian, Richmond, Recycle
S. Silly Putty
T. Terrorist, Trauma
U. Urn
V. Vilma
W. Why?
X.
Y.

I skip Q and Z because I've done these lists before and have yet to fill in a word for Q and Z. After I'm done, I go back and add Alibi Al to the "A" line and Leg-breaker to the "L" line.

I sit and stare at the list for an hour. I add: Player's Club Card, Ashes, and Neighbors, to their respective spots. I cross out: Lousy Weather, Cats, Kittens, and Deceased. I then draw arcing lines to connect certain words with others. Russian and Mob go together, as do Cash and Gambling, and Ashes and Urn. I don't have to draw a line from Silly Putty to Terrorist since one follows the other. For some reason, and I have no clue why, the word Buick pops out at me.

I go to bed hoping the electrical impulses of my brain go to work while I sleep, and I wake up with the entire case figured out.

***

The next morning, it doesn't happen. Who was I kidding?

CHAPTER 16

"You know who is the loneliest mobster in the Chicago Mafia, Sherlock?" John Bruski, my old friend, asks.

"No."

"Guido Bratusso."

"Who?" Tiffany asks.

John explains, "Guido was a hit man for the mob, and his assignment one afternoon was to put a bullet into the skull of one Ben Eto, a fellow Mafia guy who had turned rat in exchange for an immunity deal. Word had it that Ben had information, innuendo, and enough actual evidence to put boys as big as the Big Tuna, Jackie the Lackey, and Baby Fat Larry behind bars for years.

"So, Guido follows Ben to a hotel in Lincolnwood. He waits for him to finish his lunch, and when Ben goes to get in his car, Guido approaches him, pulls out his gun, and orders him to his knees. Guido puts his .25 caliber, pistol to the guy's brow, pulls the trigger, and Ben Eto falls into a heap next to his new car. Guido checks to see blood gushing from Ben's skull, smiles at his handy work, and hightails it outta there."

"How does that translate to being lonely?" Tiffany asks.

"Well, what happened was Guido must have put his gun too close to Ben's head and the bullet ended up merely bouncing off Eto's thick skull, knocking him out, and causing a bloody mess in the parking space.

"Ben Eto wakes up in a hospital bed a few hours later and his first call is to the Feds. He fingers Guido, and within an hour, the shooter's behind bars. By the next morning, every newspaper and TV station in town has Guido's face prominently displayed."

"I still don't get the lonely part," Tiffany confesses.

"He becomes lonely because half of Guido's family didn't know he was in the Mafia, much less a hit man, and were so ashamed they wouldn't have a thing to do with him. The other half of the family knew what Guido did for a living because a lot of them did the same thing, and they were so ashamed that

Guido was such a bad hit man they didn't want anything to do with him either.

"I don't think Guido's had a letter or a visitor since he went into the joint over twenty years ago."

John "Bulldog" Bruski is never without a story to tell. Although now retired, Bulldog was a fixture of TV news in Chicago for more than thirty years. Clad in a well-worn trench coat, he covered the Mafia in Chicago like Ernie Banks covered shortstop. Whenever a hit happened, a robbery took place, or the Feds cracked down, John "Bulldog" Bruski was there live on the scene. He covered trials, mafia wives, plots, and stings. He became so knowledgeable and recognized on all things criminal, it was rumored the Mafia would sometimes ask him for advice.

Tiffany and I are sitting in his living room Monday morning.

"What can you tell us about the Russian mob?" I ask.

"Those guys are mean."

"The Italians hate 'em?"

"Despise them," John says. "In Russia, they got so many thugs there's not enough thugging to go around so they smuggle guys in over here, set them up doing extortion schemes, burglaries, and whatever else. Sophistication is hardly their strong suit."

"Where do they hang out?"

"They used to frequent the baths on Division, but mostly they're out by O'Hare."

"Ever heard of a guy named Levenchenko?"

"They're all named Levenchenko, Sherlock."

I have one more thought before we leave. "Ever hear of the Hollerback Funeral Home?"

"Of course. I loved the name."

"It closed."

"Too bad. I covered a hundred stories from that place."

"Do you know what happened to the owner?"

"Frank, no."

"Do you think maybe he did freelance, 'under the table' work in the place?"

"Let me tell you, Sherlock, if people could holler back from Hollerback, I'd have enough stories for a year of special reports."

***

"Where to now, Mr. Sherlock?"

"We have enough time to swing by Vilma's house before we have lunch with Alibi Al."

"Why do they call him Alibi Al again?" Tiffany asks.

"That's another one you'll have to figure out by yourself, Tiffany."

"This is getting exhausting, Mr. Sherlock."

Twenty minutes later, Tiffany pulls up in front of Vilma's house. "Are we going in?"

"No. We can't. Eddie Floyd would have us in court in a heartbeat."

"Then what are we doing here?"

"Drive around back to her garage. I want to see her Buick."

"Are you thinking of buying one? Anything would be better than that thing you drive."

"Let me tell you, Tiffany, while all the fancy cars have frozen solid in their garages this winter, my Toyota has started up every time quicker than a gas burner on a short order grill."

"The day's not over, Mr. Sherlock."

I have Tiffany pull up in front of the open garage. I get out, walk to the back of the car, and check the metal frame around the license plate. It reads Ray Buick. I proceed to the driver's side, flip the latch on the door, and discover it's locked. I use my sleeve to defog the window, and peer inside to the dashboard. I should have known the odometer would be electronic and feel stupid seeing it dark. I next try to see the VIN number through the front windshield but fail at that too. I am able to get the make and model from the sticker below where I can't make out the VIN number. Vilma drives a new Buick Regal Luxury Sport Sedan. Lucky her.

This should be enough. I get back in Tiffany's car.

"Don't get a Buick, Mr. Sherlock. Those are like old people's cars. Get a Lexus or a BMW."

"Don't worry, Tiffany, right now I couldn't afford to buy a skateboard."

"You can't ride a skateboard in the snow, Mr. Sherlock. Maybe you should get a sled."

"Thank you, Tiffany."

***

Al Landeen is waiting for us in the Salt and Pepper Diner on Lincoln.

"I hope you don't mind I went ahead and ordered," he informs us as we sit across from him in a back booth.

"Is that the Sergai file?" I ask, pointing at the manila envelope on the table next to his deluxe sandwich plate.

"Yep." He hands it over to me. "Be careful, I happened to get a little mustard on it myself."

"What are you eating?" Tiffany asks Al as I page through the file.

"Corned beef on rye."

Tiffany takes a closer look. "Are those little bits of corn or is that just fat around the pink meat?"

"The fat is what gives it its flavor," Al informs Tiffany.

"Is that why you put so much mustard on it?"

"No, the mustard brings out the flavor of the rye."

"It's more like corn your beef and die," Tiffany says.

I read through a very sketchy police report and find little of interest, but I do find a Xerox copy of Sergai's green card. The likeness is lousy, but it is the first glimpse I've had of what the guy looks like. He's no Cary Grant."

The waitress comes over.

"If you order a deluxe sandwich, you get extra fries," Al tells Tiffany. "And feel free to splurge; this one's on me."

Tiffany studies the menu as if it were the Rosetta Stone. "I'll have the tuna burger, grilled, hold the bun, extra pickle, fresh fruit instead of fries, carrot slices instead of the slaw, a half of a red pepper, two radishes, one stalk of celery, balsamic vinegar on the side, and a cup of low-fat chicken broth."

"You want the chicken broth first, or should I bring it all together?" the waitress asks, scribbling down the order.

"First."

"You?"

"I'll have a turkey sandwich on wheat, no mayo," I order and add, "Free-range turkey if you have it."

"Good for you, Mr. Sherlock."

"Sorry," our waitress apologizes. "It's too cold for the chickens to range free this time of year."

Before the woman leaves our table, Al tells her, "Make his a deluxe and give me his fries."

I continue to page through the file. "It makes no mention of Sergai being married."

"Why would it?" Al has a point.

"There's also no Xerox of his passport."

"If he has a green card, he wouldn't need a passport," Al says, munching on his last handful of fries.

"He spells his name with a 'c' instead of a 'k.'"

"Them foreigners don't know how to spell, Sherlock."

I get to the TSA report. "It says he was going to Omaha. Who goes to Omaha in late December?"

"Omaha-ians," Tiffany answers.

"It says he was going on business but doesn't say what business he was in."

"Entrepreneur," Al says.

Our food comes, and Al digs in on my fries since his plate is now clean. "Why are you so interested in this guy, Sherlock?"

"He was the husband of a woman suing Richmond for the PTGD."

"What's PTGD?"

"Post-traumatic grief disorder."

"What the heck is that?"

"She's claiming she's had so much grief after her husband died she's no longer capable of working."

"I didn't know you could do that."

"Neither did anybody else, until she did it."

"And we have to stop her before she makes a mountain out of a whole hill," Tiffany says.

"How'd he die?" Al asks.

"Broken heart."

"Was it induced?" Al asks.

"What do you mean?"

"These guys have been known to wire 'em up, turn on the juice, and let the heart do belly flops."

"That doesn't sound very nice," Tiffany says.

Al finishes my fries before I take a bite of my sandwich. "He probably knew something they didn't want anybody else to know. So they dusted him."

Tiffany munches away on her carrot sticks while she tries to scrape the greasy butter off the tuna. She sees the picture of

Sergai. "No amount of mousse is going to help this guy's hair," she remarks.

"If he was detained by the TSA, there would have to be a video recording of the incident. Have you seen that, Al?"

"No, but it's not my fault. It hasn't come on Netflix yet." He laughs at his own joke.

"Why don't you see if you can get a copy?"

"I could probably do that."

Tiffany's phone goes into a frenzy. She punches the screen a few times and reports, "Mr. Sherlock, we got to go."

Al pipes up, "Check, please."

Tiffany says, "There's a meeting we have to be at." Tiffany turns up her nose. "And Bree's going to be there. Yuck."

The waitress lays the check in front of me, but Al picks it up. "I got this." He pulls his wallet out of his pocket opens it, "Oh my Lord, can you believe this? My wife must have cleaned me out of cash and not told me about it. I hate that." He flashes the empty leather before us. "Hey, this isn't my fault, the woman has no scruples when it comes to money." He pauses. "Could you help me out here?"

"Why don't you use that?" Tiffany says pointing to Al's plastic.

"His credit card's overdrawn," I say. "Don't you remember?"

"Not that one," Tiffany points to the card in the wallet. "That one. It's a debit card. I saw an ATM right outside."

Al suddenly looks like he's coming down with food poisoning. "I don't trust those machines. I don't think they're safe. Criminals could steal your personal information."

"I use them all the time. I'll show you how." Tiffany gets up and helps Al out of the booth.

I watch as Al takes the debit card in his hand and nervously follows Tiffany out the door.

Two minutes later, they're back inside. Al has a relieved expression on his face. "Whew."

"The machine wouldn't take the card," Tiffany says. "It kept kicking it back out."

"Let me see it."

I take it from Al. The card has a fold across the right side. Wonder how that got there?

"Not my fault those machines don't work. I told you they

were trouble." He shows his empty wallet one more time, pushes the check to our side of the table, and says, "I promise, my turn next."

***

When Tiffany and I walk into the Richmond conference room, Saul Rabinowitz, aka TV Eddie Floyd, sits on the right, Bree Bisonette, pronounced Biz-o-nay, sits at the head of the table, and Houston Twitchell, Esq., his attractive female assistant, and nerdy computer geek kid sit on the left.

"What's going on?" I ask.

"Vilma's attorney has refiled the case, changing the amount of damages," Bree tells us.

"You can do that?" I ask.

"Sure, why not?" Eddie answers.

"He's gone from one hundred twenty thousand to five hundred thirty thousand," Bree explains.

"Why?"

"Incapacitation," Eddie answers.

"Her head came off?" Tiffany asks.

"Extended incapacitation." Eddie explains, "She could be out of work for decades, not years."

Before I can speak, Eddie says, "Now, if you would prefer to avoid a long, dragged-out court proceeding, the firm of Eddie Floyd and Associates would consider a settlement."

Bree is about to speak but looks to Houston, who is being whispered to by his lady.

"I'm waiting," Eddie says.

Houston leans away from the woman, looks at the computer screen pushed before him by the kid, and says, "No."

"I assure we will be more than fair, negotiate in good faith, and save all concerned valuable time and money," Eddie says.

Twitchell takes more counsel/whispering from his associate, pauses to see the next message on the computer, and says, "No."

"If that's the way you feel about it, fine," Eddie says in a huff, packs up his things, and heads for the door. "I'll see you in court."

Bree, Tiffany, Houston, his minions, and I sit for a few seconds. I break the silence. "That was quite a devastating argument you put up, Houston."

Houston listens to his woman's whisper and says, "Yes."

Bree sits back in her big chair, gets a smug look on her face, and turns to Tiffany. "Being the lead detective on the Kromka case, can you give us an update on your investigation?" Bree adds a snarky smile to her question.

Tiffany returns the smile with a vicious sneer. "Well, Miss Biz-o-nette, I, with the help of Mr. Sherlock, have found a number of inadequacies in the case so far."

I'm thinking, *we have?*

"Would you like to expound upon them for us?" Bree continues.

"No." Tiffany smiles at Houston as if to thank him for the answer.

"Well, expound anyway, Tiffy," Bree says.

I go to Tiffany's rescue. "We are going to need some additional information on the life insurance policy on Vilma's husband Sergai."

"Why?" Houston asks after a prompt from his muse.

"Because I—we—feel the key to the case is Sergai, not Vilma."

Houston listens to a whisper and asks, "Why?"

"Because why would she sue for more money after being awarded five hundred grand in cash?" I return.

"Greed, a hunger for money, a pot of gold at the end of a rainbow due to the guy dying," Bree answers.

"Interesting you would come up with that scenario, Miss Biz-o-nette."

"Oh, before I forget, Tiffy," Bree says, "I have a favor to ask before you leave."

I break in. I have to get this back on track. "Bree, could you tell Selma Warma we'll be calling for additional information on the Kromka case?"

"Do it soon, her retirement party is this Friday afternoon."

"Could you bring her in now?"

Bree goes to her phone, dials the extension, speaks, and in a few minutes, Selma Warma enters the room.

"Yes?"

"I know you have a lot of finishing up to do, but I need to know if Sergai Levenchenko had other life insurance policies besides Richmond's when he died."

"I don't remember."

"Could you find out and let us know?

"Of course."

"Houston," I ask, "anything you need?"

Houston hears a whisper, reads from the kid's computer screen, and says, "No."

The computer slams shut, the steno pad closes, and the three from Hickel, Belittle, Twitchell, and Mitchell exit, leaving only three in the room, two of which are quite volatile.

"Oh, Tiffy," Bree says, "I understand you'll be seeing Jamison this evening?"

"I call him daddy."

Bree pulls out of nowhere a folded pair of boxer shorts and socks. "Your daddy left these at my place. I'm sure he won't mind that I had my laundress add a bit of fabric softener to give him a little more fluffy comfort during his long, hard days at the office." She hands them to Tiffany.

If looks could kill, Bree would soon be on the "ready-to-be-made-up" gurney at the Pyre/Lament Funeral Home, Crematorium, and Mausoleum, and Tiffany would be helping Thelma with just enough blush.

CHAPTER 17

Tiffany not only gets mad at Bree but stays mad at Bree. "I'd like to take that biotch, ring her neck so hard all the Botox pops out of her, and she's left with more wrinkles than a linen blouse at the bottom of the drawer."

"Calm down, Tiffany."

"I can't. I hate her. I bet if she got hit with a bucket of water, she'd melt."

"Hating someone is never the answer to anything, Tiffany. Go to your spa," I tell her. "It's the only thing that will calm you down."

"But I have to work the case. This is all the more reason I have to show Daddy I'm worth more than a trip down the runway in the latest Givenchy."

"Take it easy, Tiffany. You don't want to be hyped up when you see your dad tonight."

"I want to be able to tell him something good."

"Try telling him you love him."

"That's not going to solve the case, Mr. Sherlock."

I pause to give the conversation a break. "Why don't you let me go it alone the rest of the day? I promise I won't discover anything new until you're back with me."

"Well, if you promise, Mr. Sherlock."

I give her a pat on her shoulder. "Your dad loves you, Tiffany. Don't ever doubt that. Just go and have a good time."

"Thanks, Mr. Sherlock. I'll try."

I take the 'L' home. The apartment is freezing so I go through the usual rigmarole to get the place out of the arctic blast.

Once toasty, I pick up the phone and call Ray Buick.

"Service, please."

"Service."

"Hi, my name is Elmer Kromka and my mother bought a Buick Regal from you not that long ago and because she's starting to lose it a bit, I need to know when she last had the car serviced."

"Spell the name for me," the guy says on the line.

I do. There is a pause. I can hear his fingers clicking on the computer keyboard.

"She had it in for her six-month inspection a month ago," he says.

"That's a relief. Could you transfer me to the credit department?" I ask the kind sir.

"Hold on."

The connection is made and soon I hear, "Credit department."

"Hi, my name is Boris Kromka and my mother, Vilma, purchased a Buick Regal from you about seven months ago. I've come into a little money, and for her next birthday, I'm thinking of paying off her note on the car. Could you tell me the balance?"

"Sure."

The clicks on the computer keyboard are a little softer this time. "There is a balance of twenty-six thousand six hundred and forty dollars."

"Wow, that much?" I exclaim. "I thought she put down, like, twenty grand

when she bought it."

"No, she put down five, plus the trade-in on her old car."

"Well, I'm not sure I have that much money."

"It was a nice thought," the lady tells me. "None of my kids would ever do that for me."

So, Vilma bought the car before she married Sergai with five grand in cash. Bingo.

For the next twenty minutes, I fill out index cards and pin them up on *The Original Carlo.*

My cell phone rings. It's Tiffany.

"Are you better?" I ask right off the bat.

"I've decided to channel the negative energy I'm using to hate Bree into positive action."

"That's great Tiffany. What are you going to do?"

"I don't know. You have to give me something good to do, Mr. Sherlock."

I'm at a loss, besides getting renewed at her Re-New-Me Spa, I can't think of a lot of other choices. "Exactly what kind of action were you considering?"

"Action on the case, Mr. Sherlock, on the case," she explains.

I can't come up with many new ideas on that either.

"Well—"

I hear an odd sound. "Wait, hold on, Tiffany." The sound repeats two more times. My memory flogs. I rush to my Navy bridge coat and pull out the GPS Chappie loaned me. I get back on the phone. "Where are you right now, Tiffany?"

"I'm in my car, just north of North Avenue."

"Vilma's headed your way." I watch the GPS screen intently as I speak. She's on Belmont, turning right on Elston. Pick her up and follow her."

"This sounds exciting, Mr. Sherlock. I will."

I stay on the phone until I hear, "There she is. I got her."

"Don't get too close. I don't want her to see you."

"I got this, Mr. Sherlock. I got this."

"Call me back when you find out where she goes."

"Ten-four."

For all I know Vilma is making a run to the PetSmart.

I'm not sure if bulk will translate into understanding, but I tack up another twenty new recipe cards on *The Original Carlo.* I am arranging and re-arranging when my phone rings again.

"I'm at the bank, Mr. Sherlock."

"Aren't you supposed to be following Vilma?"

"She's at the bank."

"Is she at the teller window?"

"No, she's in the vault."

"What is she doing in the vault?"

"I don't know. I asked, but the guy wouldn't let me in the vault with her even after I told him who I was and that my dad is a big, big customer."

"The nerve of the guy."

"Oh, wait, wait. Here she comes."

"What is she doing?"

"She's folding up hundred dollar bills and putting them in her purse."

"Mad money," I say.

"No, Mr. Sherlock, I'm not mad anymore."

I hear through Tiffany's phone, "Hey, aren't you the lady who was at my house the other day?" No doubt about it, it's Vilma. "Are you following me?"

"No," Tiffany tells her.

"You have an account here?"

"No."

Bad answer, Tiffany.

"You're harassing me."

"No, I'm not. I'm in line for the ATM."

"There's no ATM on the vault floor."

"I got some bad directions from the teller." Tiffany does not think well on her feet, her butt, or her hands.

"I'm going to tell my lawyer, Eddie Floyd, and he's going to punch you out."

"Just get out of there, Tiffany," I tell her over the phone.

"Bring him on, I can handle that wimp," Tiffany yells at Vilma. "I've got a designer belt in Crab Macau." She obviously didn't listen to me.

"Let her go, Tiffany, just let Vilma go."

"Sorry," Tiffany says to Vilma, "I can't fight with you now. I have to take this call."

A few seconds transpire. "Okay, Mr. Sherlock, she's gone. Do you want me to follow her?"

"You think you can follow her without her knowing you're following her?" I ask Tiffany.

"No problem."

I click off my phone and go back to *The Original Carlo*.

A good detective will never rule any scenario out. He can take the most absurd, inane, ridiculous line of reasoning and consider it along with the most obvious. The further out his wacky idea may be, the better it usually is because it will open his mind to other intricacies in the case he may not readily see.

As I stand here and rearrange the recipe cards, the most logical line of reasoning stares me right in the face. Vilma and Sergai find each other and readily realize they have something each other wants. Vilma wants a new car and Sergai wants a pass to get into the USA. They strike a deal, and for lack of a better term, we'll call it a marriage of financial convenience. Vilma gets ten grand and Sergai gets a green card. To make their borsch kosher, they find a cheap trailer to take up "residence" in the eyes of the immigration department, and basically continue on their merry ways, Vilma with her cats and Sergai with his crimes.

All goes well for the happy couple until Sergai gets caught trying to carry explosives into Omaha. Why and for what reason, I'll probably never know. Whether Vilma knows about this or not, I'm not sure, but in the eyes of immigration, trying to smuggle exploding Silly Putty onto an airplane is not a sign of a good citizen or a good marriage. To complicate matters, nature takes its course right to the newlywed's happy trailer home and obliterates it with a tornado. Since Sergai is not seen at Vilma's Ridgeway house, obviously he's laying low and off the radar, which is another negative sign in the first year of marriage. I have a feeling Vilma gets wind, regular not tornado, of Sergai's inadequacies as a crook, and to cover herself, takes out a life insurance policy on his well-being for her future well-being. And true to form, Sergai goes down brokenhearted, possibly by his own people. "Probably knew something somebody didn't want him to know," in the immortal words of Alibi Al Landeen.

Sergai gets cremated, Vilma takes the urn home to share with her cats, and finds herself suddenly rich. Whoopee! She starts or increases the time spent in her number one pastime, gambling. She gets more use out of her Players Club Card than a dozen busloads of senior citizens with two-for-one spin coupons.

Vilma gets fired from her job, more for lack of salesmanship than depression, and spends more and more time at the casino. Soon she sees her money start to ebb, and to her credit, she decides to do something about it. She files an absurd lawsuit, saying she is in the throes of incapacitating depression. Vilma must figure this money will be as easy as the life insurance money, but it doesn't happen that way. Tiffany and I show up. Vilma is forced to lawyer up with Eddie Floyd, who won't take the case for fifty percent of the measly one hundred thirty thousand Vilma is asking, so he quadruples the amount, hoping Richmond settles for half, and he picks up an easy quarter mil walkin' around money. It is all so simple, logical, and easy to assume.

But what is my first rule of life? Never assume anything.

I have to take this out of the box. What else could it be?

Number one: How about if Vilma marries Sergai for ten grand, takes a life insurance policy out on him, and uses five of the ten grand he paid her to have him snuffed? Number two: How about if Vilma is tied into the Russian mob and the entire caper was set up by them: marriage, hit, life insurance, the whole ball of wax? Number three: This is all part of a terrorist plot, Sergai is only collateral damage, and Vilma merely got lucky? Number four: How about if Sergai was out to set Vilma up, and she was to be part of some sinister plot to transport Silly Putty explosives across the country? The whole caper gets screwed up when Sergai gets detained by the TSA for wearing his belt through the metal detector. And finally, number five: How about if Sergai had a weird fetish for women who like cats?

My phone rings. It's Tiffany.

"Guess where she's going, Mr. Sherlock?"

"Casino."

"How'd you know that?"

Besides having the GPS right in front of me, it was a pretty easy guess. "She goes to the bank, pulls out cash, and goes to the casino to lose it."

"Mr. Sherlock, you never cease to amaze me."

"Thank you." Her compliment is really not much to be proud of, but you take what you can get in life. "You can turn around, Tiffany. Go home, have a nice dinner with your dad."

"Ta-ta, Mr. Sherlock, ta-ta."

CHAPTER 18

The moment she picks up the phone, I know something is wrong. "What's the matter, Tiffany?"

"Daddy had to cancel. He said his four o'clock ran into his five o'clock, and his five o'clock ran into his five thirty, and his five thirty ran late, then they all went out for drinks, and I should check with his secretary to reschedule."

"I'm sorry, Tiffany."

"I bet if I would've had something to tell him about the Kromka case, he would have made time for me. Instead, he blew me off like lint from a belly button."

"You feel pretty rotten, don't you?"

"Yeah."

"I'm sorry."

There is a pause. I tell her, "I know what would make you feel better."

"Seeing Bree Baguette put on thirty pounds?"

"No."

"Bree's feet swell up, and the only shoes she can wear are duck boots?"

"Don't be mean, Tiffany."

"I can't help it; I hate her."

"What you need is a bath."

"A bath? Me?"

"Yes."

"Milk or regular?"

"Neither."

"Mr. Sherlock, you're either losing it or you're getting real weird on me all of a sudden."

***

At the turn of the last century, there must have been a large population of Russians and Eastern Europeans living around Division Street west of Milwaukee Avenue because that's where they built the Russian Bath building in 1906. It is a huge concrete edifice with stonework and design from the Eastern

Orthodox School of Architecture. I have no clue how many renovations it has gone through, but it still operates in much the same fashion as it did one hundred years ago. Although today, besides Russians, Turks, and Armenians, it has become a *go-to* spot for North Side yuppies wanting something different than a Re-New-Me spa.

Tiffany and I arrive before lunch on Tuesday.

"What is this place?"

"I'm surprised you don't know," I tell her as we enter the small office, stomping the snow and ice off our boots on the pad past the door.

"Why would I?"

"Because it's the new cool thing to do when it comes to communal bathing."

"I've never been one to share skin moisturizers, Mr. Sherlock."

"What we're actually here for is to find someone who knew Sergai Levenchenko or Vilma."

"And you expect me to do that without my clothes on?"

"Just this once."

"Mr. Sherlock ..."

"You said you wanted to do some positive action, Tiffany. Now, you can find out something about our most wanted and get cleaned and refreshed at the same time."

"Can I help you?" the young woman who works the entry desk says as we approach.

"We'd both like the full treatment," I tell the nice lady.

"Have you been here before?"

"No. We've had a lot of baths but none of this variety."

"May I suggest the venik technique?"

"Sounds good to me."

"Are you sure, Mr. Sherlock?"

"Trust me," the lady tells Tiffany. "You're going to love it."

Tiffany is still a bit skeptical. She asks the lady, "I'm not going to end up a Communist, am I?"

We are given a locker for our valuables, an optional bathing suit, slippers, a funny looking hat, and our veniks, an odd-looking tree branch with a number of twigs attached. The nice woman directs me to the left and Tiffany to the right, where the first stop will be to "undress and take a nice shower."

"I thought we were here for a bath?" Tiffany questions.

Inside the locker area, I strip down, take a quick shower, and proceed down the hall to the banya sauna/steam room. The only item I'm wearing is the funny hat, which reminds me of the one Chico Marx wore in the movies.

An attendant meets me before I enter the hot room, hands me a couple of towels, and takes my venik, which he immerses into a bucket of water. Inside, the steam is so thick I have a hard time adjusting my eyes but manage to find a spot in the first row of tiered wooden benches, which face the pile of hot rocks stacked like cannonballs. "The higher you sit, the hotter it gets," the man informs me with an accent as thick as the Volga River in February.

I can hear a number of voices, some in English and some, I suspect, in Russian. I listen. The English conversation concerns the best ways to avoid commitments with women you are sleeping with, and the Russian conversations—I have no clue. After about fifteen minutes, the attendant offers me hot tea, and again I have no clue why. I sit and sip for another ten minutes, and the attendant approaches once more, "Ready?"

"Guess so."

The guy lays me down on a wet, sheeted table, tells me to relax, and starts whacking me with the venik like a boss man whips a galley slave. At first it hurts, at second it hurts more, but on the third or fourth slap to my backsides, it starts to feel pretty good. He turns me over and starts on my frontside. I can't believe it. This is great. He whacks me front, back, and sides from my heels to my head, with the exception of my privates. Once all the way through, I'm as loose as a goose. I haven't felt this good since an ex-doctor for my bad back overdosed me with muscle relaxers.

"Get up," he says, helping me off the table. "Dis way."

He leads me out of the steam room, down a hallway to a small pool, and tells me to "Jump in. Feel good."

After having someone whip you with a birchbark branch and having it feel great, I have all the trust in the world in the guy, so I dive right in.

I don't know how those Swedish guys feel going from the frigid snow to the sauna, but I do know the opposite feeling. The water is freezing cold. I almost shoot out of it at a greater rate of speed than when I shot in. After about thirty seconds, and I can breath once again, a tingling sensation comes over my entire body, and I feel as rejuvenated as a repentant sinner at a revival meeting.

"Time to get out," he tells me and leads me back into the sauna/steam room where we repeat the entire process.

During my third whisking, which is what I'd call whipping, I ask him, "Like your work?"

"Can't beat it."

"The guy who told me about this place is a guy named Levenchenko, know him?"

"Know lots of Levenchenkos."

"Sergai Levenchenko?"

"Sure."

"Seen him lately?"

"Don't remember."

"Ever meet his wife, Vilma?"

"Not here."

That makes sense.

"Remember what he looks like?" I ask.

"If he your friend, why would you want to know what he looks like?"

Good point.

"I just wondered because there's a lot of Levenchenkos out there."

I can feel the guy back off. I can also feel the tree branch hitting me much harder.

"We might be all together in here," he says, and I immediately think all together in the all together. "But we don't talk much."

"What goes on in the banya, stays in the banya," I say.

"Yeah. Now roll over."

After my last dunk in the cold water, I am given a robe and led to a sitting room with tables and chairs. It reminds me of a small café. Men and women are sitting around drinking beer or vodka and eating snacks. There is a menu on the table if you'd like a bliny, shashlik, or plate of stroganov. I pass.

Five minutes later, Tiffany enters and sits down next to me. "Mr. Sherlock, I feel wonderful."

"Did you find out anything about Sergai?"

"Who?"

"We're here to find stuff out about Vilma's ex-husband."

"I was having such a good time getting whiskeyed I forgot

all about him."

"Well, at least you got your mind off your troubles."

"I just thought of something that would really make me feel good, Mr. Sherlock."

"What?"

"Me giving Bree Biotch-o-nay the old venik treatment, but I'd use a much bigger birchbark without any twigs on it."

***

We are in the Russian Bath's parking lot when I notice my phone has a message. I dial one and listen.

"Bree wants to see us, Tiffany."

"Yuck."

"You don't have to go if you don't want to," I tell her.

"I hate her."

"It does you no good to hate anyone, Tiffany."

"I know, but I still hate her. She's trying to take my daddy away from me."

"No, she's not."

"Yes, she is. I can see it right through her phony eyelashes."

"After we meet with Bree, we also have to go see Chappie today," I tell her.

"Give me a minute, Mr. Sherlock, so I can figure out what's worst."

"Plus, we don't have much time; I got to pick up my kids at school today."

I leave my car in the bath lot, and Tiffany drives us to the Aon Center. She parks in a handicapped spot in the underground parking lot, and we take the elevator up to the lobby floor.

They have a clever way of elevating people skyward in the Aon Building. Each elevator car is actually two cars stacked on top of each other so when one stops on an even floor the other stops at an odd floor. Thus, there is also the need for a two-floor lobby. We're at the odd floor lobby, and being around 1 p.m. the place is packed with workers returning from lunch. I am standing next to Tiffany, minding my own business, when I feel something hit me in the back of my neck. Not hard, not painful, but I could never miss the feeling. I turn slightly around, and I get hit again, this time right in the middle of my forehead. I look around to search for the perpetrator, see no one, and peer down on the ground to discover two folded paper airplanes lying at my feet. This is strange. I reach down, pick up the paper projectile, and just as I am unfolding, a man comes out of nowhere and says to me, "Richard Sherlock?"

"Yes."

"You've been served."

The man smiles and calmly walks away.

"Who was that, Mr. Sherlock?"

"Hopefully, no one associated with my ex-wife."

The elevator comes and goes as I finish unfolding and read the two pages.

"What's it say?" Tiffany asks.

"It is a cease and desist order from Eddie Floyd."

"Does Eddie Floyd detest you?"

"He went to court and convinced a judge we are needlessly harassing his client, causing her undo stress and worry. And we are now no longer allowed to get less than two hundred feet from her."

"I'm not sure that's a bad thing, Mr. Sherlock. I could smell cat on her from two hundred feet."

The elevator comes. We crowd in with a ton of people. "You know, Mr. Sherlock—"

I interrupt her, "Don't talk in elevators, Tiffany."

Of course she doesn't listen. "After this case is solved, do you think I could get a cease and detest order to keep Bree away from my dad."

"You'd have to ask Houston Twitchell."

"Yes."

As we enter Bree Bisonette's office, it is once again hate at first sight between Bree and Tiffany.

"Jamison felt so bad about not being able to see you on Monday night, Tiffy."

"Really?"

"He was so distraught all he wanted to do that night was cuddle."

Tiffany's nostrils flare, eyes bulge, and ears almost steam.

"Your daddy's quite the spooner," Bree adds.

I catch Tiffany before her perfectly manicured nails scratch out Bree Bisonette's eyes.

"All right, all right, stop you two."

Bree stands back as I hold Tiffany back.

"Why do you two have to constantly snipe at one another?" I ask.

"Because she's an evil witch trying to pit my dad against me," Tiffany shouts.

"If anyone's the pits, it's you, Tiffy."

"I've heard what I think you're saying about me to my dad."

"Like what?"

"You said I was from the shallow end of the gene pool."

"I said no such thing," Bree says. "You want me to repeat some of the comments you've made about me?"

"Sure, go ahead."

"You said I've had so many facelifts that when I smile my socks go up."

"I did not."

Bree goes on, "It is difficult for me to understand how you, who's had more plastic surgery than an entire cleft palate hospital ward, could question the one time I have a small amount of reconstruction."

"One time?" Tiffany retorts. "You've been cut on more times than a whole tuna by a sushi chef."

"Stop. This is doing no one any good."

"She started it."

"No, you started it."

"Did not."

"Did too."

"Stop!"

"You want to take the place of my mother," Tiffany spits at her.

"If there is one thing in the world I don't want, it's to become your mother."

"Enough!"

My shout is enough to ring the bell to put an end to the round and hopefully the fight. "May I remind you two we are in the middle of a case, and it is not going well."

Their pause continues, so I continue. "Eddie Floyd went to court to keep us away from Vilma, and if that's not enough, we still haven't figured out Sergai, or have any factual evidence of wrongdoing to fight this in court."

The two are breathing a notch or two beneath where they were a minute ago.

"Did Selma Warma get back to you on the liens against Sergai's insurance settlement?" I ask Bree.

"No, she's been real busy with people taking her out to celebrate her retirement," Bree admits.

"Has Houston Twitchell got back to you on his next moves?"

"I asked," Bree says, "and all he said was 'no.'"

"This is not looking good, people," I conclude. I feel like I'm at the end of my rope. "Maybe we should settle with Eddie Floyd and be rid of the whole mess?" I say, more thinking out loud than talking.

"And let all those other people start claiming PTGD?" Tiffany says. "Daddy will have a coronary."

Tiffany is right. What was I thinking?

"I agree with you," Bree says. "Let's get this settled and behind us."

"What should we do, Mr. Sherlock?"

I contemplate the problem for a few seconds, coming to a better sense of my senses. "Maybe we should quit playing defense and start playing offense."

"How?"

"Yeah, how?"

"We've got to put this case into our corner instead of Eddie Floyd's."

Neither speaks, which is good.

"If we can prove Vilma married Sergai so he could get a green card and she could buy a new car, immigration would step in, and we'd be out of the woods."

"I never thought of that," Bree says.

"I did," Tiffany says, "but I've been waiting for the right time to mention it."

"Or, if we could prove Vilma married Sergai, discovered he's in the Russian mob, buys a life insurance policy on him, and either waits for him to get bumped off or pays for someone to do the job."

"Who cares? Let's just settle," Bree says.

"Or maybe Sergai is this weird guy who has a thing for women with a lot of cats?" Tiffany wonders.

I pause. "The point here is that Sergai is still the key to figuring this out. Vilma's not depressed. The only depression she feels is when she loses playing the slots. She didn't get fired for being depressed; she got fired because she couldn't upsell customers from the standard lube job to the deluxe."

"So what do we do?" Bree asks.

"Resurrect Sergai, or at least find out who he was."

"How?"

"First I have to know where Sergai had the physical required by Richmond before the policy was granted."

"I can get that," Bree says.

"I need to get Houston Twitchell to call off Eddie Floyd. If I can't get near Vilma, my hands are really going to be tied."

"Yes," Tiffany says.

"And I need you two to quit fighting. You two are worse than my kids."

"I wasn't fighting," Bree says. "I was defending my honor."

"The only honor you got is to honor my father," Tiffany fires back.

"Stop! Don't start this again."

Neither speaks.

"I want you two to agree to a truce. No more name-calling, insults, sniping at each other, and being so darn mean to one another."

Neither still speaks.

"Come on ..."

"Well," Tiffany says, "I will if she will."

"I will if she will too," Bree follows.

"All right, shake on it."

The two come face to face. Bree puts her right hand out. Tiffany backs off. "I'd rather air kiss."

"Me too."

Oh, jeesh.

***

We're in Tiffany's car, going north back to my car. It is past 2:30 p.m.

"I'm giving you the choice, Tiffany."

"Ralph Lauren or Yves St. Laurent?"

"No. You can either go see Chappie or pick up my kids from school."

"That's not a pick, Mr. Sherlock, that's better of all evils."

Tiffany drops me off at my car. "You know where their

school is, right?"
"Yes."
"And don't stop for any junk food."
"No problem there."

***

Chappie is wearing a turtleneck sweater, which makes his neck look like the section of a boa constrictor where a barnyard's worth of dead chickens now lie.
"Where's Tiffany?" He asks.
"She's picking up my kids from school."
"Too bad, I was looking forward to seeing her. I don't get a lot of ten-plus model types coming to see me."
"Neither do I."
I sit next to him, but before we begin, his mother comes downstairs with two glasses filled with ice and lemon wedges.
"Thanks, Mom, but you forgot to pour the ice tea in," Chappie tells her.
"I thought something was missing," she says before retreating back up the stairs.
"Got anything for me, Chappie?"
Listings of data appear on the big screen in front of us. "Here's all your Levenchenkos, but I can't seem to nail any of them as being your Levenchenko."
"That's not good."
"There is no recorded deed of a Levenchenko owning a trailer in Plainfield."
"He was probably renting."
"I have no employment records or filings with the State of Illinois for a Sergai Levenchenko the way you spelled his name."
"These guys come over here and work for cash so that isn't odd," I tell him.
"And no arrests."
I tell Chappie of the TSA incident, and he tells me, "If they didn't arrest the guy, there would be no record to find."
This is frustrating, to say the least.
"This guy is as elusive as Waldo in a Jackson Pollock painting," I complain.
Chappie says, "What you might do is check with Richmond

if any claims were filed by either of them for the losses they sustained when the tornado wiped out their trailer."

I'll get Selma Warma right on that one.

"You might also check the passenger manifest for his flight to Omaha the day he was caught. Maybe he had buddies with him."

I'll try Alibi Al for that one, but won't expect much.

Mom brings back the glasses, this time filled with something more brownish than tea-ish.

"Be careful, dude, she gets chocolate Ex-Lax and ice tea mixed up quite often."

I leave the drink alone.

"I did find some interesting items concerning Vilma Kromka."

"Good. What?"

"She's Latvian, not Russian."

"Close enough."

"She was brought over here by her mother when Carter was president."

"That's not odd."

"And she made her living as an actress for a short period of time."

This is interesting.

"She was a Homemakers' girl."

Homemakers was a 100-year-old-plus furniture store chain owned by the John M. Smythe Company, "That's Smythe with an 'e.'" It went out of business about ten years ago. I often sing the melody I remember from seeing their TV commercial a few million times, "Home-makers ... Home-makers ..."

"She did it for about six months," Chappie says. "But she was no Shelly Long."

Shelly Long was a spokesperson for the chain before she hit the big time playing Diane on the TV show *Cheers* and Carol Brady in the Brady Bunch movies.

"I couldn't find another posted roll where she was ever credited again," Chappie finishes.

"Fame is fleeting."

"She was also married twice before Sergai."

My ears perk up.

"First husband died. The second she divorced after he deserted her. No kids in either."

"How did the first guy die?"

"Couldn't find that out. There was no obit anywhere."

"When?"

"Eighteen years ago."

"I know this sounds crazy, Chappie, but is there any way you could find out if he was interred or processed at the Hollerback Funeral Home in Logan Square?"

"You're kidding, right?"

"No."

"Why?"

"We might be working with a black widow here."

CHAPTER 19

The wind has picked up, and the temperature has fallen below zero, but I'm snug as a bug in a rug as I motor through traffic on my way home. I can't help but notice a number of new and newer cars with hoods up and cables running out, getting jumped by tow trucks or other cars. I'll have to make sure to mention to my car's skeptics how well my Toyota has performed in this winter's deep freeze.

My spirits have also perked up, although finding out that someone you thought was merely a deadbeat insurance scammer could actually be a cold-blooded killer is hardly a reason for celebration.

The traffic is horrible on the way north, and I don't get home until close to six. I walk in the door to find culinary chaos.

There are enough cardboard containers scattered around my living room to feed the Chinese Red Army. Kelly, Care, and Tiffany, each armed with chopsticks, are moving from one container to the next, sampling each box of suey, chow mein, dim sum, and dumpling like critics at an Asian foodie festival.

"What are you doing?" I say before I get my coat off.

"Tiffany says we have to improve our Pilates."

"I think she meant palette," I correct.

"So far," Care says, "I like the noodles the best."

"You know," I tell them, "Chinese food isn't good for you. The fat content is through the roof."

"It's not Chinese, Mr. Sherlock, it's healthy Thai."

"What's the difference?"

"One says *healthy* on the menu and one doesn't," Tiffany tells me as if I'm an idiot.

"Duh, Dad," Kelly says and adds a slight noise from her nose.

"Was that a sniffle I just heard, Kelly?"

"No."

"Then what was it?"

"A little spice went up my nose."

She sniffles again.

"I don't think so."

"The spice is still there."

She sniffles for a third time.

"I told you, Kelly, to bundle up and zip up your coat, but you don't listen to me, and now you're getting sick, and it's going to get worse, and you're going to miss school and fall behind, and then you're going to have to go to summer school, which you will hate, and I'm the one who's going to have to listen to all your complaining."

"And we won't get to go to camp," Care adds to my list.

"If you'd listen to me, do what I tell you, life would be a lot easier, Kelly."

"Oh, Mr. Sherlock, lighten up," Tiffany says.

"Stay out of this, Tiffany."

"Maybe if you bought her a fur, she wouldn't need to bundle up."

The solution to any problem Tiffany encounters almost always has the word *buy* associated with it.

I hang up my coat, get out of my boots, and get in the feedbag line. Being last to arrive, my chopsticks go all the way to the bottom of the containers of the most popular items. The pad thai, fried rice, and potstickers are gone, but plenty of the chim chum, khao phat, and mu phat sato sits waiting for me to dig in.

I have no clue what I'm eating. It could be sautéed python or chicken beaks for all I know, but I have to admit it's better than my turkey tetrazzini.

After we eat, we pick our cookies and read our fortunes. Kelly's: *A closed mouth gathers no feet*. Care's: *He who laughs last is laughing at you*. Tiffany's: *Person who argue with idiot is taken for fool*, very fitting for my protégée. But mine is the best: *Wise husband is one who thinks twice before saying nothing*. If I only knew then, what my fortune is now, I probably would be paying a lot less alimony.

I order the girls into the bedroom to do their homework while Tiffany and I clean up after dinner. Actually, I clean up, and Tiffany gives me hints on how to do it more efficiently. "If I were you, Mr. Sherlock, I'd get a maid to do that."

"Is this advice part of your management capability, Tiffany?"

"Some people are born to manage, Mr. Sherlock, and some people only manage to get born."

I don't think she got that right.

The girls either didn't have a lot of homework or their texting thumbs are on strike because they join us as I put away the last dish. Timing is everything in life.

"Why do you have all these cards on your ugly painting, Mr. Sherlock?" I hear Tiffany ask from the front room.

"It's not ugly, Tiffany, it's art."

"Okay, fine, it's ugly art."

"That's *The Original Carlo,*" Care informs Tiffany.

"Why don't you just take a big sheet or blanket to cover it up?"

"That's what Dad uses to figure out crimes," Care tells Tiffany.

"Really, they don't have a phone app for that?" Tiffany questions.

Kelly helps explain, "He puts up all the stuff he knows about the case on the cards, keeps moving them around until something makes sense, fills in blanks if he has to, and solves the case."

"So, it's like a do-it-yourself Clue game?"

I enter the room. "Colonel Mustard in the library with the candlestick."

I sit on the couch as the three girls stand in front of the Carlo.

"This isn't right," Tiffany says, removing the two middle cards from the painting.

"You don't think Vilma and Sergai were married?" I ask.

"Yes, but you have them going in different directions."

"Because I think they married each other for money."

"What's so strange about that?" Tiffany asks.

"Immigration frowns upon it."

Care moves around a few cards. "How about if Sergai is actually a secret agent, and he's using Vilma to infiltrate the CIA?"

"Hey, that's good," Tiffany says.

"How about if Vilma married Sergai, then found out he was really a woman, and that's when she gave up on men and started in on the cats?" Kelly wonders.

"Or," Tiffany says, her mind whirling, "how about if Sergai had an identical twin brother, and Vilma was actually married to two men at the same time?"

I previously mentioned the aspect of taking the case out of the ordinary and into the extraordinary to help your mind fill in the blanks in the obvious. I'm not sure if the theory holds water after these three suppositions.

I take a few blank cards, fill them out, stand, and join the girls. "I found out today that Vilma had two other husbands."

"What's the matter with that?" Tiffany again asks.

"And one died." I tack up that card.

"So what?" Care asks.

"Two husbands out of three dying in the prime of their lives, one of which I know was perfectly healthy," I explain. "Wouldn't you consider the odds to be a little steep for that to happen?"

"Not when she's living with all those cats," Tiffany says.

"You think Vilma might have knocked them off for the insurance money, Dad?"

"Maybe."

"Then why would she be suing now for the grief disorder money?" Care asks.

"Because she's gambled away all her other insurance money."

"And," Kelly finishes the thought, "she can't find anyone else dumb enough to marry her."

"You want to be married before your pump is overprimed," Tiffany offers her words of wisdom. "Remember that little dudettes."

"I think we're onto something here, Dad," Care says.

"We should look on Match dot com, and see if she's trolling for a hubby," Kelly says.

"Or Cat Lovers dot com," Tiffany adds picking up her phone and punching the screen.

"Or consider this," I'm thinking out loud, "Sergai's not dead."

"What?"

"No way."

"The lady at the funeral home dressed him up," Tiffany says.

"No, the Hollerback guy did the embalming."

"But didn't the guy we talked to say they had a service?" Tiffany remembers.

"Even if they did, it could have been a closed casket."

"We all saw his ashes at the house," Care says. "Tiffany had the urn thing in her hand."

"How do you know they were his? Ashes are ashes, dust is dust," I say and begin to wonder if I've been hanging around Tiffany too long.

"Vilma didn't seem to me like the murdering type," Kelly says.

"Maybe she didn't have to. Maybe she paid someone to do it."

"Where'd she get the money?" Kelly asks.

"From what Sergai paid her to marry him so he could get a green card."

Tiffany tells Care to help her remove all the cards from the Carlo. "We better start over; this is getting really complicated."

"And also please consider," I say, then pause for effect. "Sergai was a member in good standing in the Russian Mafia. Don't forget to throw that into the mix."

They look at me like *Stop Dad, we can only handle so much.*

"And last but not least," I say, holding one more recipe card, "Vilma in her youth made her living as an actress."

"Oh my God."

All three females in the room are now thoroughly stumped. They sit and stare at the almost empty *Carlo*. A pile of cards lay on top of the coffee table.

"Where do we go from here, Dad?" Care asks.

"To bed, two of you have school tomorrow."

Kelly sniffles.

"There's some Children's Tylenol in the medicine chest, Kelly. Take some."

"I hate that stuff, Dad. It makes me hurl."

"Take some anyway."

I shuffle the kids off into the bedroom for showers and sleep. They hug Tiffany before retiring. "Goodnight, Tiffany. Thanks for buying us dinner. It was so much better than anything Dad would have cooked."

"Ta-ta, little dudettes."

The girls go off into the direction of the bedroom and bathroom for their showers.

Tiffany stands and drops the two recipe cards remaining in her hand. "Maybe you're right, Mr. Sherlock, we should just give her the money and be done with it."

"Really?"

"I'm so confused I don't know which end should end up."

"Believe it or not, I actually think we're making progress."

"You're kidding?"

"Think about it."

"I hate thinking, Mr. Sherlock."

"Come on, I'll walk you to your car."

I kick my slippers off and step my bare feet into my duck boots. I throw on my jacket instead of my coat since I am only going to be outside for a few minutes.

As I follow Tiffany down the three flat's two stories, she says to me, "If you had a doorman, you wouldn't have to do this Mr. Sherlock."

"It's late, Tiffany, and I don't mind."

"Revelry's not dead because of you, Mr. Sherlock."

"So to speak."

At the front door, I double the doormat up and push it against the jamb so the door can't shut and automatically lock. Tiffany's Lexus is about fifty yards to the right. I walk her to her car. "We'll meet at the Richmond Clinic on Clark Street tomorrow morning, Tiffany."

"Okay, what time?"

I'm about to say nine thirty but say, "Eight forty-five," instead, considering Tiffany runs on Tiffany time.

"That early, Mr. Sherlock?"

"The early bird gets the worm."

"Who'd want a worm?" Tiffany asks, getting into the car.

"Drive carefully."

I watch her fishtail out of the spot and up the street, shiver when a blast of wind hits me, and hurry back up the icy walk to the front entry door.

"Ec-cuse me, buddy." A rather large gentleman with a neck the size of my waist says as I approach.

"I don't have any money to buy whatever you're selling. Sorry."

I try to push past him to get to the door, but he blocks my way.

"I sad ec-cuse me."

"You're excused, now would you mind letting me into my building?"

“You’re not ec-cused.”

“I didn’t do anything to be excused for,” I try to reason with him.

“Dat’s no ec-cuse.”

“Why not?”

“Cause you not.”

I can feel my toes icing up inside my boots. “Can we go inside; it’s freezing out here?”

“Compare to Moscow, nice out.”

The guy is as wide as the door, but I try to push past him anyway. He belly-butts me backwards.

“What do you want? I don’t have any money.”

“Why you ask about Sergai?” he asks.

“Sergai who?”

“You know Sergai.” The way he speaks, I’m not sure if it is an answer or a question.

“Sergai Levenchenko?”

“Yeah, dat Sergai.”

“When?” I ask.

“Other day?”

“I don’t remember the topic coming up. You must have me mistaken for somebody named Boris or Natasha.”

“No, you.”

My fingers are now as frozen as my toes. “Okay, fine, I was looking for Sergai.”

“Why?”

“I work for the lottery. He might be holding a winning Powerball ticket, and I want to know if he wants his two hundred million monthly or in a lump sum.”

“Sergai don’t want some lump,” he informs me.

“Fine, I’ll put that down on the form. Now, can I go inside?”

“Not yet.”

“Why not?”

“Not done.”

“Not done with what?”

“With Sergai.”

“I don’t know Sergai. I’ve never met Sergai. I’ve never run into him, and if I did, I wouldn’t know him because I have no clue what he looks like.” Oddly enough, I’m not lying.

“Den why you ask about him?”

“I’m curious.”

"Why?"

"I know his wife."

"Sergai's wife?"

"Yes."

"What's her name?"

"Vilma."

"Sergai don't got no Vilma wife."

"Then I guess we both got the wrong Sergai." I pause. "It was nice meeting you. Maybe we can get together again in the spring?" I pause again. "I bet you're a Cub fan."

The guy reaches out, takes a hunk of my flimsy jacket into his hand, and pulls me close to him. "You don't be asking about Sergai no more." He pulls me closer. I can smell the beets on his breath. "You got dat?"

"Consider it done."

He pushes me away. I stumble backward, unsure of my footing since my feet have become a couple of ice blocks.

"No more Sergai for you," he says, turns, kicks the folded mat back into the small lobby, and lets the door slam shut. "Spakoinoy nochi." He slams past me like a bowling ball taking the tenpin out for a spare, knocking me into a three-foot snow bank, and proceeds down the walkway.

I lift myself out of the snow, hustle to the door, and twist the knob, but the knob won't twist. I'm locked out.

My fingers are so cold I have to hit the door buzzer with the butt of my hand.

No answer.

No answer to my second through the next ten tries. The kids must be in the shower and can't hear the buzzer in the kitchen.

The frostbite is past my feet and working its way up my ankles. I trudge down the walk, through the space between my building and the building next door, and all the way to the back stairway, which hasn't been shoveled since the first dusting in November. I know now how Edmund Hillary felt going up Everest for the first time as I slip and slide up long flights of stairs. Finally, at my back kitchen door, I knock. Knock again. And knock once more. I can see inside the bathroom door is open so the kids must be out of there and back into the bedroom or the front room. They both probably have their earbuds in and are either talking on their phones or listening to what they refer to as music.

I knock again. Nothing. I pound as hard as I can without shattering my frozen hand into a million pieces.

No answer.

I give up.

Going down the slippery stairs is harder than going up. I take most of the trip on my butt.

I get back to the front of the building. I have to use my elbow to ring the buzzer; my fingers are popsicles. It takes three rings, but finally I hear a voice.

"Who is it?" It's Care.

"It's me, open up."

"Who's me?"

"Your father. Hit the button, open the door. I'm freezing down here."

"Why?"

"Because it's twenty below out."

"My Dad told us never to let anyone in if we don't already know who it is."

"I'm the guy who told you that. Let me in."

There is a pause. I'll bet Care is conferring with her older sister.

The next voice I hear through the small speaker is Kelly's. "Hello."

"Kelly, it's your father. I'm locked out. I'm about to undergo hypothermia. So, would you please hit the button and let me in?"

"We have to be sure it is you. If it's not you, and we let you in, my real dad will really get mad at us."

Oh jeesh.

I can hear them discussing, but can't make out what they're saying. Finally, Kelly asks, "What's your mother's maiden name?"

"Why would you want to know that?"

"That's what they always ask at the bank and stuff," Care explains.

"Just let me in."

"What's her maiden name?"

"Wolenski."

"Wait," Kelly says. They confer again. "That was a bad

question because we don't know what her maiden name is either."

I'm about to freeze to death for a lack of name recognition.

I push the button again and yell, "I happen to know, Kelly, you're sniffling, coming down with a cold, merely pretended to take the Children's Tylenol, and are going to be in big, big trouble if you have to miss any school the rest of this week."

"Yep," I hear, "that's Dad."

The buzzer buzzes. I push the door open. My life is saved.

By the time I get upstairs, I'm getting some feeling in my feet.

"What were you doing downstairs, Dad?" Care asks.

"I walked Tiffany out to her car and got locked out of the building. I almost froze to death out there."

"Well," Kelly says, "it serves you right. You should have worn something warmer than that jacket you have on. Did you have it zipped up all the way?"

There is nothing worse than having your own life lessons slap you in the face. "I wasn't planning on being outside for that long."

"You always tell us to be prepared at all times, Dad. 'Failure to prepare, is preparing to fail.'"

"Thank you, Care."

I might as well get this over with, "Kelly, do you have any words of wisdom to add?"

"Yes," Kelly says. "Never date anybody who drives a van."

I work so hard to instill knowledge in my children, and this is the thanks I get.

I put on a pair of thick wool socks and stroke my feet with both hands. I'm rubbing so hard I wouldn't be surprised if the wool ignites.

"Dad," Care asks, "how much insurance did Vilma get when Sergai died?"

"Half a mil."

"Really?"

"That's a lot of money," Kelly says. "How much insurance do you have, Dad?"

"Why, Kelly? Are you thinking of knocking me off so you can buy a new pair of shoes?"

"No, but now that you mention it, I would like to get a new pair of leather boots."

"Check with me in the spring when they go on sale."

"I won't want to wear them in the spring, Dad. And by the time winter rolls around again, they'll be out of style."

"Life's tough, Kelly. Get used to it."

I can once again feel the tips of my fingers. It takes a near-death experience to remember it's the little things that make life worthwhile.

"All right, time for bed."

"Already?"

Care and Kelly tromp into my room, and before they share my bed, each performs the newest must-do ritual of every teenager and preteen, which is plugging their cellphones into their chargers.

"Good night."

"Good night, Dad."

I kiss the girls, tell them I love them, and send them off to dreamland.

Back in the living room, I sit on the couch, which will soon be my bed, and look up at *The Original Carlo*. It's a mess. What connections I may have had are now irreparably broken. Most of my recipe cards are scattered on the coffee table or strewn haphazardly on the floor. I should pick them up, but I don't. I should also add a new card reading: *Russian mobster stops by and threatens my life*, but I can't find a pen. It was probably a mistake to allow the girls to scramble the cards the same way Tiffany makes one of her kale, kumquat, quinoa power shakes, but you never know what someone might come up with.

I must stare at the empty *Carlo* for twenty minutes and don't come up with a new or even different thought. My fingers and toes may no longer be frozen, but my mind remains in a deep freeze.

CHAPTER 20

Next morning, I consider making the girls a leftover chim chum and mu phat casserole for their lunch, but I settle for PB&J, Ritz cracker sandwiches, which are the only items I find in the cupboard. I add a small bag of walnuts I bought some time back, my last celery stalks, and half a lemon for each. They're going to hate me when they open their bags to eat, but the Donner Party would have been thrilled to get such a meal. I write on their napkins *Bon Appetit and I Love You.*

I rustle them out of bed at 7 a.m., pour bowls of granola cereal, and smell the milk before pouring it on. "Eat."

"Dad, are you going to let us be there when you solve the case?" Care asks instead of eating.

"I haven't solved the case yet."

"Will you wait to solve it until we're available?"

"No."

"It's only until this weekend."

"I don't have you this weekend." I stop, think, and ask, "Your mother didn't write me one of her notes telling me she has to switch weekends at the last minute, did she?"

"Not yet," Kelly says.

"Come on, get your coats on. We're going to be late."

As we hustle out to the car, I once again have to remind my oldest, "Would you zip your coat up, Kelly."

Kelly sniffles before she answers, "Don't forget I'm not the one who almost froze to death last night, Dad."

The kid inherited that attitude from her mother, not from me.

The Toyota starts up with more vigor than the Chicago Marathon, and I'm one of the first in the drop-off line at their schools. "Don't forget: Learn something new every day, girls."

"Yeah, right, Dad."

***

Tiffany time is usually forty-five minutes past any scheduled time, but today she's more than sixty. I sit in my

Toyota with the engine and heater on in the parking lot of the Richmond Medical Clinic, which is referred to by patients as Richman/Poorman's Doc in the Box. I read all the material I have on the case so far and reread it again.

No matter how many times I go over it, all the roads in the case lead back to Vilma being the hub of the guilty wheel. She was the one who'd gain if Sergai married her, if Sergai died, and if Sergai's grief caused her undo hardship. Although she didn't impress me as being the smartest puppy in the litter, maybe all the acting lessons in her youth are finally paying off. But if she is smart enough to pull this off, how can she be so dumb to lose all her money playing the slots in Buffington Harbor? Heck, any gambler worth his ante knows slots have the worst odds in the place; she should be playing craps for Chrissakes. Plus, the fact of the matter that any photo, painting, or hieroglyphic of Sergai, either living or dead, has not yet surfaced screams to me that only Vilma would benefit from such an omission.

There is one item I have to check out. I call Chappie.

"Yo, dude."

"I still need help," I tell him.

"You've needed help since the day I met you."

"When it comes to me needing help, Chappie, there's no end in sight."

"And speaking of ending, when is this going to end?" he asks.

"I have no clue."

"What do you need to know now?"

"I have to find out how Vilma's first husband met his fate."

"Easier said than done, dude."

"Please?"

"I'll see what I can do."

"Thanks."

"How's Tiffany?"

"Tiffany's Tiffany."

"Say hello for me."

The second I hang up, Tiffany is knocking on the passenger side window. I reach over and open the door. "Get in."

"No way. Your car is disgusting."

"I'll take function over fashion any day, Tiffany."

"Funk went out of fashion a long time ago, Mr. Sherlock."

I grab the files, climb out of the car, and join Tiffany. We walk to the entrance of the clinic. "A little later than your usual later, today, Tiffany."

"I couldn't sleep last night."

"Why not?"

"You got me all confused about this case, Mr. Sherlock, and I kept getting flashbacks to that ugly painting in your apartment."

"Art is in the eye of the beholder, Tiffany."

"Well, I think the artist must have had something in his eye when he painted that thing."

The waiting area of the Richmond clinic is chock-full of sick people. There are runny noses, fevered brows, rashed skin, hacking coughs, and pink eyes. I feel like I'm running through a germ gauntlet as we make our way to the reception desk.

"What's your problem?" the receptionist, dressed faux-nurse, asks.

"My name is Sherlock—"

She interrupts me. "So, you got a weird name. What do you want us to do, surgically remove it and give you a new one?" After her query, she adds, "This look like City Hall to you?" The woman rips off a hunk of doughy sugar from a fried hunk of cholesterol and squashes it into her mouth.

I've only had the pleasure of visiting one other Richmond Medical Clinic since Mr. Richmond is too cheap to add me to the employee plan, but I do remember the exact same attitude from the front desk staff. The only way this woman would make you feel better is if you turned around and left.

"You don't look sick to me," the woman chews as she speaks.

"I'm not."

"If you want to sell us something, you have to contact the main office," she informs me and adds, "But I wouldn't be counting your commissions for a while. We've been using World War Two surplus bedpans for the past three years."

"My name is Richard Sherlock, and I work for Richmond Insurance—"

She cuts me off again. "Do you have your Richmond Insurance ID with you?"

"No."

"Then I can't help you."

"What I'm here for—"

"Here's what I would do if I were you," the lady tells me. "I'll put your name down, and you go home. You'll be better off waiting there than waiting here getting infected with more diseases. If you don't feel better in six or seven hours, come back, and I'll see what I can do getting you in to see a nurse."

I try to speak, but this time Tiffany interrupts me.

"Hi. I'm Tiffany Richmond. That's Richmond as in Jamison Richmond's daughter, Tiffany."

The woman removes her name badge.

"And Mr. Sherlock and I are here to go through some files on one of the past patients."

The woman stands up. "Welcome to the Richmond clinic. So nice of you to stop by. Would you like some coffee or part of my apple fritter?"

"No. You can fritter away your fritter by yourself."

There are a few catcalls from the sickies seeing us go into the clinic area before them, but the woman silences them by pointing to Tiffany and calling out, "Boss's daughter."

The now-kindly receptionist leads us to a small office where another poorly paid health-care professional sits behind three stacks of files, typing furiously on her computer keyboard. "This is Tiffany Richmond," she repeats, "Richmond as in Richmond, and she needs help."

"What can I do for you?"

"I need to cross-reference the corporate file with the actual file on a patient of yours named Sergai Levenchenko." I finally get to speak.

"Let me see the file."

I hand it over. She types the name and number into the computer, gets an odd look on her face, gets up from her chair, and says, "Follow me."

We are led into a windowless room in the back of the building, which seems bigger than the Library of Congress, although I've never stepped foot into the Library of Congress. There must be fifty thousand manila folders in the stacks. We end up in the middle of the room with the L's. "Look up there," she says, pointing.

I'm the tallest, so it makes sense for me to do the reaching. In a few seconds, I pull out six Levenchenko, or similar Levenchenko-spelled, files. "Are these the actual doctor's notes and results from the appointments?" I ask.

"Yes."

"Is all of this information transcribed and put into the computer?" I continue asking as I separate the files.

"Not everything," she says. "Only serious issues."

"Thank you."

She takes the hint, hands me back the file I originally gave her, and leaves us alone.

"This what we're looking for Mr. Sherlock?"

"Hope so."

Of the six I pulled down, three of them are from Levenchenkos over the age of sixty. One is a female. A *Sergai* in Russia must be like a *Leslie* in America. Of the two remaining in my hand, one is Sergai Levenchenco, the other is Sergei Levenchenko. I open both and hand the original file to Tiffany. "Let's compare."

Neither home address matches either Ridgeway Drive or the Plainfield Estates. Neither has a picture of the patient. Both men are in their mid-thirties, one thirty-six, the other thirty-two, each about the same height and weight, dark hair, and dark eyes. Both type O positive. Sergai with an "A," came into the clinic twice, once for a checkup and once for veisalgia. Sergei with an "E," came in once for a checkup. I could quickly call my hypochondriac friend "Wait" Jack Wayt and find out what the word *veisalgia* means, but I'd merely be giving him yet another disease to contract.

"I think this is our guy, Mr. Sherlock."

"Why?"

"His blood pressure of 154 over 110 and his heart rate of seventy-six matches on all the files."

"Very good Tiffany. I'm proud of you for pointing that out."

Tiffany beams. "Don't forget to tell my dad."

"Everything else is pretty similar," I say.

"Yeah."

"Except the doctor's signatures." Neither of which is legible.

"I was going to say that next, Mr. Sherlock."

I keep the Sergai and Sergei files, and we walk back to the lady transcribing in the office. "Excuse me," I interrupt her work, putting the files before her. "Are either of these doctors available?"

She looks closely at the signatures. "Both gone."

"These files aren't that old."

"Doctors come and go out of this place faster than the patients. They get hired, and after a few weeks, they start looking for another job."

"Overworked and underpaid?"

"Just like me."

We turn to leave but turn back.

"By the way, what's veisalgia?" I ask.

"In my neighborhood, it's referred to as the Irish flu."

We turn to leave again.

"I can't let you take those with you," she says. "They have to stay on the premises."

I take one last scan of the pages, hoping the cold weather hasn't frozen my photographic memory, and hand the files back to her. "Thanks."

We merely wave our goodbyes to the receptionist, but she responds with a "Come back anytime. I'll put you in the front of the line."

Tiffany covers her mouth as we reverse gauntlet through the germ zone, whose population has grown by leaps and moans. I merely hold my breath.

It is said that germs can't live in subzero weather, and I certainly hope that is the case because we're hit by a Canadian Clipper the moment we step outside. I can almost feel the evil germs fall from my body like sweat from a nose in a steam room. Finally a positive associated with this bitter cold weather.

"Where to next, Mr. Sherlock?"

"We've got to go look at some property."

I move my car to a nonmetered spot in the street, and we take Tiffany's car to the Hollerback Manor, once the Hollerback Funeral Home, in Logan Square. When we arrive, Tiffany sees the place in the midst of construction renovation and says, "I prefer new."

The same gentleman as before answers the door, but this time he's covered in plaster dust. "Come back to make an offer?"

"No."

He sees Tiffany standing beside me. "This isn't the mother of those kids you had with you, is it?"

"No."

"I didn't think so." He turns to my protégée. "Hi, I'm Lou."

"Tiffany."

"Please come in to my humble abode."

"You got a lot to be humble for," Tiffany says. "This place is a mess."

"In a few weeks, it's going to be a palace."

"I can barely wait for the grand opening."

I try to make my next comment as casual as possible. "You mentioned last time I was here there was some stuff from the previous tenant still in the basement."

"Yeah."

"We'd like to see them."

"Why?"

Tiffany answers, "I'm a psychic, and I'm channeling a dead relative of mine, and if I can make contact, he might be able to give me tips on what lottery numbers to play next week." I certainly didn't expect this comment.

Even through the plaster dust covering Lou's face, I see skepticism.

"If I win, I'll cut you in for twenty percent," Tiffany adds.

"Follow me."

We have to climb over sheets of drywall and bags of concrete to get to a back stairwell, which makes the stairway in Chappie's house look like it belongs in Tara.

"Watch your step," he tells us.

The floorboards of the steps creak like high-pitched toads, and the bannister is as wobbly as an alcoholic with a bad case of veisalgia. When we reach the bottom, our host pulls the chain on a hanging light bulb. At least now we can see the cobwebs in front of our faces.

"This will be the last floor in the house we renovate. We're thinking about doing it as a man cave," Lou says proudly.

He opens the door to a room and ushers us inside.

He pulls another chain on a light bulb.

"This is charming," Tiffany says.

The room is quite large, but so filled with everything mortuary it seems small. There are vases in all shapes and sizes, many chipped or broken, fake flower arrangements, candelabras, a couple old pews, kneelers, three-fourths of one coffin, hundreds of books stacked in stacks not on shelves, and boxes and boxes of what I suspect are unused prayer cards. There are no file cabinets or banker's boxes anywhere to be seen.

"I'm starting to feel vibrations," Tiffany says, closing her eyes and raising her hands like a swami. Her fur coat parts to reveal her physical assets as she chants, "Ohhhh, Ohhhhh, spirit of Sergai, speak to me."

Lou stares at her. "I'm feeling some vibrations too, but not the same kind I bet you're feeling."

"Could you maybe give us a minute?" I ask.

Lou leaves us alone. "Good luck in the netherworld."

Once he's gone, Tiffany comes out of her trance. "I am getting some vibrations, Mr. Sherlock."

"Really?"

"Yeah, this place gives me the creeps."

I'm careful as I move around the room. "Forget about the big stuff, just go through and try to find the files or anything with *Sergai* or *Levenchenko* on the outside."

With years of dust, spider webs, dirt, dead bugs, and insect excrement covering everything like crops dusted with DDT, it's tough to find or read anything. I'm trashing around the books section as Tiffany tiptoes around stuff she refuses to touch. "I'm not going to find any skeletons, am I, Mr. Sherlock?"

"Only if you look in the closets, Tiffany."

I wipe about a pound of gunk off the spines of a stack of thin books and see an obscured Levenchenko on one in the middle. I carefully pull it out, but not carefully enough because the stack tumbles over like a tree falling in the forest everyone can hear. I give the book an additional blow and read the inscription on the cover: *Guests.*

"I found something."

"Is it alive or dead?"

I open the book and read. There are about twenty lined spaces on the third page, filled out in black ink. Each has a name. On the first page is Sergai's name and *May he rest with the angels* in a fancy script. The remainder of the book is empty of any markings.

"What is it?"

"It's the sign-in book from the viewing."

"Anybody we know?"

I run my eyes down the list. "No."

I turn the book over and see on the spine a date that would pretty much correspond to when Vilma said Sergai died. Tiffany examines my find. "Is Vilma's name in it?"

I open it back up. Read. No Vilma.

"Maybe she doesn't know how to spell her own name?" Tiffany surmises. "Is there an *X* on any of the lines?"

"No," I reply. "But if she was the one giving the party, she wouldn't necessarily sign."

"Kinda like not singing *Happy Birthday* at your own party?"

"Exactly."

"If I die, and this is all the people who show up for my funeral," Tiffany remarks, "there's going to be some real hell to pay."

Tiffany's phone rings. I'm surprised she can get a signal in the basement of a mortuary. She must have an *anywhere/anytime* cell phone plan.

"Hello." She listens. "Are you calling to ask me 'How I feel?'" She listens. "Then why are you calling?" A few more seconds go by, and she hands her phone to me. "It's Doctor Lunay. She's mad at you, or she's acting out her past life aggressions."

I take the phone. "Dr. Lunay ... Calm down. You don't have to scream. I can hear you just fine." I pause. "You're screaming again." I hold the phone away from my ear, and I can still hear her loud and clear. She screams some more. I'm finally able to edge some final words in, "Okay, we'll be right over." I hang up and hand Tiffany back her phone. "Guess what?"

"Lunay has gone loo-nay."

"So to speak."

We make our way back up the rickety stairway without falling to our deaths, although it would be extremely convenient to die while visiting a mortuary. Our rehabber host meets us on the first floor.

"Thanks."

"Talk to anybody while you were down there?" He asks.

"Yeah, a psychiatrist," Tiffany tells him.

"What did he say?"

"He asked, 'How do you really feel?'" Tiffany tells him.

I show him the book. "I'll bring this back after we do a séance at home."

"Sure, you don't want to put a bid on this place?" Lou asks.

"I'd like to think about it some more."

He turns to Tiffany and asks, “How would you feel about a cocktail after work?”

“Sorry, I don’t go out with guys who are in rehab.”

CHAPTER 21

"How could you do that to the poor woman?"

"Please, calm down."

"When you are dealing with a person stuck in the sixth stage of grief, you are dealing with a very vulnerable human being," Dr. Lunay continues to scream.

"Just tell us what happened," I plead. "Calmly."

"She comes in for her regular appointment near catatonic."

"What did you expect?" Tiffany tells more than asks. "The woman lives with thirty cats."

"I could tell immediately she was on the brink of a serious hypomanic episode."

"How?" I ask the shrink.

"BDD."

Dr. Lunay is so worked up I have a hard time distinguishing her letters. "Better Business Bureau?" I verbalized my guess.

"No," Dr. Lunay shouts back at me. "She had definite symptoms of body dysmorphic disorder."

"What's that?"

"She becomes overwhelmed with the thought that everything about her appearance is defective."

"Did she pass by any mirrors on her way into your office?" Tiffany asks.

"No."

"So, what happened next?" I try to move this along.

"I can sense she is on the edge of a panic attack brought on by a depersonalization disorder."

"And—"

"I begin to sense an avoidant personality disorder brought on by obviously something you said or did."

"Me?" I question.

"Yes, you."

"I didn't do anything."

"She's become paranoid schizophrenic with you following her around, asking questions, doubting her love for her now dead ex-husband."

"Are you sure?"

"Yes, I'm the doctor."

I should thank her for reminding me, but I don't. "Then what happened?"

"Vilma had an IED."

"I had one of those once," Tiffany says. "But I didn't trust it and went back on the pill."

"An IED is intermittent explosive disorder." Dr. Lunay is so upset she's shaking like a cheap cell phone on vibrate.

"She exploded?" I ask the doc.

"No, she went into an autophagia episode."

"What?" Tiffany asks. "She went gay for a day?"

"She began biting herself," Dr. Lunay explains in her own agitated state. "This is a classic psychotic disorder brought on by excessive stress and anxiety."

"What did you do?"

"I tried to stop it."

"Did you?"

"Yes."

"How?"

"I re-channeled her aggression."

"Where?"

"To me."

I'm thinking that was a pretty selfless act by the doc. "And that worked?"

"For her."

"That's good."

"But she bit me." The good doctor rolls up her sleeve and shows us the teeth marks on her upper arm.

"Overbite," Tiffany remarks checking out the bare shoulder.

"Did you know a human bite is over one hundred times more infectious than a dog bite?" I don't know how I know this, but I do.

"I'll remember that the next time I want to get even with someone, Mr. Sherlock."

"I don't know what you said or what you did, but you have brought on seriously unstable conditions for this poor woman." Dr. Lunay is beside herself in anxious anxiety.

"Vilma didn't seem so worked up when she was playing slots in the casino when I saw her."

"These types of panic attacks can come on instantaneously

and without warning." The doc might need to see a shrink to calm down after our meeting.

"So, what did you end up doing?"

"I had to call the paramedics, who sedated her and transferred her to Northwestern for further observation."

"Vilma's in the loony bin?" Tiffany asks.

"In my office, I prefer the term 'psych ward.'"

I take a short pause before I ask, "And you're blaming me?"

"Yes."

I take another short pause. "Did Eddie Floyd happen to call you after this happened?"

"Yes."

Gee, I would have never guessed.

"And you told him exactly what you've just told us?"

"Yes."

I have a feeling I'm going to be hearing real soon from Eddie Floyd, Esquire, aka Saul Rabinowitz, with a revised settlement offer.

Dr. Lunay starts wagging her index finger in my face. "You should be ashamed of yourself."

"Why?"

"Driving the poor woman into convulsive fits of fugue."

"Fits of fugue sounds like one of those punk rock bands," Tiffany says.

"I'm sorry if I did something wrong, but I really don't think it was me. Vilma might simply be acting."

"Yes, acting out her aggressions," Dr. Lunay almost shouts and adds, "on me."

"She used to be an actress, if you didn't know," I inform the doc.

"The woman was obviously stricken with cyclothymia periodically interrupted in a period of hypomania with a delusionary folie a deux."

"It could also be a case of pulling the wool over your eyes, Doc."

"There's no way," Dr. Lunay retorts. I was with her; I saw with my own eyes the symptoms she displayed. I'd stake my professional reputation on my diagnosis."

"That and a couple bucks will get you a ride on the 'L'."

Before we exit her offices, Tiffany looks at the spent and exhausted Dr. H. Oliva Lunay and says, "You might want to consider signing up for your own *manage your anger, anger management plan.*”

CHAPTER 22

"Calm down."

"This entire case is exploding in our faces," Bree screams almost as loud as Dr. Lunay.

"Calm down."

"Eddie Floyd is all over us. He's going to revise the amount of damages to over one million!"

"That's just another negotiating tactic on his part," I tell her.

"Jamison says we should settle."

"My daddy said that? I don't think so," Tiffany says.

"Let's just give her the money and get the whole thing over with." Bree is adamant.

"I don't think that's a good idea," I say. "How do you vote on the matter Houston?"

Richmond Insurance's lead counsel, Houston Twitchell, doesn't listen to his lady or his geeky helper at his sides. He speaks right up and says, "No."

"And I vote no too," Tiffany says. "That makes you a minority, Miss Biz-o-nette."

Bree turns to Tiffany. "It's pronounced Bis-o-nay."

"Right now it's pronounced loooo-zer."

"Knock it off," I tell the about-to-battle females. "You two have a truce, remember?"

Bree and Tiffany exchange dirty looks but back off.

"Let me handle Eddie Floyd." I say this and look to Houston and his entourage. "Is that okay with you Houston?"

The lawyer accepts whispered council and written counsel off the laptop, turns to me, and says, "Yes."

I take a breath. Bree is not happy, but Tiffany is happy because Bree's not happy.

"For all we know, Vilma could be faking it," I tell the group. "This is all a game Eddie Floyd is playing to force us into a settlement, and that's the last thing we'd want to do."

I see out of the corner of my eye Houston's lady whisper in his ear.

"Yes," Houston says.

"I need more time," I tell the group.

"Why?" Bree asks. "If this goes any longer, we could be up to two million."

"There's pieces of hanging fruit that haven't yet fallen," I say as poetically as possible. "We still don't even know what the husband looked like."

"What difference does that make?" Bree asks.

"Maybe nothing, maybe a lot. There's too much still going on, too many pieces that have no connection, and more questions than answers; just give me more time."

"How much more time?"

"I don't know."

"That's not a good answer," Bree responds.

"No," Houston agrees.

There is only one way to get these people off my bad back. "Listen everybody ..." I doubt if they will listen, but it never hurts to ask. "This could be a lot more than just an insurance claim. We could be on the trail of a black widow serial killer."

Everyone in the room except Tiffany, who probably thinks I am referring to a person killing spiders crawling around a power shake, is silent. "Eewww, gross," she says.

"We're meeting with a cold case detective this afternoon to see if we can tie Vilma or Sergai to a number of missing persons in the past." I decide not to mention the detective is Alibi Al Landeen, whose interest in cold cases usually concerns *cool ones* instead of criminals.

"Hang in there," I plead with them. "I'll be back to you tomorrow with an update, I promise."

No one responds. Fearing no one listened to me, I am about to repeat my plea, but I hear a voice.

"Yes."

"Thanks for the vote of confidence, Mr. Twitchell."

***

We are not due at the Belmont police station until 12:30. I tell Tiffany to take the expressway toward O'Hare.

"Where are we going?" she asks.

"Mrs. Lament called and said she wanted your opinion on the shade of eyeliner for a person she's working on."

"I can't blame her."

As Tiffany drives too fast on the icy highway, I take out the guest book from Sergai's viewing. Something strikes me as odd about it. I don't know what. It just seems wrong.

"What's the matter, Mr. Sherlock?"

"I'm having a brain freeze looking at this book."

"Don't let that bother you; I get those all the time."

There is one grieving family ahead of us in line waiting and one family at the lady in black's desk. I wave to Blackie and point to where Tiffany and I are heading. She gives me a sad look, which is the look she gives everybody.

I knock before entering. "Hello. Anybody alive in there?"

I open the door and see business has remained brisk since our last visit. There must be six or seven bodies in the embalming queue. Cold weather stops a lot of activity, but evidently dying isn't one of them.

Titus Pyre is inserting a tube into a customer when he turns and sees me. "Mr. Sherlock."

"I hope we're not disturbing anyone."

"No, our customers are pretty much past the point of being disturbed."

Tiffany immediately makes her way to where Thelma Lament poofs up a bouffant. "I just love what you've done with her lip liner."

"Thank you," Thelma says. "I get so few compliments in my work; it's so nice to actually hear one for a change."

"Mind if I do her nails?" Tiffany asks.

"Be my guest."

Titus turns on the juice, and I see the guy on the table swell up. "Titus, I promise nothing will come back to haunt you, but I need some answers."

"That ghost thing is really overblown, Mr. Sherlock," he says. "What can I do for you?"

"What was the problem between you and the Hollerback Home?"

"We didn't see eye to eye on things."

"Which means ..."

"I felt their way of doing death was more deadly than ours."

"Hollerback did a lot of *family* business, didn't they?" I put particular emphasis on the word *family*.

"We all work with families."

"Mafia families."

He turns off the spigot as a little embalming fluid backs up and out of the customer. "The Hollerback clientele was a bit different than ours."

I continue, "A great place for disposing of bodies would be a funeral home, wouldn't it?"

Titus gives me a look as if to say, "Yep."

"It would be tough to trace cremated remains, wouldn't it?"

"I'm not sure how much DNA can be retrieved from a person's ashes," Titus admits.

"Kinda dumb to do a Jimmy Hoffa burial under a stadium when you can fry the remains and let the wind do the rest."

Titus takes a break from the stiff, puts his gloved hands on his hips, and says to me, "For years, Hollerback used a crematorium on the South Side. The EPA put them out of business, and he came to us with a 'deal we couldn't refuse.'"

"So Hollerback was sending over folk you didn't have paperwork for?"

"Yes."

"Or had multiple burn-ees in the cardboard coffins?"

"I should have known not to get involved, but our business was getting killed during the recession."

"No pun intended."

"We offered cut-rate deals, no money down, six months without payments. We even started burying people standing up to increase our available plots, but even that didn't put any new life into the business. I was forced to do something."

"Do you have any idea of who or how many questionable bodies you may have handled?" I ask.

"Absolutely not. Hollerback did all the preparation; we only did the cooking."

"Bon appetit."

I think for a few seconds and ask, "Then why do you think Hollerback would have kept a file on Sergai if it was a body he wanted to dispose of with no trace?"

"I don't know."

"Well, I certainly can't ask Sergai, can I?"

"It would be difficult."

I look over to see Tiffany doing a superb job with bright red fingernail polish. If she ever decides to change careers, she may have a real future in the exciting world of mortuary makeup.

"How did you ever get out of the deal with Hollerback?" I

ask Titus. "Once you're in the family, you usually stay in the family."

"Fred, the guy who owned Hollerback, one day just up and left. I heard he packed up, put the property up for sale, and moved to Costa Rica or somewhere."

"And it was over?"

"The deal was as dead as a coffin nail."

I have to wait for Tiffany to finish up, and I take that time to assure Titus our conversation is dead and buried. He thanks me.

Thelma thanks Tiffany, "You put so much life into our clients; I and they can't thank you enough."

"My pleasure."

***

I find it very difficult walking into a police station. For me, it has been impossible to get used to no longer belonging or feeling welcome in a place where I once entered every day, had a desk to go to, friends to greet, and donuts to share. I used to know every name and face, what everyone did or was supposed to be doing, who to help, and who to avoid, but no longer. Police stations were my life for close to twenty years, a second home, which I spent more time in than my first home. It was where I was taught, challenged, succeeded, and failed, a place where all the tools of my trade were at my fingertips. If I had a question, I'd know where and who to go to for an answer. It was the one place on earth, I felt totally comfortable. A police station was my refuge, man cave, and where I knew I belonged. And in one fell swoop of a right cross, the door slammed shut, and I was *persona non grata*. I miss it terribly.

The Belmont station is one of the best in the city. It has a command center, media room, high-speed computers, and enough high-tech bells and whistles to play a police symphony.

"Can I help you?" a desk sergeant I've never met asks.

"Richard Sherlock to see Detective Al Landeen."

"The Richard Sherlock who punched out Captain Borrello?"

I nod my head.

"Let me shake your hand," the sergeant says, reaching over his desk.

"Are you, like, famous around here, Mr. Sherlock?"

"More like infamous."

"Is that like being famous inside someplace?" Tiffany asks.

"So to speak."

The sergeant picks up his phone, dials a few numbers, asks, waits, hangs up, and says to us, "Al's going to be late."

"How late?"

"He said it isn't his fault. He said he was driving in and ran out of gas because his wife forgot to fill up the tank."

Tiffany and I wait in the chairs off to the left. I see a few cops I used to know come in and out of the building but decide not to say hello.

Ten minutes later and twenty-five minutes late, Al comes in the door holding his right hand.

"You're late," Tiffany tells him, as if she should talk.

"It wasn't my fault. I told my wife to get gas."

"Couldn't you see the gauge was on empty?" I ask.

"No," Al says, "because I've picked up this tic in my left eye from all the stress you've put me under, Sherlock, and couldn't see down in that direction."

"And you were driving?" I ask.

"My other eye was on the road where it should have been." Al takes a pause to massage his hand and asks, "Did the pizza get here yet?"

"Here he comes now," the desk sergeant announces.

As we wait for the Giordano's guy to enter, Tiffany asks Al, "What happened to your hand?"

"I saw on old friend in the parking lot, and when we shook hands, he squeezed mine so hard I think he broke a bone."

"That'll be twenty-two fifty," the kid says as he takes the pizza box out of the square, portable warming blanket.

"I hope you guys like anchovy deep dish," Al says.

"I'll pass," Tiffany says.

I make absolutely no move toward my wallet, as there is an uncomfortable lapse of activity from Al.

"That'll be twenty-two fifty," the kid repeats.

"Don't worry," Al says to us. "I got this. It's my turn."

Al starts to reach into his pocket for his money but instead lets out a horrible scream of agony. "Oh, the pain."

"What's the matter?" Tiffany asks.

"My hand's so swelled up, I can't get it into my pocket. Reach in there and help me out, would you?"

"I'll pass."

"You, Sherlock?"

"This Peter Piper isn't going to be picking your pocket, Al."

"Then I won't be able to get my money out. Hey, it isn't my fault some guy put my hand in a vice grip."

Tiffany ponies up for the pizza.

"My turn next time, I swear," from Alibi Al's lips to God's ears.

When we finally get to the tape room, the videotape guy has the tapes racked and ready for viewing, but Al has to have something in his stomach, or he'll get dizzy. "It isn't my fault I have hypoglycemia," he tells us.

We wait for Al to down two slices of deep dish, anchovy pizza, which makes the room smell like an Italian seaside cannery. Thankfully, his swollen hand had a miraculous recovery, and he's able to handle the fishy, cheesy slices like a sideshow juggler. I decide to try a piece. When in Rome ...

The TSA supplied four tapes for our viewing pleasure. The first two are the wide shots of the screening area where passengers put their carry-ons on the conveyor belt, take off their shoes and metal objects, and either pass through the metal detector or enter the glassed-in oval where you put your hands over your head, and your body is scanned. It is a grainy picture taken from at least a twenty-foot distance and difficult to distinguish facial features. Luckily, it's not crowded, and each passenger going through the procedure is easily seen. There is a time code in the lower right hand corner of the shot; the pictures were taken at 13:38.

By the way, if you want to avoid crowds at O'Hare, one of the busiest airports in the world, try to travel in the early afternoons. Most of the flights going out are out by noon, and most of the flights coming in don't come in until after three. Travel inside the early afternoon window, and life will be a little easier.

Tiffany, Al, who is now on his third deep dish slice, and I sit elevated in the center of the room. The video guy below and in front of us controls what we see on the two screens using a computer keyboard. We have to wait about a minute or two for who we suspect is Sergai Levenchenko to come into the shot.

If you can avoid it, never get behind older women, mothers with little kids, a fat guy in a suit, or a techie; each takes forever to get through the line. The best person to stand behind is a thin guy in a rumpled suit; he's a professional salesman who's on and off planes every week and knows all the tricks of the traveling trade.

After about thirty seconds, Sergai, our lead in the movie, puts his carry-on bag, which looks to me like it would be way too big to fit into the overhead compartment, on the conveyor. He reaches over to take a plastic, rectangular container and removes stuff from his pockets, which I can't make out due to the camera angle. He takes off his shoes, adds those to the box, moves forward, makes sure his items go on the final section of the conveyor, and walks to the metal detector. He waits for the signal to pass, and when he goes through the tall rectangular passageway, two lights come on the upper support of the unit. The TSA guy on the other side asks something, then motions for Sergai to take off his belt and return to the starting point on the other side. Back to square two, Sergai places his belt on the conveyor but is now instructed to go through the bigger scanner, which he does, raising his arms as if he is playing Simon Says. The TSA agent gives our traveler a nod and ushers him to the spot where the conveyor outputs the smaller baggage.

To the left, we see everything has stopped: the conveyor belt, Sergai's belt, Sergai, and obviously Sergai's bag inside the screener. Two TSA agents on the other side of the machine are joined by three other TSA agents, and all congregate across from Sergai at the output point of the scanner, which someone has flipped back on. One of the agents physically lifts Sergai's bag off and carries it about ten feet down the aisle to an inspection table. Sergai follows and words are exchanged, but it's a silent movie, and I can't read lips. The five agents circle the table and are joined by four other agents. I don't know who is left to man the other lines of inspection, but if you were going to try to smuggle a bazooka onto a jetliner, now would be a good time.

From this point on, there is really little to see except nine TSA guys huddled around a table as if they're playing a game of Three-card Monte. Sergai is held way back out of the way, but he is allowed to put on his shoes and belt, and stuff his stuff back into his pockets. During the entire tape, we still haven't got a good look at the star of the show. If I were Sergai's agent, I would demand more close-ups.

The tape continues with not much else happening.

"You want to see this again, or do you want to see act two?" the operator asks. He seems pretty bored with the silent movie and will probably give it no stars in his review.

"Let's go to the next tape," I instruct.

Al burps a few times as the operator magically makes the pictures change before our eyes. "How do you like it so far?" Al asks.

"I'm hoping for a twist before the movie ends."

"No, I was talking about the anchovy pizza."

I took one bite that was enough.

"Pass it down, I'll eat it," Al says.

The next tape is a one-camera shot of one half of a small interview room. Sergai is led inside. This is the first good look we've had at our boy.

It's hard to gauge height, but I'd say 5'8" give or take an inch; maybe 160 to 175. Dark hair, not thin and not fat, thirty-five-ish, could use a shave, and has a diamond stud in his left earlobe. The most distinguishing feature is a beak-like nose, which, with his dark features, reminds me of a raven.

"What do you think, Tiffany?"

"Not somebody I'd ever go out with."

Sergai is seated at a table facing the camera. I can't tell how many TSA agents are in the room, but two pass through the camera shot to the other side of the room. We listen as many TSA questions are asked, but most are garbled and hard to understand. It doesn't really matter since Sergai answers, or attempts to answer, in Russian; garbled or non-garbled, nobody understands a word. This goes on for a few minutes. Sergai remains quite calm. The only movement he makes is to remove a pack of cigarettes from his pocket, take one out, light it up, and inhale at least a pound of cancerous particulate.

"They should have arrested him right then and there," Al Landeen speaks up. "It's against the law to smoke anywhere but a designated smoking area at O'Hare."

"Too bad, Al, you missed your chance at a big bust."

I watch Sergai puff away on the Marlboro and get a thought. "Didn't Vilma tell us Sergai didn't smoke?"

"Yeah," Tiffany says, "but I know he did."

"And how do you know that?"

"Because when I opened his urn, it was filled with cigarette butts."

"What?"

"Why do you think it stunk, Mr. Sherlock?" Tiffany says to me. "There's nothing more stinky than stale cigarette butts."

"Well, make it a point never to stop by our house a night my wife cooks eggplant, and I eat way too much," Al tells her.

"There wasn't, like, human remains ashes in the urn?" I question.

"How would I know? I'm not some kind of ash expert." She pauses. "At least not in that sense."

"Al, do you have a copy of the Sergai picture you had the first time around?"

"I could go get it, but do you really need it?"

"Would you, please?"

Al reluctantly gets up and exits the room. Tiffany and I continue to watch the exciting program as the TSA agents ask questions and Sergai answers in Russian, hardly dialog that is compelling. "I don't think this is Vilma's guy," I say.

"Me neither," Tiffany says. "I can't see the two as a couple."

I contemplate this whole exercise as being a waste of time and effort. I ask the operator, "Did any paperwork come along when they sent the tapes over."

The guy picks up a padded manila folder and hands it up to me, "See for yourself."

I reach inside the large envelope and pull out a few pieces of paper. The first two are reports made the day of the questioning, the third is a date stamp on a copy of a picture of the Silly Putty eggs, which do display the Silly Putty logo. The last page is a Xerox copy of Sergai's green card. I take a long look at this one. The picture of Sergai on the card is lousier than the shot of him in the first set of TSA tapes.

Al comes back into the room and lays down the page with the picture of the much younger Sergai before us.

"Could you stop the tape?" I ask the operator as I see Sergai look up at his questioners.

He does so, and I ask, "Could you zoom in on his face?"

Again, he obliges. I hold Al's paper in my hand to the left, the copy of the green card on the right, and compare the two with the frozen zoom shot on the screen.

"What do you think, Tiffany, same guy?"

"The only way they could be the same is if the guy on the right had a reverse nose job."

CHAPTER 23

"We're not doing real well on this case, are we, Mr. Sherlock?" Tiffany asks as we leave the Belmont Station.

"No."

""Do you have any new ideas on Vilma?"

"No."

"Do you think you've found the right Sergai yet?"

"No."

"Mr. Sherlock, you're sounding more and more like Houston Twitchell."

"Oh, no."

I motion for Tiffany to turn east on Belmont.

"I sure wish you could come up with something I could tell my Dad and take credit for, so he'll start to have a better opinion of his daughter."

"Tiffany, I'm trying my best."

"If I don't come up with something, he's going to marry that awful Bree Biz-o-bitch, and I'll be replaced."

"That's ridiculous, Tiffany. If there is one person in the world who can't be replaced, it's you."

"But I already have to fight for time with my dad. With her around, it'll be almost impossible, or worse yet, I'll have to share. I hate sharing, Mr. Sherlock."

"You're looking at the situation all wrong, Tiffany."

"How else can I look at it? The woman is horning in on my territory."

"You have to accept that your dad has the right to a relationship with another woman besides you and your mom."

"That's what Facebook is for, Mr. Sherlock."

"Your father's relationship with Bree is much different than the one he has with you."

"Duh. Hers is much better."

"Tiffany, your father loves you. He just doesn't know how to show it."

"He could start by showing up once in a while."

***

The psych ward, as Dr. Lunay would refer to it, is located in the Northwestern Memorial complex in the Streeterville section of the city. If you're going to go nuts, at least you get to do it in a fancy neighborhood.

We meet TV Eddie Floyd, aka Saul Rabinowitz, in the lobby.

"This is highly unusual, Sherlock."

"Seeing is believing, Eddie."

"The more time that passes by, the more it's going to cost you," he informs me. "I've already increased the kitty to one point five million and added lifetime health benefits without a deductible to the total. No judge in the world is going to rule no on health benefits for the mentally disturbed."

"Interesting you use the word *kitty* in reference to Vilma," Tiffany points out.

"What do you say, Sherlock? One mil up front, health benefits, and five grand monthly stipend for the first five years?"

"No." I wonder if I picked this negotiating tactic up from Houston Twitchell.

"You're making a big mistake here, Sherlock."

"Let's go take a look, Eddie."

Tiffany and I wait as Eddie goes to the lady at the reception desk and either gives her some legal mumbo jumbo or tells her outright lies to get us inside. Whatever he says, it works because a few minutes later an orderly, dressed in scrubs, comes out and leads us inside the floor.

Maybe there is a part of me who expected a bit of Camp Delta at Gitmo inside, but I see no long hallways with cell-like doors lining the corridor. There are no arms stretched through the bars, clamoring noisily with their tin coffee cups against the cold steel, or twisted contorted faces inside, jabbering nonsense as they pull on their hair or contort their bodies into faux yoga poses even yogis couldn't twist into. Instead, the first room we pass is a dayroom. Patients sit watching Jerry Springer on TV, playing board games, or sleeping. There are orderlies hanging around, and two nurses wheel a cart from one person to the next, handing out small cups of pills and water to wash them down. Everyone seems calm, contented, and happy to be there. The craziest people in this room are the guests on the Springer show.

We continue out of the dayroom and into a section arranged with the nurse's station in the middle and the patient/treatment rooms circling. I don't count as we walk around, but there must be at least nine or ten rooms in the pod. Each has a see-through glass wall, although pulled curtains could block the view. We stop at the farthest room from the nurse station. The curtains are drawn, and we can't see inside. The orderly cracks the door open and taps before entering. He asks, "Mrs. Kromka are you awake?"

I would have said *decent*, but that's just me.

"Vilma, may we come in?"

There is no answer. We enter.

Vilma sits up in her hospital bed, her eyes wide open but with a blank expression on her face. She is staring at the TV, which happens to be playing an Eddie Floyd commercial.

"I'll come out of our corner swinging."

"Hey look," Tiffany says, "that's you."

"And we never settle when we know we got the other guy on the ropes."

Eddie should take a bow but doesn't.

The four of us circle the bed, and Eddie points at the comatose Vilma, "Seen enough, Sherlock?" Eddie asks. "Is this enough to get you to the negotiating table?"

"No."

I turn to the orderly. "Is she medicated?"

He picks up the chart from the back of the bed and reads, "Some, but not a lot."

Jerry Springer comes back on the TV. One woman calls another woman a "ho and a half," and the two go at it like a couple of over-caffeinated pit bulls. They thrash around the floor like untrained UFC cage fighters, madder than the aforementioned pit bulls until Jerry's behemoths pull them apart.

Vilma has no reaction to the action on the screen. The orderly picks up the remote, mutes the sound, and says, "I've seen this one; it's a rerun. The one on the left smacks the one on the right a good one right before the next commercial. Want me to keep it on?"

"No thanks."

Disappointed, the orderly kills the TV.

I move closer to the edge of the bed. "Vilma."

No response.

"Vilma Kromka."

Nothing.

"Let me try, Mr. Sherlock." Tiffany comes to the other side of the bed, leans toward Vilma, and says, "Meow." She repeats the phrase a few times and adds a hissy spitting sound to the last "Meooooowwwww."

Vilma blinks a few times, but that's as good as it gets.

"Seen enough, Sherlock?" Eddie presses. "It's obvious the woman is in dire mental straights. And it's all your fault."

I start to respond but stop. What would be the point? I'm stuck. I know it, and Eddie knows it.

"Okay, Eddie, put together a package, send it over to Richmond, and we'll go from there."

"Can I try just one more hiss, Mr. Sherlock?"

"No, I think you've meowed enough, Tiffany."

The orderly leads us out of the room. I'm the last to exit, and leave Vilma's door slightly ajar. I allow the others to walk ahead of me. I stop hearing the door fully close behind me, wait a few seconds longer, and return to the room.

I walk in on Vilma out of bed, seated by an open window. She has a cigarette to her lips, inhaling like a sump pump, and blowing the smoke out the open portal.

"Keep smoking, Vilma, and you could end up in the hospital." I warn her, smile, and leave the patient to her own worst devices.

I decide not to mention my findings to Eddie; he may or may not find out. Either way, I have one negotiating tactic in my back pocket. I don't mention Vilma's lapse to Tiffany either. She may get her hopes up and go running to tell her dad and Bree she's broken the case. Sometimes silence can be your best friend.

By the time we're out of the hospital, bid Eddie adieu, and are at the handicapped spot where Tiffany parked, it is close to five o'clock. "Had enough for the day, Tiffany?"

"Only if there is no place else we have to go."

I look inside the car and see the guest book on the seat. "There is an old friend I wouldn't mind dropping in on."

"Where?"

"Evanston."

"Nobody lives in Evanston except old people and students,"

Tiffany informs me.

"Which one would you prefer?"

"Neither."

***

Phoebe and I have known each other for a number of years. We have an odd mutual admiration for each other's work. Although she's been out of prison a good twenty years, that doesn't mean she's in any way reformed. She lives in a senior citizen high-rise in Evanston named the Georgian.

As we enter, Tiffany asks, "What are we doing here, Mr. Sherlock? Are you trolling for a near-death cougar?"

"No, Tiffany."

"Whew. You had me worried there."

We enter the dining room where the residents sit four at a table, some in wheelchairs, some in sit-able walkers, and others in regular chairs. On each table are big bowls of mac and cheese, mashed potatoes, creamed spinach, and what I suspect is some sort of pulverized meat.

Tiffany takes one look at tonight's menu and says, "It's ABC food, Mr. Sherlock."

"What?"

"ABC food," she explains, "Already Been Chewed."

Phoebe, who has or is pushing eighty, sits way in the back of the room. She is admonishing some goat-bearded guy to get his dentures off his plate and put them back in his mouth. "That's disgusting, Harry."

"Ah, shut up you old bitty," Harry responds.

"Phoebe."

"Sherlock, what are you doing here?"

"I need some of your expertise."

"You need more than that, Sherlock."

"Who's the little lady?" Phoebe asks, eyeing Tiffany.

"This is Tiffany. She's my assistant."

Harry rises out of his wheelchair as fast as he can, get's in Tiffany's face, and says, sans dentures, "I'm Harry, but all the little ladies call me 'Harry, da Man.'"

"Sure they didn't say, 'Man is he Hairy'?"

Phoebe rises from her chair. "Come on, let's go upstairs. I can only take these old geezers so long before I start getting

Alzheimer's by osmosis."

Phoebe's ninth floor apartment has an unobstructed view of the lake, one bedroom, one bath, a kitchenette with only a fridge and microwave, and a den/living room with an oversized TV on one wall. Hanging on the remaining walls in the room are framed antique letters, autographed book pages, and signed historical documents.

Tiffany stops at one of the smallest but oldest. "Is this really signed by George Washington?"

"Of course it is," Phoebe tells her. "I got an Honest Abe Lincoln over there." She points.

"These must be worth a lot of money."

"They're all for sale if you got cash," Phoebe informs her.

I pull out the guest book from Sergai's viewing. "There is something about this book that's bothering me, Phoebe."

She takes the book in hand. "What?"

"I don't know; that's why I'm here."

Phoebe opens the book, pages through the first sheets with the titles and signatures, thumbs through the remaining pages quickly, closes the book, checks out the spine, and opens again to the signature page. "A friend of yours?"

"No."

Phoebe holds the page up to the light, views it from three different angles, slaps it shut, and tosses it back to me. "You got to be kidding, right, Sherlock?"

"Kidding about what?"

"What's wrong with this book."

"No, I'm not." I'm being honest.

"This is either an insult to my professional intelligence or you're really losing your touch."

"Fine, Phoebe, I'm losing my touch. What's wrong with the book?"

"Look at it."

"I have."

"Look at it some more."

Tiffany comes over and sits next to me as I open the page listing Sergai's name.

"Do I get a clue?" I ask Phoebe.

"No. Look."

I flip to the sign-in guest signature page.

"Could I get a clue?" Tiffany asks.

"No."

I peer closely. "It's all in the same ink?"

"Oh course it's in the same ink," she says. "Haven't you ever been to a funeral?"

I think back to my morning with Roscoe Jarbeaux.

"There's always a pen next to the guest book," Phoebe spits out.

I remember Roscoe didn't have a guest book; if he did we would have had to chip our names in with an ice pick.

"Think, Sherlock," Phoebe orders and adds, "you think too, little assistant lady."

"I let Mr. Sherlock do most of the thinking when we're on a case," Tiffany explains.

I peer down so hard on the page I'm getting a headache. "I don't know. Phoebe, tell me."

"You're not much of a detective anymore are you?"

"Guess not. I'd love to quit and get a real job," I admit.

"You should come and work with me. These old geezers downstairs still have checking accounts and are ripe for the picking."

"No thanks." I pause, "Come on, Phoebe, tell me what's wrong with the book."

"I can't do that. It's as plain as the nose on your face."

"Would you tell me?" Tiffany asks. "My nose is perfect; I've had it done twice."

Too much information, Tiffany.

"No."

"Please," I beg Phoebe.

"Tell you what, Sherlock, and I'm only doing this for your own good, if you can't figure it out by tomorrow morning, call me. I'll tell you, but you're going to feel dumber than an arsonist with no matches when you find out."

Oh jeesh.

We drop Phoebe back at the dining room where soupy ice cream is being served. "I'll call you," I assure her.

"I hope not," she assures me.

On our way out of the building, Tiffany remarks, "She's a very interesting woman. What's her last name?"

"I don't know. I've always just called her Phoebe the Forger.

CHAPTER 24

The wind blowing off the lake is colder than a divorcee who didn't get a dime.

I get in Tiffany's Lexus. I'm a shivering mess. I clutch the guest book in one hand and squeeze so hard I almost bust the spine. I hate it when I can't figure something out, and knowing a clue is as obvious as a wart on a witch's nose, it makes me even crazier.

"Are you not having a good time, Mr. Sherlock?"

"No."

"What's the matter?"

"I'm cold, confused, and can't come up with a clear, concrete clue."

"Oh, Mr. Sherlock, I've been there. I know exactly how you feel. One time I was trying to pick between a Harry Winston platinum tennis bracelet and a pair of diamond drop earrings, I couldn't remember which one was considered more *over the top*, and I didn't know which to buy."

"What did you do?"

"I bought the Winston. It was bigger. One lift of my wrist and nobody could miss it."

"And they say size doesn't matter."

I return to my sedentary state of mind and body.

"What would make you feel better right now, Mr. Sherlock?"

"Some good news."

"Really, I was thinking more along the lines of a trip to the spa or another one of those Russian baths. I loved that tree branch whisky thing."

I take out my phone. I dial his number. He picks up immediately.

"Yo, dude."

"Chappie, did you find out about Vilma's first husband?"

"Sure did."

"How'd he die?"

"Lung cancer."

"Really? Damn."

"What?" Chappie questions. "You were wishing for a brain tumor?"

"No, but some brand of murder would have been nice."

"If he was a smoker, in a way he kinda murdered himself."

"Did he have a life insurance policy with Richmond?"

"No."

"Did he have money or assets that got passed to Vilma?"

"Not that I could find."

This is not good news.

"Thanks, Chappie."

"Am I done here? Should I send you my bill?" he asks.

"Sure, but send it to Tiffany. God knows I can't pay it."

I turn off my phone, jam it back into my coat pocket, and again sit staring at nothing for I don't know how long.

"Excuse me, Mr. Sherlock," I hear Tiffany ask. "But are we just going to sit here in the car all night?"

"No, Tiffany. Why don't you take me home."

Tiffany pulls the Lexus out of the spot, winds down to Sheridan Road, and goes south. At the bend of the road at the cemetery separating Evanston from Chicago, the iced-over tree branches on the east side reflect the lights of the oncoming cars and sparkle like Christmas decorations.

A beeping goes off from where I sit.

"Is that that cheap phone of yours, Mr. Sherlock?" Tiffany asks excitedly. "Answer it. It may be the big break in the case we're waiting for."

I pull the phone out of my pocket. It's as silent as a frozen church mouse.

The beep keeps beeping.

I dig in my other coat pocket and pull out Chappie's GPS. Its screen is lit up. I watch the red dot on the screen move over a small street map.

"Vilma's either home from the loony bin and on her way to the casino, her Buick is getting stolen, or someone she knows is taking her wheels out for more cat food."

"Tell me which way, Mr. Sherlock, and I'll be on her like Armani on a supermodel."

It takes about seven minutes, and we connect with the Buick near Andersonville. "That's him."

"How do you know it's a guy, Mr. Sherlock?"

"Because I looked in the window and saw a guy driving."

"Good move."

"Don't get too close."

"Ten-four."

We follow our prey north. We stop when he stops at a liquor store. When he gets out of the car, we get our first good look at him.

A swarthy fellow, dark complexion, 5'8"–5'9", a bit of a gut, thirty to thirty-five in age, he could use a haircut, and has the type of beard that makes him look as if he needs a shave an hour after he shaves. He's wearing jeans, a black leather jacket, and a pair of go-to-meeting shoes that don't fit with the outfit.

"Look familiar, Mr. Sherlock?"

"Maybe."

"Who do you think it is?"

"I'm hoping for Sergai."

"Sergai?" Tiffany can't believe it. "If that's Sergai, we're looking at a zombie."

Our man comes out of the store with a twelve-pack in his left hand and a large bag in his right. He dumps both into the backseat of the Buick, climbs into the driver's seat, starts it up, and takes off.

"Get on him, Tiffany."

We follow a few car lengths behind. He turns west on Devon Avenue. He's soon in the Pakistani and Indian neighborhoods. "You didn't see a dot on his forehead, did you, Mr. Sherlock?"

"No, Tiffany."

The Buick proceeds west. In about three more miles, he turns right, goes one street, turns right again, and drives into a six-space parking area in front of a square, unlabeled building."

"Should we park across the street and wait for him?" Tiffany asks.

"No, with all that booze, he could be in there for hours. Pull up behind him and stop, but keep the car running."

As our man retrieves the booze booty from the back seat, Tiffany pulls up right behind him. I roll down my window. "Excuse me, could you tell me where to find the Udupi Palace restaurant?"

"No."

I get out of the car but keep the door open. "We're lost."

"Too bad."

I stand maybe twelve feet away facing him. We've already had the chase, I might as well do the cutting. "You look familiar," I tell him. "You're name wouldn't happen to be Sergai, would it?"

"Sergai who?"

"Sergai Levenchenko."

"Why you ask?"

"I talked to a Sergai once at the Russian baths, but it was in the sauna. We were both naked, and there was a lot of steam so my memory is a little cloudy, so to speak."

The guy puts the beer and the bag on the hood of the trunk and steps my way. "You know Sergai?"

"No, but this lady I know does, Vilma Kromka."

"How you know her?" he asks.

"I met her in a casino."

There is a pause as he processes the information. "Sergai was her husband," I add.

"I know," the guy says.

"You know Sergai?" I ask.

"Used to."

"Not any more?"

"He died."

His answer kills my first suspicion. "Well that's certainly a good reason for not keeping in contact."

As he gets closer, I can see an odd lump on the left side of his zipped up jacket. It could be a gun. I hate guns. I make more conversation. "Since we seem to have a mutual friend," I explain, "how do you know Vilma?"

"My sister."

"Really? I didn't know she had siblings."

"And I didn't know she knows you." His left hand goes to the base of his neck, and he slowly pulls the zipper down.

"Small world, isn't it?"

"You don't look like Vilma's type to me."

I jump back into the car as he reaches into his coat. "Tiffany, time to go."

"Wait!" He yells.

"Don't worry, we'll Google the Udupi," I say quickly. "Thanks anyway."

Tiffany floors the Lexus, and she lays enough rubber to empty a plantation.

Out of pistol range, Tiffany says, "That guy was scarier than Chappie showing up as your blind date."

"Don't be mean, Tiffany."

"You have to admit Vilma's bro was a little on the scummy side."

"Yeah, but I'm sure he's a lot of fun at book club."

Four miles away from our supposed Sergai, Tiffany is still driving like a pizza delivery guy on a deadline. "You can slow down, Tiffany."

"The guy didn't look a lot like Vilma," she says. "Maybe they had different fathers?"

"Maybe."

"I wonder if he's into cats too."

"I was going to ask him that next," I tell her.

Tiffany reverts to only breaking the speed limit by ten or so miles per hour.

"You actually thought Sergai might still be alive, Mr. Sherlock?"

"I did until about ten minutes ago."

"Why?"

"Wouldn't you think there would be at least one picture of the guy getting married, or in Vilma's house, or standing in front of his trailer before the tornado hit?"

"Maybe he was just camera shy," Tiffany suggests and adds, "or really, really ugly."

"No, it doesn't fit."

"How about the guy in the TSA airport video?"

"I'm pretty sure that's not our Sergai."

"Who do you think that was?"

"Some silly Sergai puttying around with an explosive personality."

My humor goes over Tiffany's head like a coherent thought.

"Now you think Sergai is back among the dead?" Tiffany asks.

"Yeah. Titus cooked him to a crisp."

"Mr. Sherlock, can I ask you something off the subject?"

"Sure, Tiffany."

"Where am I going?"

I look up and see we're in the middle of a forest preserve. "Sorry. Turn around, it's time to take me home."

Tiffany finds the expressway and aims for the city.

"Biotch-o-nay Bree is going to dinner with my dad again tonight," Tiffany says. "Her hot topic will probably be how lousy we're doing on this case."

"I'm trying my best."

"I don't need your best, Mr. Sherlock. I need something to convince my dad I'm smart."

"I'm working on it."

"Well, work harder, okay?"

The pressure rises to a crescendo. Lucky me.

Tiffany drops me off at my building a little after nine.

Inside my igloo, I suddenly realize I didn't call my kids. I pick up my phone and dial. Care answers. We talk. She tells me about how mad the kids are because they have to stay inside the gym after lunch instead of being able to go outside. I remind her that it's a part of winter in Chicago, and there is not much you can do about it. After we speak, I ask her to get Kelly, but Care says she already went to bed.

"Is she sick?" I ask.

"Kelly is always sick," Care says. "Sick in the head."

"Does she have a cold?"

"I don't know, Dad. Around here, I try to stay away from her as much as possible." Care says. "She's a real pain in the butt."

"Don't say butt, Care."

"Should I say ass? That's what she says I am, 'a pain in the ass.'"

"No. That's another word we don't use."

"Like suck?"

"Exactly."

She says, as if this is a *rote* lesson, "Ass, suck, and butt are no-no words. Let me repeat that to be sure I got it right: Ass, suck, and butt; ass, suck, and butt; ass, suck, and butt."

"Go to bed, Care."

"Why? I'm not tired."

"Good night. I love you."

As my place heats up, I search the cupboards for something to eat. I consider opening the one can of stewed tomatoes I find, heating them up, and serving them over some very old rotini with a June 2009 *eat-by* date stamped on the back of the box. I decide it will be safer to go hungry this evening.

I boil water, make some tea, retire to the living room, and

sit on the couch. *The Original Carlo* stares down on me like Mrs. Thrumble, my teacher, did when I got caught tying square knots with the pigtails of Mary Jo Johnson, who sat one seat ahead of me in the third grade. The recipe cards are in front of me, strewn like oversized confetti on the coffee table. I gather them all together, straighten them into one 3x5 stack with the writing facing the same direction, and flip through slowly. I separate the blank cards and place them in their own pile. Once the stacks are completed and neat, I begin to fill in the blanks. I write one card for Vilma's brother, one for Vilma faking it, one for TV Eddie Floyd, one for Vilma's lung cancer husband, and one for Fred Hollerback. I would like to fill out one more card with the address where I met up with Vilma's brother, but I have no more blank cards, and I forgot to write down the address. Blank index cards will be yet another item that won't be on the shelf when I go to the store when, and if, the weather ever breaks.

I put all the cards in one pile and flip through one more time. I find the Vilma card, but I don't find the Sergai card. These were the hubs of my wheel when I first pinned them up on the *Carlo*. Tiffany must have taken it home with her as a souvenir. I stand up and start over, covering the work of art with scribbled-on recipe cards, leaving a hole where the Sergai card would belong. It takes me about twenty minutes. I sit back down, stare at the mess another twenty minutes, and don't come up with one new thought or idea. I get up and pace back and forth, which isn't much of a pace since the room is the size of a jail cell. I stop at the window, feel the cold air coming through. I look outside.

Oh jeesh. More snow. Just what Chicago needs, more snow.

CHAPTER 25

I don't sleep well.

I don't wake up well either because when I look outside, I see another three-inch blanket of snow. I'm sure a lot of people marvel at the pristine beauty of the freshly fallen white stuff, but I've had it. I'm totally, absolutely, positively sick of snow and can't wait for it to melt.

I make the coffee, do my back-stretching exercises, and before I go in and take my shower, I bundle up, go outside, and dig out the car. A half hour later, the Toyota fires up like a fancy backyard barbecue in late spring, and I'm on my way.

My first stop is a return trip to where I was last night. I forgot to notice or take down the address of the building. The place certainly hasn't changed much in the ten hours I've been gone. The only real difference is all six parking spaces are empty. I park across the street and stay in the car with the engine and heater running.

It's a boxy building, one story, with its front door off to the right. The windows on the street side are half-windows, high up on the wall so no one walking by can see inside. There are no windows on the other two sides of the building that I can see. The address numbers are the silver, shiny, paste-on variety, stuck on the front door, right above the in-the-door mailbox. The place doesn't impress me as one that would get a lot of mail.

The neighborhood isn't residential or industrial, more a hybrid of the two. Other surrounding buildings probably manufactured products no one uses anymore and haven't gotten around to being reconditioned for other uses or torn down. I don't see a lot of workers rushing inside anywhere to get to work.

I take out my cell phone and call Al Landeen.

"Cold cases," the voice answers.

"Is Al Landeen in?"

"You're kidding, right?" the male voice says. "It's eight in the morning."

"Sorry, I don't know what I must have been thinking."

"Try around ten. If he can't come up with an excuse, he

usually comes in around then."

"Could you have him call Richard Sherlock?"

"The Richard Sherlock who punched Captain Mario in the face?"

Will this ever end?

"Yes."

"What do you need? I'll help you."

I give the detective the address of the building and ask him to run it through the system.

"Sure."

I wait.

"Moscow Social Club."

Pretty much what I suspected.

"Thanks."

"If you get anything on it," he says, "please let us know."

"I'll tell Al."

"No, call me. I'm Jeffries."

Next stop is breakfast because I'm dying of hunger. I have the three-egg omelet special at a little diner on Foster. It used to be said that truck drivers knew all the best places to eat, but with only fast food franchises lining our interstates, this has gone by the wayside. Now, the only professions with such a culinary expertise are cops and restaurant critics.

My morning journey continues. I arrive a little after ten and park across from Vilma's house on Ridgeway Avenue. The lights inside are on. She must no longer be insane and is back home enjoying reruns of Jerry Springer.

I'm here because I am seriously considering approaching Vilma with a deal. Since I caught her faking mental illness, I'm now dealing the cards. I'll offer her ten grand cash in exchange for her dropping the PTGD, the monthly stipend, the half million settlement, and Eddie Floyd. Vilma has no idea of how much I know or don't know about the case, and if I position it correctly, she might take the money and run. Heck, she wouldn't even have to get married for this ten grand. I'll keep the fact that I know her brother is a hood with the Russian mob as a final deal closer. Maybe this whole mess can all be over in a few cold heartbeats. If she is a husband serial killer, I am doing a great disservice to society and her next hubby, but I am so sick of this case I could scream.

I'm just about ready to get out of the car when my phone

rings.

It's Alibi Al.

"Sherlock, I got good news for you."

"What?"

"We found that Sergai guy you're looking for."

I'm stunned. I can't believe it. This doesn't make sense.

"Where?"

"Northwest Side."

"Where on the Northwest Side?"

"Dumpster behind a 7-Eleven just off Higgins Road."

"What was he doing in a dumpster?"

"Not much."

"Was he homeless?"

"No, he was dead."

"Dead?"

"Frozen solid."

It is hard to believe I'm hearing what I'm hearing. "The guy froze to death in a dumpster?"

"No, somebody whacked him, threw him in the dumpster, then he probably froze over."

I'm thinking, how can my already dead guy get murdered?

"How'd you know it was Sergai?"

"Green card."

I get the address from Al.

"I'm on my way."

***

A murder scene at a 7-Eleven is actually quite convenient; there's fresh coffee, donuts, awful snack foods, warmth, and the latest editions of newspapers all right there.

By the time I arrive, there are miles of yellow crime scene tape separating the back parking lot from the front parking lot. The owner or manager either put up a great fuss or the cops fully understood his plight because the front parking spaces remain available for customers. The cop cars with their flashing lights are either parked illegally in the street or slightly down the block. I park about a block away.

As I approach the tape, I can't see Alibi Al anywhere. I go back out front and look in the 7-Eleven, and he's not there either. "Anybody see Al Landeen?" I ask a group of sipping uniformed officers.

"I think he went to breakfast," one tells me.

Another officer adds, "Again."

"Who's the officer in charge?"

"Clemons."

I return to the back lot. The CSI techs are hard at work with cameras and sample kits.

"Excuse me, is Clemons around?"

"Over there."

I go under the tape and am careful not to disturb any evidence left on the snowy pavement. It seems quite dumb to me, seeing what the techs are doing. Not only is the whole area covered with salt pellets but if it warms up enough today, the snow will melt, and any evidence will run right into the sewer.

"Clemons."

"Sherlock, how you been?"

"I'm surprised you'd remember me."

"You're a tough one to forget, Sherlock."

"Landeen tell you I was coming over?"

"No."

"I'm a private on this case."

"Working with Alibi Al?"

"Yeah."

"Too bad."

We walk toward the dumpster, which has been turned on its side. The contents spilled out onto two parking spots and spread out. The techs are sifting through the wadded paper, cups, half-eaten snacks, wrappers, fruit peels, doggie bags, and other assorted disgusting residue.

"Where's the body?"

Clemons says, "They loaded him up twenty minutes ago and took him downtown."

"Was he shot here?"

"No."

"When did they think he got dumped?"

"At lease six or seven hours ago," Clemons says. "Although it's tough to estimate when the guy's a block of ice."

"Who found him?"

"Some homeless drunk was dumpster diving looking for half a donut when he came across a frozen foot. If that wouldn't be enough to get you to stop drinking, I don't know what would."

"How'd he look?" I ask.

"The victim or the homeless guy?"

"Victim."

"There was no doubt about this one. I suspect they whacked him in the forest preserve, wrapped him up, and dumped him in the middle of the night when business was slow."

"How'd you ID him?"

"He had a wallet."

"Any eyewitnesses?"

"Guy said he saw a late model car."

"Was it a Buick?"

"Nobody knows what a Buick looks like anymore, Sherlock."

We walk around a few more minutes, but there isn't much to see. Almost all crime scenes are worthless. It only takes about an hour of wind, rain, snow, newly dumped trash, other cars parking, and a few dumpster divers to ruin any clues that might be present.

I have one last question. "What they use?"

"It looked like a .38 to me."

When you get hit with a .38, there's little doubt.

"Thanks, Clemons."

"You're welcome, Sherlock. Good to see you again."

I go back to my car, start it up, get the heater going, and call Al.

"I was just at the crime scene; where were you?"

"I had to go back home and take my grandkids to school."

"I didn't know you had grandkids, Al. Actually, I don't remember you having any kids at all."

"We adopted some after you left the force. It was my wife's idea."

"Where's Sergai now?"

"On his way to the morgue to thaw out."

"I have to see the body, Al," I tell him. "Why don't you meet me at the morgue in a half hour?"

"Sorry, Sherlock, no can do. My skin breaks out when I get around too much formaldehyde. It isn't my fault, the condition's hereditary." He pauses. "Why don't you go, and we'll meet for lunch later? And this time, it'll be my treat."

CHAPTER 26

Luckily, I have an old friend at the morgue named Jellyroll.

"Sherlock, I'm busier than a one-armed gravedigger after a street gang war," he says, seeing me make my way up the ramp, past all the vehicles parked in the loading area.

We have to weave our way inside the building.

The place is packed. Two or three toe tags sticking out of covered and uncovered, overloaded gurneys. This would be "ca-ching" heaven for Titus Pyre.

"Remember that heat wave we had a few years back when people got cooked inside their brick flats? Well, this cold snap's giving it a run for its money," Jellyroll says.

"What are you doing with the overflow?" I ask.

"The city rented refrigerated trucks to keep up. The parks department doesn't know it, but we got 'em parked in their warehouse lot."

"When it's twenty below, they rent refrigerated trucks?" I wonder out loud.

"Alderman must have a brother-in-law in the trucking business." Jellyroll has never been one to mince words.

"I sure would hate to be the coach who goes into one of the trucks searching for hockey pucks."

We make our way into the 'processing' area of the unit. This is where the bodies are identified, tagged, and labeled for autopsy, holding, dispersal, burial, or cremation.

"What can I do for you, Sherlock?"

"A Sergai Levenchenko came in this morning. They found him in a Northwest Side dumpster last night."

"And what can you do for me?" Jellyroll asks.

Nothing in life is free. I hand him a twenty.

Jellyroll retrieves a clipboard, reads down the manifest, and says, "The good news is he's checked in. The bad news is you got to find him."

He escorts me into a room off to the left. The label on its door reads: Police Procedural. It is a big room with stainless steel, built-in cabinets lining the outer wall, and tables, the kind you'd see in a school cafeteria or social hall, arranged in rows end to end. Seeing what is currently on the tables, I am sure I will never have dinner in an Elks Club again, no matter what the special of the day may be.

"He's here somewhere, Sherlock. Happy pickin's." He hands me a pair of latex gloves.

"You're not going to help?" I ask my old buddy.

"Sorry," Jellyroll apologizes. "And don't be takin' any of them cell phone pictures. I don't need no body of mine showin' up on that Internet thing."

I have finally found someone with less Internet savvy than I.

Jelly leaves to tend to more dead. I start at the last table in the last row and begin toe tag checking. I try not to touch anything but the tag itself, but with some of the victims, I have to do a little uncovering. Many of the bodies are still clothed, covered in their own blood, and fresh from their recent demise. Some are naked, washed, and with bullet holes or stab wounds clearly visible. Males outnumber females by a hefty margin, which should tell you something about our society. The males also win in the *gruesome nature of the deaths* category; yet another aspect to make you proud to be a man. The place stinks to high heaven, or low hell in this case.

I'm about fifteen bodies in without getting a Sergai bingo when my cell phone rings. I fumble to get it out of my coat pocket.

"Hello."

"Mr. Sherlock, where are you?" It's Tiffany.

"Tiffany, it's not ten yet. What are you doing up so early?"

"You sound funny. You in a cave somewhere?"

The stainless steel must me echoing my voice like in a spelunker's cavern. "No, I'm at the morgue."

"What are you doing there?"

"Looking for Sergai."

"What would he be doing there?"

"Being dead."

"But you said he was already dead months ago."

"I know."

"Is he deader?"

"Could be."

"So," Tiffany tries to understand, "you can be dead, deader, and deadest?"

"No."

"Mr. Sherlock, you're not making any sense."

"Neither is this case, Tiffany."

There is a short pause in the conversation.

"Mr. Sherlock, Bree Boobs-on-a-broomstick Biz-o-nette called. You have to be at Richmond in an hour."

"Why?"

"Eddie Floyd is coming in to cut a deal."

In all the craziness, I forgot what I mentioned to Eddie about coming up with a settlement offer. And now I don't want one. "Can you hold him off?"

"Me? No way."

"Is Houston Twitchell going to be there?" I ask.

"Bree said she called him and he said no."

Why does this not surprise me?

"What should I do, Mr. Sherlock?"

"Wait for me, and don't you or Bree agree to anything until I'm there."

"Can we agree that Bree is a horrible excuse for a woman, and we wish she would get deported to Alaska?"

"You can't get deported to Alaska, Tiffany."

"Okay, someplace cold and miserable without cell phone service?"

"Tiffany, don't be mean."

I hang up and go back to finding the right toe tag in a sea of bodies. I quit counting the times I almost lose my three-egg omelet breakfast. This is utterly disgusting. The more I search and uncover, the more I shudder at man's inhumanity to man. Finally, in the middle of the room, covered with a blood soaked plastic sheet, a toe tag sticks out reading: Sergai Levenchenco.

I take a breath as deep as the putrid odor around me will allow and slowly peel back the sheet from his head to his upper torso. Somebody wanted this guy not just merely dead but really dead. There is a hole in his head, one in his shoulder, and three in his chest; one right though the aorta. If the shots didn't kill him, he would have died from lead poisoning.

I stand back. First thing I notice is his nose. It's been broken a few times, but there's no beak. The second thing I notice is his hair; it's dark but receding. Maybe the guy in the TSA video had recently quit using Rogaine and reverted to having a widow's peak, but I doubt it. I move closer and get above his face so I can see him at the same angle as the one photo of the younger Sergai Al Landeen had. Nope, this isn't him either. Last but not least, I look for similar genetics to Vilma's brother and strike out there too.

I look around to be sure I'm the only one in the room; I am. I take out my cell phone, punch around until the camera screen comes up on the screen, and snap a few head shots for a possible photo album. I ask him to smile, but he must not be in the mood.

I cover him back up. Goodnight Sergai. Enjoy eternity.

I find Jellyroll back in the main room directing an ambulance crew to "put him anyplace you find a spot."

"Jelly, what came in with Levenchenco to identify him?"

"I don't know."

"Could you see?"

"You got another twenty?"

It takes my last twenty and ten minutes, but Jellyroll shows me the copy of a copy of Sergai's green card. Yep, it's him, same guy that's on the gurney but without the holes and looking much better alive than dead, at least until Thelma and Tiffany get a crack at him.

I study the ID carefully, "Can I get a copy of this?"

"You got another five bucks?"

Copy made. I'm escorted through the maze of bodies to the door I first entered. "Thanks, Jelly."

"You're welcome. Stop by when we're not so busy. It's nice to have somebody around here who talks back."

***

I arrive at Richmond a little before eleven. Even before I give her my name, I ask the receptionist, "Has Eddie Floyd showed up yet?"

"The guy on TV?"

"Yes."

"No." She hesitates and asks, "When he does show up, will he be wearing his boxing gloves?"

"If he is, remember to duck."

I enter the conference room and find the two females seated. At first I think this is a positive, but with one listen I prove myself incorrect.

"You should try shopping at Mervyns," Tiffany says with a snide look on her face. "They have such a good selection for the more mature woman."

"Oh really," Bree says smiling. "Did you stop in on your way to the teenybopper section at Forever 21?"

"No, my Grandma Moomah's birthday's coming up, and the two of you dress so alike—"

"By the way, I'm invited to the party. Are you?"

"I see you two are enjoying yourselves," I say to break their method of not breaking their *no insult* truce.

Tiffany continues as casual as can be, "I was talking to my dad the other day, and he mentioned that he was just using you for sex, Bree." Big smile.

"Well, all I can say is he sure is getting an enormous amount of enjoyment, and all the feelings are mutual." Bigger smile.

"All right, stop you two."

The two exchange one last dirty smile.

"Where's Eddie Floyd?" I ask.

"He's late."

Tell me something I don't know. "Is Houston coming?"

"No."

Houston couldn't have said it better.

"Eddie said you wanted to settle," Bree says. "But little Miss Tiffy here says I shouldn't agree to anything."

"Except taking a powder," Tiffany tells Bree.

"I asked Eddie to put together a proposal yesterday."

"Why"

"To settle the case."

"So, what is it? You want to settle or don't you?" Bree asks.

"No."

"What happened?"

"I changed my mind."

"Duh," Bree says. "Why?"

"Just seemed like the thing to do," I skirt the issue as best as I can.

"Eddie Floyd comes in here and makes an offer because you asked him to, and you beg off. That makes no sense to me. I think we should counter."

"No."

"You're the one who called him in," Bree reminds me.

"I know."

"So, what are you going to say to his offer?"

"Nothing," I answer.

"Nothing?"

"Yes." I sound like Houston Twitchell again.

"You said you want to settle?" Bree makes the statement into a question. "I heard you."

"I know." I pause to explain. "I didn't, then I did, and now I don't."

Bree puffs up and says as forcefully as she can, "Well, I think we should settle and get this over with. It will be a small price to pay if we can avoid bigger problems in the future."

"No."

"Why not?"

"Because I don't want to settle with Eddie," I say. "I want to settle with Vilma."

"You just said you didn't want to settle," Bree shouts at me. "Would you make up your mind?"

"No." Houston Twitchell would be proud of me.

"Men," Bree says and sighs.

The phone on the side table rings. Bree gets up, picks it up, listens, and says, "Send him in." She sits back down. "He's on his way. This should be good."

"Let's hear what he has to say. Don't talk until he has all his cards on the table."

"It doesn't feel like we're going into this playing with a full deck," Bree says.

Tiffany says to Bree, "Something you're probably used to, Bree, since you don't play with a full one either."

"Coming from you, a yo-yo who can't spin, that's quite a compliment, Tiffy."

"Enough!"

Eddie enters carrying a loaded briefcase. He's not wearing boxing gloves. It would be too difficult carrying a big briefcase wearing ten-ounce gloves.

"Nice to see you again, Eddie," I say in greeting.

"Don't be trying to butter me up, Sherlock. I'm only here to do business."

"Too bad we don't have a bell to ring to get us started."

"Where's Twitchell?"

"I asked if he could be here," Bree says, "but he said no."

"You have the authority to act in his absence?" Eddie asks me.

"I do," Bree says, to my utter chagrin.

"And as a member of the Richmond family, so do I," Tiffany says to counter Bree.

My group couldn't come to agree on whether it's raining if we were all standing outside under wet umbrellas.

"Go ahead, Eddie. We're all ears."

Eddie pulls out five or six legal folders from his case. He spreads them across the table. He opens the first and removes a page, holding it up for us to see from a non-readable distance.

"In the interest of fairness, I have to inform you we have a sworn statement from Dr. H. Oliva Lunay, Ms. Kromka's mental health doctor, explicitly specifying not only to her manic condition but to the added stress you people have put her under with your overt and unrelenting harassment."

"Can I see that?" I ask.

"No, it will be included in the discovery if you decide not to settle, and we have to go to trial." Eddie places it back in the folder.

"Just a peek?"

Eddie opens the second file. "We have prepared a calculation of future medical costs associated with her condition for Richmond Insurance to cover without deductibles."

This page he passes out to the three of us. There are a lot of zeros on his projection.

"Isn't Vilma still covered by her Lube-in-a-Jiffy policy?" I ask.

"No, she was dropped when she was fired for being too depressed to do her job."

"She was fired, Eddie, because she couldn't sell brake fluid to a car that couldn't come to a stop."

"That's your opinion, Sherlock, not the determination of a court of law."

"Ask the guy who runs the shop," I tell him.

"We visited and have a sworn statement from a fellow employee stating that Vilma was working in a depressed, demoralized frame of mind."

"Did he sign it before or after you ordered the premiere

lube with all fluids flushed and new wiper blades front and back?"

Eddie ignores my question. He pulls out yet another page. "And due to Ms. Kromka's incapacitation, a number of debts have piled up, which will require immediate payment."

I read the page carefully. "I don't see any debts from local casinos listed. How'd ya miss those, Eddie?"

Eddie ignores me once again. He passes out one last piece of paper. "And in conclusion," he says, "Ms. Kromka has most generously waived her prior demand for a monthly stipend for the next five years in her, and our, desire to bring this matter to a final resolution—"

"What a great human being," I interrupt.

Eddie finishes his summation, "And instead, will settle for a one-time payment of one million one hundred and fifty thousand dollars."

Eddie's done.

"Deal!" Bree shouts out.

"No way."

"We'll take it," Bree says.

I out-shout her with, "We'll take it under consideration, she's saying."

"No, I don't," Bree says.

"Yes, you do," Tiffany corrects her.

"He didn't even mention the elimination of PTGD in any future cases, Bree," I inform her. "What about PTGD, Eddie? Does it disappear?"

"No." Eddie's now sounding like Houston Twitchell.

"No?" I ask. "Are you going to try to make PTGD the next whiplash?"

"Start negotiating, and I'll let you know."

"We want to come to an agreement," Bree tells him.

"No, we don't," Tiffany counters.

"Yes, we do."

"No, we don't."

I take a deep breath. "Eddie, in the words of Arnold Schwarzenegger, 'I'll be back.'" I pause and add, "To you."

Eddie, angry as a tormented pit bull, packs up his briefcase. "You got twenty-four hours or the price is going to skyrocket."

"Eddie, thanks for stopping by."

Once Eddie is out the door, Bree speaks up. "We should

take the deal."

"No way," Tiffany says.

"Why not?"

"Because if you want to do it, it must be the wrong thing to do," Tiffany responds.

"Sherlock, you have to realize what this is doing to my department. The claims people have always been the shining apples of Richmond Insurance, but this lawsuit is causing serious workplace anguish and anxiety for people under my watch."

"I'm sorry to hear that, Bree, but there is no way we're going to take that deal." I could inform her of catching Vilma during a break in her performance, but I'm afraid of what Bree might do with the information. "We need a little more time."

"You've already had a lot of time." Bree is getting more emotional. "You and your dimwit assistant are waiting for a light bulb to go on, but your lamp isn't plugged in."

"Who you calling a dimwit, dimwit?"

Truce ends.

The two square off again. I get between them. "Listen, it's Friday tomorrow. We get through that day, we have the weekend to work the case," I plead with Bree. "If I can't break it by Monday, you can do what you want."

"No, twenty-four hours is noon tomorrow. If you don't have something by then, I'm calling Houston Twitchell, and we can end this nightmare!"

CHAPTER 27

A lot of jokes are made about cops spending more time eating than in the pursuit of criminals. And, I have to admit there is a modicum of truth to the humor. Cops, especially detectives, do spend a lot of time in a lot of restaurants, but a lot of it is because it is very difficult being a police detective. The thrills of victory over the criminal element are few and far between from the frustrations faced on a daily basis. Being a detective is a very disheartening career. Even if you do solve a case, you still have to go to trial and be battered and basted on the stand by slimy defense lawyers. And if the perp does get convicted, he's usually back on the street before you hit your next pension level. Worst of all, if one slime ball does get locked up, there's hundreds more chomping on the bit to do the same crime. The point here is a good meal in the middle of a frustrating day is a bit of a welcome relief for a hardworking, well-meaning police detective.

Be that as it may, some police detectives abuse the culinary privilege. Alibi Al Landeen is the poster child for this category. Tiffany and I find him seated in a booth at Shaw's Crab House, a very nice seafood restaurant owned by Lettuce Entertain You, a group of eateries in Chicagoland known for their clever promotions.

"Where have you two been?"

"Sorry, Al."

"I almost wasted away to nothing waiting for you two."

A little hard to believe seeing a beer, half-eaten bread plate, an empty bowl of mussels, and a full bowl of mussel shucks on the table.

"Sit down, let's order," he says. "And don't forget, it's on me."

Tiffany orders the crab salad. I go for the grilled grouper.

"I'm sorry I couldn't join you at the morgue, Sherlock. My stomach would still be doing somersaults if I inhaled all that formaldehyde."

"Can't say that I missed you, Al."

"Did you get a picture of the deceased?"

I take out my cell phone, punch around to the picture gallery, pull up Sergai postmortem, and pass it across the table.

Al refuses my phone. "Let's wait until after our dessert."

"I want to see," Tiffany says.

I hand her the phone, she gives the photo a long gaze, and says, "I bet me and Thelma could make this guy look better than Channing Tatum."

"With Sergai in the morgue, I'm gonna transfer the case from a cold one to a solved one," Al informs us. "Chalk up another winner for Detective Al Landeen."

"I wouldn't be opening up the file drawer just yet, Al."

"Why not?"

"Still to come could be bigger fish to fry."

"Are we talking minnows or flounders, Sherlock?"

"Maybe a whale."

Our food is served. Tiffany nibbles at her salad. I savor each bite of the delicious white fish, and Al cracks into a lobster the size of Maine.

"What have you got, Sherlock?" Al asks between dips into the drawn butter.

"A woman who did her husband in for the insurance money."

"That's no whale, more like a trout in a overstocked farm."

"She's tied into the Russian mafia, who has had a flurry of activity as of late."

Al cracks a tail with his oversized nutcracker, and the shell pieces fly across the table like an exploding grenade.

"She might seem dumb as a cheap vodka, but I suspect she can name enough names to fill a Moscow phone book."

"What do you want me to do?" Al asks.

"Right now, nothing."

"I can handle that."

We finish our food. Tiffany and I beg off dessert. Al has a piece of key lime pie. When the check comes, to my surprise, Al grabs it and pulls it toward him. "I got this."

"Thanks, Al."

"My pleasure." Al pulls out of his coat pocket a stack of coupons. The first is: *Buy one fish, we'll float the other*. The second is: *The key to your key lime pie*. The third is: *Something fishy's going on*. The final slip he places on the pile is a *Lettuce Entertain U Lunch Scratcher* with a jackpot of three fishes showing. He puts them all in the leather check folder, slaps it shut, and pushes it out for the waitress to grab. "Since I bought lunch, why don't you guys leave the tip?"

***

I have Tiffany drive me to my car, which is parked on the other side of the band shell in Grant Park. I got lucky and found an unmetered spot. She double parks.

"Should I meet you somewhere?" she asks.

"No."

"You want to assign me something to do?"

"No."

"What then, Mr. Sherlock?"

"I don't know, Tiffany. I'm at a loss on what to do next."

"You are?"

"I can't make any sense out of any of it."

"I thought you thought Vilma was a breakfast serial killer?"

"I did, and I do, but with so many pieces of the puzzle not connecting, I don't know for sure."

"We only have until tomorrow at noon, and Bree is going to give Eddie the password to the Richmond ATM machine."

"I know."

"Mr. Sherlock, we have to solve this case. This is my big chance to impress my dad and make that Bree Bizzy Breasts-o-Nette look like a total boob."

"Tiffany, you got to ease up on the Bree bashing. It doesn't do you any good to be mean."

"Fine, I'll do that, but what are you going to do to solve this case?"

"Right now, think."

"You got to do something more than that," Tiffany raises her voice. "Trust me, I know from experience thinking is not going to help us now."

***

Every detective or person in the sleuthing business I've ever met, although Tiffany may be the exception, has a way of thinking things through. Some drive around in a car for hours, some may sit in a warm tub, some may visit and revisit the scene of the crime. One guy I used to know years ago would spread all his case notes in front of him and fill in all the o's and a's with a lead pencil. Sometimes these activities help; most of the time they're a waste of time.

I usually go in front of *The Original Carlo* and move the cards around and around until one connects with another, and another, and another. Since I've already done this with this case until my eyes crossed, the activity would be pointless now. I get in my car, fire it up, and head up Lake Shore Drive. I get off at Montrose, go east, and park the car just south of the deserted, iced-over harbor. Mine is the only car in the lot.

I have no clue what the temperature may be, and I don't want to know because it would be too scary to know. I strap down my furry hat, shove my gloved hands into my pockets, and walk toward the water. There is a stretch of lakefront that goes for a few hundred yards. It has a dirt path, which is now covered in snow, and boulder rocks against the shoreline, many of which have graffiti messages of lover's love. On the opposite side is an area, which is seldom used. It's too small to play soccer, too pitted and rocky for little kids, and too potholed to ride bikes. Even in the spring and summer, this stretch seems desolate. If there is a spot in Lincoln Park that could be considered off the beaten path, this is the place.

I pace south along the path until I get to the turn, turn around, and pace back to Montrose Harbor. After an hour, I lose track of the number of turns I've made. I keep my pace up to help stay warm, although there is little I can do to keep my face from hurting from even the mild wind off the lake.

I contemplate every aspect of the case over and over. My problem is that I can't convince myself that Vilma, who will never be a candidate for the Mensa society, is smart enough to pull off such a caper. I also can't give myself enough reasons why Richmond Insurance paid her off after Sergai's demise. Why wasn't I called to investigate that case? The number of Sergai/Sergei's is also problematic, but Levenchenko is a pretty common name in Eastern Europe. And the whole idea of using post-traumatic grief disorder as the basis for a medical claim seems absurd from the get-go. Back and forth, back and forth, I quit pacing when I can no longer feel my toes.

I get in the car and drive home.

***

"Hi, Care."
"Hi, Dad."
"Did you learn something new in school today?"
"No."
Care goes on to tell me who she sat with at lunch, that she hated going to the gym for recess, and that the janitor from her school got locked in a stall in the girl's bathroom. Everybody on the second floor heard his screams and thought it might be some pervert inside.

I listen, comment a few times, and when she's done, I say, "Let me talk to your sister."

Kelly comes on the phone and sniffles.

"Are you sick?"

"No."

"I heard you sniffle, Kelly."

"It's that landline you use, Dad."

"You know, when you get sick, Kelly, you're hardly pleasant to be around."

"That's not true."

"Yes, it is, and you know it is."

She doesn't argue.

"When you were out today, did you dress accordingly and zip up your coat?"

"Yes."

"Are you sure?"

"Dad, I'm not sick, so give it a rest."

I pause to give it a rest. "What do you have planned this weekend?"

"A bunch of us are going out to play Frisbee football in the snow."

"Kelly, you're going to freeze to death doing that."

"One day you complain I don't get enough exercise, and now you're telling me I can't go out. Make up your mind, Dad."

"There is a time and a place for everything, Kelly."

"I know, that's why we're playing in the park on the weekend."

"Did you tell your mother you're doing this?"

She hesitates. "Maybe."

"Kelly."

"Mom's going to a spiritual awakening this weekend, and I

don't want to screw up her mantra."

Oh jeesh.

"I don't want you to go flopping around in the snow and catch your death of pneumonia."

"It's a Mom weekend, so you can't tell me what to do."

I hate it when she plays that card. "I'm only thinking what's best for you, Kelly."

"Then quit thinking so much; you're making me crazy, Dad."

"I don't want you to get sick."

"I'm not sick!"

I give up. I don't say a word.

"Did you solve the case yet, Dad?"

"No."

"Why not?"

"Because I've run out of things to think about."

"That's hard to believe."

I tell her I love her and hang up the phone.

The remainder of the evening I sit or stand in front of *The Original Carlo* and since I have no more blank cards to add, I shuffle and reshuffle the ones pinned up over and over again. The Vilma card stays in the middle. I have to imagine the missing Sergai card next to it.

Before 10 p.m., I'm exhausted and don't bother watching the news and the weather for tomorrow. If you are a Chicagoan living here in the wintertime, you always watch the late news and never tune out before the weather segment. Tonight, I make an exception and go to bed at 9:55.

I fall fast asleep in minutes. Two hours later, I'm wide-awake. So much for the good night's sleep.

CHAPTER 28

I can't sleep. I toss and turn like cookie dough in a mixer for hours. I check my clock about every ten minutes to see how much sleep I'm missing, which makes me more tense, angry, and wide awake. Many times, instead of seeing the actual time, I see *12 noon, Friday* on the display. I consider getting up a thousand times but only get as far as sitting up once before I convince myself I have absolutely nothing to do if I do get up. I finally fall asleep but have no clue when.

I awaken at 9:12 a.m. The sunlight is shining into the apartment like a prison searchlight. I must have been hit in the head with an iron skillet because I went out like a light. I haven't slept this well or this late since the morning after my bachelor party. I feel great, rested, and most of all, warm. I open the drapes, pull up the blinds, and look outside to see a beautiful morning. The snow on the sidewalks is melting faster than a kid's ice cream cone in July. I stand back and let the sun hit me like an eco-friendly space heater, and a wave of energy pulses through my entire being like someone inserted a whole new set of batteries into my electrodes. I don't even pull on my robe. I go straight to the kitchen, plug in the coffee, go into the front room, get on the floor, and start my back exercises even though my back isn't hurting. In the middle of a cat/cow, I look up at *The Original Carlo* and stare at the Vilma card alone in the middle, and I almost go into shock.

As Tiffany would say, "Oh my God."

I don't even have to move the cards around. Suddenly, I'm making sense out of nonsense. Answers are answered, connections are connected, and new questions are queried. Thoughts are flooding into my brain like a plague of locusts swarming into a cornfield. I run to the dining room table, grab the guest book from Sergai's viewing, open to the third page, and can't believe I missed this. It's as plain as the beak on one of the Sergai's noses.

I go to the computer, find the number, check my watch, subtract a couple of hours and decide to call anyway. I catch them just after they wrap up the last ceremony of the night. I get exactly what I need.

I drink one cup of coffee, don't bother to scavenge for food, and take a quick shower. I'm out the door in record time.

The first steps outside are wonderful. The sun hits me with warmth not felt since October. I barely need my coat. I take the Ushanka hat off my head and head toward my Toyota with a springtime vigor a budding crocus would envy.

First stop: Vilma's house. I have to make sure she hasn't skipped town. I can see a flickering TV on in the front room. Mission accomplished.

Second stop: Chappie's. His mother answers the door.

"Who are you?"

"Sherlock, I was here on Tuesday."

"What year, Tuesday?"

"Is your sister home?"

"How do you know I have a sister?"

The sister finally shows up.

"Is Chappie up?"

"No, he's down," she says. "You want to see him?"

I go down the rickety stairs and find Chappie seated before his computers.

"Hey, dude."

"Have you moved since I was here last?"

"Not much."

"You got to get out more," I tell him.

"I'm working on it."

I sit down next to him and explain my recent epiphany on the case.

"Good thinking, Sherlock."

"There is only one connection I have to prove."

"How?"

I'm not sure, but pictures would be nice."

"Pictures could be tough."

"And I need them by noon today."

"No can do, Sherlock."

"Run a Chappie on them, Chappie. One of these people is going to be connected, and I have to show how."

"Why?"

"I'm big into show-and-tells."

***

By the time I'm back up the stairs, out of the house, and into my car, it's after ten. I call Tiffany. She doesn't pick up. I leave a message, "I thought of something; call me right away."

I call Alibi Al. He doesn't pick up but another does, "Cold cases, Jeffries."

"It's Sherlock. Is Landeen in yet?"

"There's a donut on his desk, but I don't see him," Jeffries explains. "Want me to go check the men's room?"

"No, tell him not to leave. I'm on my way in. I need his Levenchenko file."

"You sound excited."

"I'm getting there." I hesitate for a few seconds, then ask, "You know a Detective Clemons?"

"Yeah."

"Could you transfer me?"

A minute of wait time and I hear, "Clemons."

"It's Sherlock. I'm not all the way home on this one, but I may have a break for you on the guy in the dumpster."

"Talk to me."

I tell him what I know, what I think, and what I'm going to do next.

He's impressed. "What do you want me to do?"

"Keep lunch open."

Tiffany calls me back. "Mr. Sherlock, it's so early; I haven't had my toilet yet."

"Make it a quick one, Tiffany. I need you to meet me at the Chicago police station on Larrabee in a half an hour."

"A half hour? It takes me twenty minutes just to put my eyes on."

"No excuses, Tiffany. The clock's ticking, and we only have until noon."

"That's right."

"And one other thing, Tiffany."

"What?"

"Thanks."

"Thanks for what?"

"It was your idea that broke the case."

"It was? That's fantastic. I knew I had it in me."

"Okay, now hurry."

"Wait, Mr. Sherlock, you got to tell me what I did."

"I can't talk now. I got to go." I hang up.

The Toyota kicks over like a freshly tuned Harley Davidson, and I head in the direction of the city. I'm downtown in record time, pulling into the police lot, and parking the car a little before eleven. I make one more phone call before going inside.

"Bree Bisonette speaking."

"It's Sherlock. We're going to need the big conference room today at lunch."

"Why?"

"We're going to settle this mess once and for all."

"Thank God." She speaks again before I have a chance, "I'm so glad you came to your senses."

"So am I."

"Wait," she says, "we can't have the conference room; we're using it for Selma Warma's goodbye luncheon."

"Can we use the one next door?"

"It's not as big."

"It'll have to do," I say.

"Do you want Houston Twitchell there?"

"Not really, but he might be helpful."

"I'll call him." She breathes a huge sigh of relief. "I am thrilled this will be settled once and for all, Mr. Sherlock."

"You might want to postpone your outright glee until it's all put to bed, Bree," I warn her. "See you at noon."

I put my cell phone back in my coat pocket, grab the file I have on the case, and climb out of the car. On my way into the station, I'm shocked for the second time today. Tiffany runs up to meet me.

"Mr. Sherlock, tell me what I did. Tell me what I did," she says, following me as we hurry toward the building.

She looks gorgeous, radiant, and beautiful. "I thought you said you didn't have time to get ready? You look perfect, Tiffany."

"Mr. Sherlock, tell me something I don't know. How did I break the case wide open?"

"By using your intuitive methods in the process of elimination."

Tiffany beams brighter than the day's sunshine. "That's exactly what I suspected. Tell me how I did it."

"Later."

We're inside. I announce myself to the desk sergeant. He calls Al, and we're in the detective dayroom in a few minutes.

"I need your entire file on Levenchenko, Al."

"You know it's classified police business," he warns me.

"Give me the file, Al."

He hands it over. I open it and find the first, younger, Sergai picture. I compare it to the one in my file, compare those two to the one from the TSA. I close the file. "I need to borrow this, Al."

"Why?"

"I need it for a meeting today at noon."

"I'm not a library. I can't go lending out evidence, Sherlock."

"Then come to the meeting."

"I'd like to, but I told my wife I'd join her today for a charity buffet luncheon for the End Obesity League."

"Well, if you can't make it, I'll ask Jeffries. I was chatting with him the other day, and he seemed pretty interested in the case."

Al looks over at his fellow detective, then back at me. "I hate that guy."

"It's up to you, Al. You want the credit on this case or not?"

Before he answers, my phone rings.

"Chappie."

"Yo, dude. I got pictures."

"Stay there, I'll be right back over." Once I utter the words, I feel dumb telling Chappie to "stay there."

Al answers my last question to him with a question. "Is lunch going to be served at the meeting?"

I hate when people answer a question with a question.

"There'll be cake at the party next door," I tell him. "I'm sure I could score you a big piece."

"Well, my wife will be heartbroken, and I won't be there to help counsel anyone with their overeating problems, but I'll change my plans if I have to."

What a guy.

I grab both files off the desk, stand, and exit with Tiffany.

"Here's what I need you to do, Tiffany," I say as we make our way out of the station. "Call Eddie Floyd, tell him to be at Richmond at noon. Tell him I'm going to settle the case, but Vilma has to be there with Dr. Lunay. Don't take no for an answer."

"No problem, Mr. Sherlock."

I give her Clemons name and phone number. "Call this guy and tell him to be there too."

My phone rings. I look at the display: Pat Nixon School.

"Hello."

"Is this Richard Sherlock?"

"Yes."

"This is the nurse at your child's school." Her voice is rising as if she's getting angry. "How could you send your child to school like that, Mr. Sherlock?"

"How?"

"She's sneezing and coughing enough to infect the entire student body."

"She is?"

"Yes, she is. What kind of a parent are you?" she yells at me. "Don't you have any respect for the other children?"

"Did you call my wife?"

"We couldn't get ahold of her."

"Look, it wasn't my day—"

She yells even louder, "I don't need to hear excuses, mister. You get yourself up here, pick up your child, and remove her before she causes an epidemic."

She slams down her phone.

I can't believe this. The timing couldn't be worse. Now, I'm mad. Wait till I get ahold of that Kelly. I'm going to give her a talking to that will scare the germs right out of her.

"Change of plans, Tiffany."

"What?"

"You're going to have to go to Chappie's."

"Alone?"

"Yes."

"Ewwww, gross."

"Don't be mean, Tiffany."

"Mr. Sherlock, I can't be around somebody who looks that bad. I have trouble being around some guys the morning after."

"You have to go. He's got what we need. I have to have it for the meeting."

"I can't."

"Tiffany, you have to start seeing people for what they are and not just how they appear. Chappie is one of the nicest, loyal, hard-working people I've ever known." The anger I'm holding for Kelly is being quickly transferred toward Tiffany. "It wasn't Chappie's fault he looks the way he does. You better start to instill a little compassion in your life, Tiffany, or you're the one who will be sitting alone not going out."

"Okay, okay. You don't have to snap at me. You know I hate being snapped at, Mr. Sherlock."

"Go."

"Could you first tell me what I did to break the case?"

"No."

Tiffany traipses off like a scolded child. I hop in my car and take off like a man possessed.

With the Pat Nixon Grammar School being adjacent to the Ann Margaret Middle School, the facilities save money by combining some needed functions. One of which is the school nurse, Cece Lancit, whose office is set right between the two schools.

I park in the drop-off/pick-up area, run into the main office to check in, and head straight to the nurse's office.

"What kind of a parent are you?" Nurse Lancit woofs at me as I enter her clinic.

"It wasn't my turn. I'm a divorced Dad—"

"No excuses."

I have a strong suspicion Cece Lancit was sick the day in nursing school when they had the bedside manner lecture.

"You're lucky she's been vaccinated, or you'd really get a piece of my mind, mister." She points her finger at me like Uncle Sam points on his poster.

"May I please see my daughter?"

"I'll get her."

I take a deep breath, promise myself not to explode when I see Kelly, stand back, and try to remain calm.

It doesn't do me a bit of good. "What are *you* doing here?" I scream out.

Red-faced, mucus dripping, throat coughing, and nose sneezing, Care says, "I feel awful."

"Care, what happened?"

"All of a sudden, my nose started to run, I started to cough, and I felt terrible."

Oh jeesh.

One kid gets all the symptoms and the other gets sick. I

can't believe my luck.

I pull Care close to me. "I'll take care of you. You'll feel better, I promise."

"My stomach hurts too."

Nurse Lancit stands facing us with her hands on her hips. "I hope this is a lesson for the both of you."

"I'm sorry, Nurse Lancit," Care says.

"It's not your fault, Care," she says and turns to me. "But don't let it happen again, mister."

"Sorry."

"You should be."

"Come on, Care, I'll take you to your mother's house."

"She's not home. She's busy getting her spirit awakened."

"How were you going to get home this afternoon?"

"I don't know. Kelly does though."

I get Care out into my car, get the heater going, and tell her to lie down in the backseat. I cover her with my coat.

"Dad, I'm hungry. Can we go to McDonald's?"

"No. What do you want to do, get sicker?"

"No, I want some French fries."

I leave Care in the car, go back into the office, and ask to see my eldest.

Kelly arrives in five minutes. She comes into the office with her coat wide open; she was at lunch outside. "What are you doing here, Dad?"

"Your sister's sick."

"I told her to zip her coat up, Dad, but she wouldn't listen to me."

I try my best to ignore her comment, but it's near impossible. "How were you getting home after school today?" I ask.

"Mom or some friend who's also getting woke up, is picking us up at five thirty. We're supposed to hang around in the tacky afternoon program they have here."

"Well, I'm taking your sister with me."

"Can I come? The only class I'll be missing this afternoon is gym."

I check Kelly out of school. She's thrilled. I look at my watch. It's twenty to twelve.

Care is laid out in the car, half asleep, sniffling, and sneezing. Kelly sits in the front with me.

"Dad, can we go to Wendy's?" Care asks between somnambulant coughs.

"No."

"Taco Bell?"

"No."

"You know you're supposed to feed a cold and starve a fever, Dad," Kelly says.

"I don't remember asking for any medical advice from you, Kelly."

"How about Burger King?" Care asks.

"No."

Care sneezes a real whopper.

"Care is really being really gross, Dad. Make her stop."

"Shut up, Kelly."

"Care, don't tell your sister to 'shut up.'"

"Dad, since it's the weekend already, can we go do something fun?" Kelly asks.

"No."

"Well, what are we going to do?"

"Yeah," Care adds, "since you won't let us eat, are we going partying with those Donner people."

I check my watch. "I have to be downtown at Richmond at noon."

"Why?"

"I got to go solve the case."

"And we get to go with you ... Cool!"

CHAPTER 29

We're twenty minutes late, but before we enter the room, I pull the girls aside and lay down the law. "You two stay on opposite sides of the back of the room. Don't say anything. And try not to infect anyone, Care."

We walk by the big conference room where Selma's party is in full swing. I should go in and scarf up a couple of sandwiches for the kids, but that would hardly be kosher.

I enter the table-for-eight conference room. "Sorry I'm late, everybody."

"The clock started at noon, Sherlock," Eddie Floyd informs me. "The price is going up as we speak."

Houston Twitchell sits at the table for eight, between his entourage. After Eddie's comment, the lady whispers in his ear, and Houston says to Eddie, "No."

"I had a medical emergency this morning I had to tend to," I explain.

Care sneezes.

"And here she is."

My girls head to the back of the smaller conference room, passing Alibi Al.

"Where'd you get the cake?" Care asks him.

"Next door. They got sandwiches over there too."

"Dad—"

"No."

I see Clemons on the other side of the room and motion for him to come over. I whisper, "Do me one favor?"

"Sure."

"Anyone who comes in the room, stays in the room."

"I can do that," he says and positions himself in the chair closest to the door.

Vilma and Dr. H. Oliva Lunay sit adjacent to Eddie Floyd. Vilma has worn a crummy housedress with what looks like mustard stains on the front that I'm sure gives a fashion statement of *depressed destitute*. Dr. Lunay chose to wear a white lab coat, with her name embroidered on the front, over her regular therapy clothes. I'm surprised she didn't bring along one of those doctor's black bags. TV Eddie Floyd is in an ill-fitting striped suit, sans boxing gloves, and he has his loaded briefcase set before him. Bree Bisonette has worn a sleek, body-hugging little black number designed to win a cleavage contest against much younger and firmer challengers.

And guess who's not here.

I'll have to stall for time until Tiffany gets here with the final pieces of the puzzle.

"I don't know why you invited all these people, Sherlock," Eddie says. "I'm here to do business."

"I'm going to settle this, Eddie. I promise you."

"Then, let's start settling. The price of the immediate payout is now one million five five fifty."

I can't help but ask, "Why do you always pick such an odd number, Eddie? Didn't you ever learn to round up?"

"All right, one million six," he says and adds, "and counting."

I position myself at the far end of the table, between my two girls, one of which is sniffling constantly. I hand her the box of Kleenex on the table.

I wait for Al to take the last bite of frosting and I begin, "Here's what I think happened, people. And, I will admit this case was more baffling than the Enigma Code. Vilma Kromka, who I must commend on her choice of wardrobe today, a *Please feel sorry for me* housedress, should have taken her talents to Hollywood. She's not only a good actress but a pretty sharp cookie."

Dr. Lunay jumps out of her chair. "What are you doing? Insulting a person in her depleted mental state is nothing less than cruel and unusual punishment."

Vilma hardly moves except for the tears welling up in her eyes. She sits with a total blank look on her face, which I have a feeling isn't hard for her to do without acting.

"Calm down, Doctor Lunay, calm down. I wasn't insulting her; I was heaping praise upon her performance in this little three-act play."

"No, you weren't!"

"Please, let me explain."

Dr. Lunay sits.

"Vilma knows a good deal and a good husband when she meets them. And, in this case, they arrived at the same time.

Sergai Levenchenko needed an American wife to ward off deportation back to Ubeakistan, and Vilma needed ten grand for a new Buick and to play the slots in Buffington Harbor's Majestic Star riverboat. A perfect couple. The pair ran off to Las Vegas where they were married by the *Old Elvis* at the Hunka Burnin' Love Chapel. Maralyn Monroe was the witness. It was the perfect marriage. For a time, each fulfilled each other's needs. Vilma proudly wore the beautiful diamond ring Sergai gave her, and they lived in a suburban doublewide out in the burbs. Life was good. Sergai, who had snuck into the USA over the border somehow, was now street legal and rising rapidly in the exciting world of leg-breaking and extortion. Sergai was a real up-and-comer in Chicago's up-and-coming Russian mob. Vilma had an office job downtown, which left her plenty of time to pull the arms of one-armed bandits. But bliss didn't last forever, and things started to go wrong. Their 'love nest' trailer got blown away by a tornado, Vilma lost her job, and Sergai didn't like spending time at Vilma's old house on Ridgeway in the city. I guess you could say, 'The bloom was coming off the rose faster than the odor off the cat litter in Vilma's bathroom.'"

"What is this all about?" Eddie Floyd yells out. "The more you talk, the bigger the price. The settlement is now up to one point seven five."

"Sherlock, hurry up," Bree jumps in to beg me.

"My patient is starting to wheeze," Dr. Lunay announces.

I sure wish Tiffany would get here.

"Bear with me, folks, bear with me," I plead. There is a second of silence, and I use it to continue. "So Vilma needs an influx of cash, and since the marriage isn't working out, and divorce can be a costly and time consuming event, Vilma decides to end the marriage in a less traditional manner, but not to make the same mistake she made when her first husband passed away. This time she loads up on life insurance policies for Sergai, just in case something awful might befall him."

To my surprise, Alibi Al interrupts, "Does anyone know if there's any more cake next door?"

"I'll check that out in a minute, Al."

"Could I have some too, Dad?" Care asks and sneezes.

"This is total and absolute absurdity," Eddie Floyd says. "The price is now one nine nine fifty-five."

"I'm almost done, folks."

"Hurry up, Sherlock," Bree yells. "You talk, our money walks."

"So, guess what happens? Perfectly healthy, Sergai Levenchenko's heart stops beating and he dies. Vilma is crushed, inconsolable, and beside herself in grief. Sergai's body, or what's left of it, is laid to rest at the Hollerback Funeral Home, where a small but simple viewing takes place. The next day, Sergai is cremated, and his ashes are placed in a very nice urn, prominently displayed on the fireplace mantle amidst all the cat clutter in Vilma's house. Vilma collects a half million from Richmond Insurance, but money isn't everything because she just can't shake the grief. Instead of getting better, she gets stuck in stage six of the seven stages of grief and heads to Richmond's resident shrink, Dr. Lunay, for help.

"Instead of helping, Vilma gets worse, so bad in fact she loses her Lube-in-a-Jiffy job, gets more depressed, and decides to sue Richmond for another big chunk of change due to what she calls PTGD.

"And here we are today."

"What are you talking about?" Eddie Floyd is up, ripping into me. "This is nothing but gibberish, unproven slander against my client. You haven't stated one fact yet. Our price is now up to two million five."

"Well, at least you rounded up this time, Eddie."

The door opens, and for my third surprise of the day, Tiffany walks into the room with Chappie by her side.

"Hello, everybody. Sorry, were late." Tiffany sees the girls in the back of the room. "And hello there, little dudettes."

"Hi, Tiffany."

"For you, who have not had the pleasure of meeting my astute assistant, this is Tiffany Richmond."

"And this," Tiffany says, "is Chappie. He's got these gross tumors growing out of his neck, but they're not his fault, and I don't want anyone staring at his neck and making him feel ugly and weird."

"Yo, everybody," Chappie says, waving to the group. "Glad I could join you."

There are no more chairs remaining. I motion for Tiffany and Chappie to come and stand flanking me. Chappie hands me a folder. I open and read quickly. I smile and hand it back.

"Two million five, take it or leave it!" Eddie screams.

"We'll take it," Bree yells back.

"No, we won't," I correct her. "Right, Houston?"

Our lawyer is counseled by his female assistant with a whisper, his male assistant via laptop, and he says, "Yes."

"Sorry Eddie." I pause. I put my hand to my chin as if I'm wondering. "When I started that story, did I say 'I think this is what happened,' or 'This is what happened'?"

Detective Clemons answers, "You said, 'I think.'"

"Oh, I am so sorry. I went on and on about what I thought happened. How silly of me. I meant to tell you what actually did happen. Anybody interested in hearing that sordid tale?"

"No," Eddie Floyd screams. "I've had enough of this drivel, Sherlock."

"Yes," Houston Twitchell counters.

"How about you, Vilma?" I ask.

Suddenly coming to life, Vilma looks up at me, "You're crazy."

"That's what you've been trying to convince everybody of."

Vilma gives me a stare that could melt icicles.

I begin again. "When Vilma's first husband died from lung cancer, and let that be a lesson to all you smokers or would be smokers, Vilma didn't get diddly-squat. It was a pot of gold that disappeared as quickly as a rainbow. She wouldn't let that happen again if she could help it. Her next husband deserted her. With her third husband, Sergai, she was going to make this marriage work no matter what. She was going to load up on life insurance policies and cash in big when he dropped dead." I look away from Vilma. "Bree, would you please go next door and ask Selma if she could join us?" I turn back to the assembled as Bree stands to leave the room. "Selma Warma can corroborate and add a lot of fun to our little meeting here."

I give Clemons the okay to let Bree out, but before she exits, I ask, "And if there are any sandwiches left, could you bring some back for my girls and another piece of cake for Al? I'm worried he might pass out from a lack of processed sugar in his system."

"Thanks, Sherlock." Al is appreciative if nothing else.

While Bree is out of the room, I mention to the remaining group, "In almost every crime, one of two things will invariably come out. The truth of the crime or the vanity of the criminal, and one of which will lead to the unraveling of the crime itself.

Correct, Detective Clemons?"

"Correct, Sherlock."

Selma and Bree, who holds a plateful of sandwiches and a corner piece of cake for Alibi Al, come into the room. Clemons gives up his seat and stands by the door.

"Everyone, I'd like to introduce Ms. Selma Warma, who retires from the Richmond Insurance Company today after thirty-five years of faithful service." I lead a small smattering round of applause.

"Take Detective Clemons's seat, Selma. He won't mind."

Selma, who obviously is not sure why she's been invited, is dressed in what is probably her most playful outfit, a red and blue striped pantsuit, which would be perfect for an oompah band recital or bingo night at the lodge hall. She sits in the seat next to Alibi Al.

"Don't stare at Chappie's neck," Tiffany tells her. "That gunk inside isn't his fault."

"I wasn't," Selma says, staring at Chappie's neck.

"Yes, you are," Tiffany corrects her.

"I asked Selma to get me a list of all the life insurance policies written on Sergai Levenchenko by Vilma. Selma, do you have the list, or could you tell us what you found?"

I've caught her off guard. "I'm sorry, but with all I had to do in my last week here," she says in a weak, apologetic voice, "I didn't get around to it."

"Really?"

"I'm so sorry."

Selma gets up out of her chair and makes her way to the door, but Clemons blocks her path.

Selma isn't happy. "I don't want to miss my party."

"Selma, why don't you stay with us?" I say. "This might prove to be an exclamation point to your career at Richmond."

She reluctantly sits back down.

"Now, to what really happened."

"Hurry up," Eddie says. "Or the price is going to three million."

"There was a Sergai Levenchenko. Matter of fact, there is a number of Sergai Levenchenkos out and about in Chicago. You see, the Russian mob has a very good business producing phony documents and loves to use the name Sergai Levenchenko." I stop, take out the copies of the different pictured green cards

I've collected with the name Sergai Levenchenko, and lay them on the table for all to see. "You might want to notice that the faces may be different, but the ID numbers are all the same."

Everyone looks quickly.

"That was the first mistake, Vilma. You should have used an oddball name like Nikita or Tsar Alexander. And secondly, if you are lucky enough to head to the altar in Vegas to do the deed one more time, you're going to have to find a new chapel." I hold up their marriage certificate. "You see, Vilma's marriage certificate was signed by the *Old Elvis* at the Hunka Burnin' Love Chapel, who is no longer there. He was replaced by the new *Young Elvis* because the chapel was going broke. No one wants to be married by a fat, greasy-haired guy busting out of his sequined outfit. And, Vilma, if you are unlucky for the third time around and your husband passes away yet again, you'll also have to find new funeral home arrangements because the Hollerback Funeral Home is now on its way to becoming a mini-mansion. And the last piece of news I have for you, Vilma, is you have to learn to leave well enough alone. If you wouldn't have started this ridiculous post-traumatic grief disorder lawsuit, you might have been home free for a lot longer. From my years of experience, I've learned that criminals, and most people in general, are invariably their own worst enemies."

"I have no clue what you are talking about," Vilma says. "I want to go home."

"So do I, but first I'd like to finish the story."

"Three million six fifty-five, Sherlock."

I ignore Eddie. "The other night, when I was at the end of my investigating rope, my assistant, Tiffany, had the brilliant idea of removing one piece of evidence from the jumbled pieces of the puzzle staring me right in the face. It was a brilliant deduction on her part." I look over at Tiffany, who is giving Bree her *I knew it all the time* smile. "Would you like to tell the group about it, Tiffany?" I ask her.

"No, Mr. Sherlock, I'm too modest. You go ahead."

"Tiffany adeptly realized that it wasn't a clue that was missing from the puzzle, but that we had too many principals in the mix."

"It was nothing," Tiffany tells the group.

"And I came to realize, with Tiffany's incredible deductive reasoning, that Vilma's Sergai Levenchenko didn't exist. He was a phantom, an apparition created out of thin air for the sole purpose of dying and leaving a half-million-dollar Richmond Insurance policy to his grieving heirs. It was a brilliant scam. Every base was covered." I pull out more pages from the folder to add to the table's show-and-tell.

"There were Sergai's health records, rent receipts from the trailer where they lived, a Nevada marriage license, a birth and death certificate, all of which were either legit or impossible to prove fraudulent. There was a guest book from the funeral showing. Vilma even brought home an actual urn, which she now uses for her personal cigarette ashes."

"It was a brilliant, well-thought-out, and well-executed plan. But all that glitters is not gold."

"First," I say as I open the guest book to the third page, "all the guests' names were not only signed with the same pen but by the same person." I hold the book for all to see. "You can see all the ends of the letter S are identical." I pause. "On the two health reports, which somehow found their way into the back room of the Clark Street Richmond Clinic, the blood pressure readings were exactly the same, 154 over 110; in real life this seldom happens."

"And if you don't keep up with Mafia talk in Chicago, there have been rumors for years that the Hollerback Funeral Home has had a very good business disposing of bodies and performing services, under the table shall we say, for mob victims. For Vilma's Sergai, they didn't even need to turn on the oven; all they had to do is supply some fraudulent paperwork. And that beautiful diamond ring Sergai gave you, Vilma, Tiffany spotted that from twenty feet away to be either from the Home Shopping or the QVC Network."

Tiffany beams even brighter.

Vilma's eyes stare at the floor.

"I wish I could give Vilma all the credit, but, and I don't mean to be mean in saying this, Vilma, you're just not that smart. Nobody dumb enough to sue on the basis of post-traumatic grief disorder could pull a scam like this off. I will admit you did a great job finding a shrink who swallowed your story hook, line, and sinker and really did believe you were as crazy as a Cheshire cat."

Dr. Lunay wisely chooses not to comment.

"And, of course," I decide to add, "you were dumb enough

to hire Eddie Floyd, who won't be throwing any knockout punches today. A scam is only good if all the pieces of the puzzle fit perfectly, and this one came close, but vanity, or too many spins of the slot machine, reared its ugly head."

My story is so preposterous the folks in the room can't wait to hear what comes next.

"Yes, Vilma had help. More likely, Vilma was only a piece of the puzzle because the real brains of the design were on the inside." I look right at Bree.

"Me?"

Tiffany almost jumps out of her seat in glee. "Did I think that too, Mr. Sherlock?"

"No, Tiffany, and it's not you, Bree."

"Damn," I hear from Tiffany.

"Before I go on, I would like to wish Selma Warma all the best in her life of retirement. I understand you're moving south?"

"Yes," she answers softly.

Chappie opens his folder and pulls out a number of photos of beachfront vacation homes. As I speak, I put them on the table for all to marvel. "A home in Costa Rica, one in Belize, a condo in Antigua, and a yacht in the Bahamas. When you want to get away from Chicago winters, you really go all out, don't you, Selma?"

Selma sits as frozen as a clogged eave.

"I don't know how long it's going to take, Bree, but you're going to have to go through every case Selma handled to find the rest of the death scams I'm sure she pulled off."

There is not a sound in the room; even Care's sniffles have stopped and Alibi Al's fork comes to rest.

"If you wouldn't have used the name Sergai Levenchenko and picked such a dumb accomplice, Selma, you might be on one of your verandas tanning tomorrow. But alas, it is not to be."

Selma sits and seems to literally shrink inside her clothing. Her face turns gaunt, her shoulders collapse inward, and her chin rests on her concaved chest.

"You said we'd never get caught," Vilma says to Selma.

"We wouldn't if you hadn't been so stupid. You idiot."

"Please, please, let's not quarrel ladies," I tell the two. "I do have to give you credit, Selma; you really had me baffled. But when another Sergai got iced, no pun intended, I said to myself, 'Too many Sergai's in the Levenchenko pot doesn't make for a tasty meal.' It all started to come together."

"And ..." Detective Clemons says.

"I'm pretty sure the Sergai who got froze out a couple nights ago in the dumpster was done in by a couple of Moscow Social Club members Vilma knows since she let them use her car to do the deed. The boys had a real good reason to party so hearty the night after the event, didn't they, Vilma?"

"Thanks, Sherlock," Clemons says, nods, and readies a set of handcuffs.

Alibi Al eats the last bite of frosting.

"I'm not sure of how far back you and Vilma go, Selma, but as soon as this meeting is over, I'm going to put my friend Chappie here on it, and I'm sure he'll find out the day and date you two met. And after that, he'll start in on every claims file you ever processed in the past thirty-five years. If that's okay with you, Bree?"

"We'd love to have you, Chappie."

What a way to end a retirement party.

"I'm sorry, there'll be no settlement today, Eddie, but if you do criminal work, I got two potential clients for you."

"No money in criminal law, but if they use my name, I'll get a referral fee," Eddie says.

"That's all folks. I would like to compliment Chappie for his outstanding work and Tiffany for being the one who broke the case wide open."

I peer down the table. I have one more question to ask. "Houston, do you have anything to add?"

The lady whispers in his ear and the kid punches the keys on his laptop, Houston considers both, turns to me, and says, "No."

CHAPTER 30

It takes a good half hour for Selma and Vilma to be cuffed and taken outside to a waiting squad car. Clemons thanks me. Alibi Al checks his watch and says, "I still might be able to catch the end of the buffet if I hurry."

"Well, Al, if you're too late, tell them it wasn't your fault and you want a coupon for a rain check."

Tiffany goes right up to Bree. "Well, Ms. Biz-o-nette, what do you think of me now?"

I interrupt. "Knock it off, Tiffany."

Bree starts to say something, but I pay her the same mind. "You too, Bree. From now on, you two are going to stop sniping at one another. It does neither of you the least bit of good. You are going to accept each other, and if you can't be friends, you will be respectful and cordial to one another. Do you understand?"

"Well—"

"Well—"

"Shake hands."

Bree puts her hand out; Tiffany doesn't.

"Tiffany—"

"Could we just air kiss, again?"

"No."

The two shake hands.

Bree suggests, "We should go celebrate."

"I can't. I have to get Care home."

"Come on, Chappie, the three of us will go," Tiffany suggests.

Chappie smiles. That is going to be one interesting table at some fancy bar.

Everyone exits. Me and my girls are the last people in the room.

"Care, do you feel any better?"

"Little bit. I'd feel a lot better if I could get some McDonald's French fries in me."

"Forget it."

"You know, Dad," Kelly says as we walk out, "that was really sweet how you made nice between Tiffany and Bree Biz-o-nette."

"It's pronounced Biz-o-nay," I correct her. "Next week, I'm going to get Bree to nominate Tiffany for the Richmond Employee of the Month."

"Cool."

I address both of my daughters, "I hope the two of you both learned a good lesson out of this."

"No, I didn't," Kelly says.

"Me neither," Care adds. "What?"

"To be a little nicer to each other," I explain.

Kelly takes a few seconds to consider and says, "No, that's not going to happen."

"No way," Care says and sneezes.

Truly wishful thinking on my part.

We get all the way to the bottom of the Aon Center to where my Toyota is parked. It has been such a warm Chicago day even the lower levels of parking are pleasant.

"Can we stop at Chuck E. Cheese?"

"No."

We pile in the car. I turn the key, and my Toyota won't start.

Oh jeesh.

The End.

Thank you very much for reading The Case of the Woebegon Widow. I certainly hope you enjoyed my novel, and if you did, please let others know of your good reading fortune. The easiest way being through cyberspace via social media networks such as Amazon, Facebook, LinkedIn, Goodreads, and Twitter. Please put in a good review to the above and to your friends, contacts, and fellow readers. It will be greatly appreciated.

About Jim Stevens

Jim Stevens was born in the East, grew up in the West, schooled in the Northwest and spent twenty-three winters in the Midwest. Jim Stevens has been writing for over thirty years. Usually without much success, but for some reason he keeps writing. Jim started writing TV series specs in the 1970s and went hungry. He segued into spec movie scripts and starved. He went into the corporate world for a twenty-five year career in broadcasting and advertising, but just couldn't drop his pencil. He found time to write plays in the Chicago theater scene, wrote, produced, and directed numerous short films, videos, and TV commercials, created TV pilots, and even optioned a few movie scripts that never saw the glare of the Klieg lights.

Jim has been writing novels for the past four years. His Richard Sherlock Whodunit series has ranked him in the top 10% of Amazon authors. He is also the author of WHUPPED, a reverse romantic comedy from many different points of view. His most recent novel, Hell No, We Won't Go, A Novel of Peace, Love, War, and Football is his first writing of a 'serious' nature.

Jim loves to hear from his readers, especially the ones who enjoy his books. He can be reached at JimStevensWriter@gmail.com

If you would like to be the first on your block to get all the up to date news on the detecting of Richard Sherlock and whatever Jim Stevens has to say, please sign up for Jim's email list. All you have to do is drop a line to JimStevensWriter@gmail.com to join a very select and fun-filled group. Don't delay, do it today!

Also by Jim Stevens

The Richard Sherlock Whodunit Series

Hell No, We Won't Go

WHUPPED

And Coming Soon:

WHUPPED TOO

Made in the USA
Coppell, TX
02 October 2024

38011738R00135